CRITICAL ACCLAIM FOR LEIGH RUSSELL

'A million readers can't be wrong! Clear some time in
your day, sit back and enjoy a bloody good read'
– **Howard Linskey**

'Taut and compelling' – **Peter James**

'Leigh Russell is one to watch' – **Lee Child**

'Leigh Russell has become one of the most impressively
dependable purveyors of the English police procedural'
– **Marcel Berlins, *Times***

'A brilliant talent in the thriller field' – **Jeffery Deaver**

'Brilliant and chilling, Leigh Russell delivers a cracker
of a read!' – **Martina Cole**

'A great plot that keeps you guessing right until the very end,
some subtle subplots, brilliant characters both old and new
and as ever a completely gripping read' – *Life of Crime*

'A fascinating gripping read. The many twists kept
me on my toes and second guessing myself'
– *Over The Rainbow Book Blog*

'Well paced with marvellously well-rounded characters and
a clever plot that make this another thriller of a read from
Leigh Russell' – *Orlando Books*

'A well-written, fast-paced and very enjoyable thriller'
– *The Book Lovers*

ALSO BY LEIGH RUSSELL

Geraldine Steel Mysteries
Cut Short
Road Closed
Dead End
Death Bed
Stop Dead
Fatal Act
Killer Plan
Murder Ring
Deadly Alibi
Class Murder
Death Rope
Rogue Killer
Deathly Affair
Deadly Revenge
Evil Impulse
Deep Cover
Guilt Edged

Ian Peterson Murder Investigations
Cold Sacrifice
Race to Death
Blood Axe

Lucy Hall Mysteries
Journey to Death
Girl in Danger
The Wrong Suspect

The Adulterer's Wife
Suspicion

LEIGH RUSSELL

FAKE ALIBI

A GERALDINE STEEL MYSTERY

NO EXIT PRESS

First published in 2022 by No Exit Press,
an imprint of Oldcastle Books Ltd,
Harpenden, UK

noexit.co.uk
@noexitpress

ISBN
978-0-85730-346-2 (print)
978-0-85730-348-6 (epub)

2 4 6 8 10 9 7 5 3 1

Typeset in 11 on 13.75pt Times New Roman
by Avocet Typeset, Bideford, Devon, EX39 2BP
Printed in Great Britain by Clays Ltd, Elcograf S.p.A.

MIX
Paper from
responsible sources
FSC® C018072

For more information about Crime Fiction go to crimetime.co.uk

To Michael, Jo, Phillipa, Phil, Rian, and Kezia
With my love

Glossary of Acronyms

DCI	–	Detective Chief Inspector (senior officer on case)
DI	–	Detective Inspector
DS	–	Detective Sergeant
SOCO	–	scene of crime officer (collects forensic evidence at scene)
PM	–	Post Mortem or Autopsy (examination of dead body to establish cause of death)
CCTV	–	Closed Circuit Television (security cameras)
VIIDO	–	Visual Images, Identifications and Detections Office
MIT	–	Murder Investigation Team

Prologue

FROM THE MOMENT THEIR eyes met he knew she was special. For the first time, he grasped the meaning of the words 'life-changing', because he understood there was no going back. He couldn't pretend he had never seen her, not even to himself. His life changed forever when she smiled at him. Her voice thrilled him because he knew she was speaking just to him, her words imbued with a meaning that no one else listening could possibly suspect. But he understood. Mesmerised by her gaze, for an instant he dared not speak for fear of breaking the spell.

'Would you like chocolate with that?' he managed to stammer at last.

She hesitated, wanting the moment to last. 'I don't know. What would you do?'

He didn't answer straight away, savouring her deference. He wasn't used to people asking him for advice.

'Yes,' he murmured stupidly.

'Okay then.'

'Coming up right away,' he muttered awkwardly. 'Kylie,' he added, trembling as he uttered her name for the first time.

Watching the way her lips curled into a shy smile as he spoke, he wanted to beg her to stay. They could sit down at one of the tables together and talk. He spent his days watching other people chattering and exchanging confidences over coffee and cakes. He and Kylie could engage in meaningful conversation just like the other customers. There was so much they didn't know about each other, so much he wanted to find out. Her hair fell across her face, shielding her eyes from him. Angry with himself for letting the opportunity slip, his sigh was swallowed by the noisy grinding of the coffee machine as she paid his colleague, tapping her card delicately against the card reader before turning away to move along the counter and collect her drink. A moment later she was gone. Time dragged until his shift ended.

The heavy glass door swung shut and fresh air enveloped him, making him shiver. A chill rain pattered on his cheeks as he hurried away, nursing his disappointment. The following day was sunny and the spring warmth gave him courage. When she returned, he was determined to speak boldly across the counter, and invite her to meet him after work so he could tell her exactly how he felt. He already knew how she would respond. He would not let his chance slip away again. But when he went back the next day, there was no sign of her. He went to work every day for a week without success, until he began to despair of ever meeting her again.

When he finally saw her, an uncontrollable song burst out of him. She was striding purposefully along the street. In a flash, he understood what had happened. He had been worried she was ill, or worse. The truth reassured him. She had forgotten where he worked and had been searching for him all week. Like him, he knew she would not rest until he held her in his arms, like he had seen on television. Heedless of the consequences, he seized his chance. Ignoring the startled shout of the manager, he tore off his apron and darted across the coffee shop. A pair of old women turned to stare at him as he hurtled past them, and a couple of girls sitting at a table near the door giggled. For once he didn't care that they were laughing at him. He would probably be fired for running out like that at the beginning of his shift, but he didn't care. He could find other employment, but he would never fall in love again.

Having quit his job without a word of explanation, he spent

a blissful day with the woman he loved. First he accompanied her to the hotel where she worked. Once she had gone inside, he waited patiently for the rest of the day before trailing her home. All the way there, he conversed softly with her. A woman who walked past him gave him a curious scowl, but he took no notice of her. Nothing could upset him now that he had found Kylie again. His mother sometimes sang a song about being on the street where he lived. That was just how he felt now. He wanted to stay there all night, singing softly, waiting for Kylie to emerge in the glorious daylight, but eventually hunger forced him to go home.

'It's gone eight,' his mother grumbled, turning to take a dish out of the oven. 'Don't blame me if your dinner's ruined. It was ready over an hour ago. Why didn't you phone me to say you were working late?'

Predictably enough, she was furious when he admitted he had lost his job.

'What do you mean?' Her normally pale face flushed with anger. 'You've only just started there. What did you do this time?'

He shrugged. 'It was the manager. He said they were overstaffed and someone had to go. It wasn't my fault. I didn't do anything wrong. I was working really hard.'

That wasn't strictly true, but his mother would never know. He crunched his way through his overcooked dinner without complaining, even though his fish fingers were hard and there was no soft potato inside his waffles.

'They only gave you the job last month,' she said.

'Exactly. Last in first to go,' he replied, quoting something he had been told when he had been sacked from his previous job. 'That's how it works. The manager said he didn't want to lose me but he had to let me go.'

'Why would they take you on and then change their minds so quickly? It doesn't make sense. If you were doing a good job, he had no business firing you.' She glared at him as if it was his fault.

He did his best to look aggrieved, although every muscle in his face was aching to smile at his wonderful memories. He hugged his secret to himself.

'I've a good mind to go down there and give that manager a piece of my mind.'

'There's no point, Ma. It's not the manager's fault. He was very nice about it. He said he was sorry and it wasn't anything to do with me. It was a decision from head office and there was nothing he could do about it. If it was up to him, he said he would have kept me because I'm a good worker. But it wasn't up to him and there was nothing he could do about it. That's what he said.'

He gave his mother a placatory smile but she scowled at him.

'That's exactly what you said last time. Did you at least ask him for a reference?'

He hesitated because he hadn't thought of that, and then he had a flash of inspiration. 'The manager said he wouldn't do it because a reference has to say how long you've worked somewhere. He said having a job for a month doesn't look good, even though it wasn't my fault I had to leave.'

His mother grunted and he continued eating his ruined dinner. It was a pity the fish fingers were so hard, because he usually enjoyed them, but these were so dry they were almost impossible to chew. He was afraid they would give him a belly ache, but he dared not complain. His mother was angry enough already. Before he finished his supper she was on at him again, telling him that he had better start looking for another job first thing in the morning. The next day he left the house early, his mother's nagging ringing in his ears. She assumed he was job hunting, which suited him fine. In reality he spent the day with Kylie.

'How did you get on?' his mother demanded when he returned

home for supper. She was in the kitchen, and he could smell his dinner in the oven. She was still harping on about him earning money. She didn't understand he had no time for that right now. He was too busy to go job hunting. When he attempted to explain, she didn't seem to understand what he was saying. It was typical of her. She never listened to him.

'I tried it,' he said. 'It didn't work out.'

'What are you talking about? You have to get a job. We need the money. My pension isn't enough for us both to live on. I do what I can, but you're young and strong. There must be dozens of jobs you could do. You can't just sit around and rely on me for the rest of your life. Have you tried the supermarket? I'm sure they have openings. They employ plenty of young people. You could at least try to get a job there.'

Her whining irritated him.

'No, Ma, I'm not getting another job and that's final.'

'You can't spend the rest of your life sitting around here doing nothing.'

'I'm not doing nothing.'

'What are you planning to do then? Because whatever it is, if you expect to stay here all day living off me, you can think again.'

He shook his head at her. She didn't understand. How could she? He scarcely understood the miracle himself.

He tried again, struggling to express his feelings. 'You don't understand. I can't get a job. I have other things to do. More important things.'

'More important than getting a job? What are you talking about?'

He drew in a deep breath before confessing he had a girlfriend. Instead of looking impressed, his mother burst out laughing.

'A girlfriend? You? What girl in her right mind is going to look twice at you?'

For once, her mockery washed over him; she had lost the

power to hurt him. All he wanted to think about was Kylie. One day, very soon, he would summon up the courage to ask her to marry him. He smiled, knowing what her answer would be.

1

JULIE WAS FURIOUS WHEN delivery men left parcels on her front step without bothering to find out if anyone was in. It had happened a few times when she was at home, so she knew they hadn't rung the bell. Equally irritating was returning home to find a parcel waiting for her on the doorstep, in full view of anyone walking past. As far as she knew, no one had yet helped themselves.

'But how would I know if something's been taken?' she complained to her sister, who made sympathetic noises.

So Julie's hackles rose when she was returning home one day and spotted a package lying beside her next-door neighbour's front step. The delivery man – or woman – must have deposited it there without bothering to knock. Even if the person delivering it had rung the bell, they obviously hadn't waited. It was outrageously unfair, because Julie knew that Doreen wouldn't be able to retrieve the package from the ground. Had it rained, the parcel could have been drenched. Fortunately it had been dry that day, although recently the month had lived up to its reputation, with seasonal April showers. Her son must already have left for work, in which case the package could have stayed outside all day, until he came home. It was lucky for Doreen that Julie was a good neighbour. Feeling virtuous, she marched up to her neighbour's front door and rang the bell several times. There was no answer. She knocked and called out. Aware that Doreen could only move slowly, Julie waited before ringing again, but there was no response from inside the house. Either Doreen was out, or else she had fallen asleep.

15

With a sigh, Julie scooped up the parcel, intending to take it home with her and return with it later, but as she turned away she distinctly heard voices in the house. Annoyed that no one inside had answered her summons, she followed the sound which seemed to be coming from the front room. Through the net curtains, she made out the flickering light of the television. Now that she was close to the window, she realised that was the source of the voices. Doreen must have turned the volume up so high, she hadn't heard Julie at the door. Annoyed, Julie knocked on the window and shouted. Still there was no response from inside the house. She bent down and squinted through a gap in the curtains, screwing up her eyes in an effort to see if anyone was there. Suddenly registering what she was looking at, she drew back with a low cry of alarm, letting the parcel fall from her hands. It landed at her feet with a soft thud.

Doreen was lying flat on her back, gazing up at the ceiling. Stooping down to retrieve the parcel, Julie peered in through the window again, shouting Doreen's name and knocking loudly on the glass all the while. Doreen didn't stir. Shaking slightly, Julie stepped further back, knocking into the bins with a clatter that startled her so much she dropped the parcel again. Telling herself that her neighbour must be asleep and she had no business spying on her through the window anyway, she picked up the parcel, which was starting to look rather dirty and battered. It was difficult to see very much through a narrow gap in the curtains anyway. Doreen was definitely lying on the floor, but there was nothing to suggest that she was in need of help. She was probably just resting. In any case, she wasn't Julie's responsibility.

It wasn't as if Doreen lived on her own. Her son would be home soon to look after her. But Julie knew that the young man might be out at work for hours. Only a few days earlier, Doreen had called out to Julie as she was putting her rubbish out, to boast that he had landed a job in town. Surprised to hear that Doreen's son had a job, Julie had smiled and nodded and congratulated her neighbour. To hear Doreen talk, anyone might have thought he had landed a highly paid post as Chief Executive of a multinational corporation. The reality, of course, was rather different. He had found employment as a waiter in a café. It was hardly an impressive position, but Doreen seemed ready to burst with pride, insisting that her son was starting at the bottom and would work his way up the ladder.

'Not much of a ladder,' Julie muttered.

'What's that?'

'I was just saying how pleased I am for him. Do pass on my congratulations.'

'Oh yes, he's a real help, my boy,' Doreen had continued, as though Julie hadn't spoken. 'He's an absolute treasure.'

Julie had nodded and smiled. 'You're very lucky to have such a wonderful son,' she had replied, hiding her true feelings because, after all, Doreen was in a wheelchair, and there was no call to be unkind.

Clutching the battered parcel, she tried not to think about her neighbour, lying flat on her back, with the television blaring beside her. It was difficult not to imagine the worst. The problem for Julie was that she had clearly seen Doreen's eyes were open, and she was lying on the floor staring at the ceiling. Something was clearly amiss. Julie regretted having gone out of her way to try and be a good neighbour, but she could no more undo her actions than she could forget what she had seen through the window. Clutching the undelivered parcel in front of her like a shield, she peeped in between the curtains again. The television was still on and Doreen remained on the floor, in exactly the same position as before, seemingly staring up at the ceiling. It was impossible to keep on pretending that nothing was wrong.

Scowling, Julie pulled out her phone. This was what came of trying to be a good neighbour.

'Hello, hello? I think my neighbour's had a fall or something.

I – I happened to catch sight of her through the window.' As she spoke, she realised that must sound as though she had been spying on Doreen. Having begun, she had no choice but to plough on. 'The thing is, I knocked on her door because someone had left a parcel outside, and no one answered so I looked in because I could hear voices, only that was just the television. Anyway, I can see her lying on the floor and she's not moving. I think she might need help if she's fallen out of her wheelchair. She probably needs an ambulance. She may have had an accident. I don't think she could hear me calling her. She didn't react. She's just lying there –'

The voice on the line asked for her address. As she hung up, it occurred to Julie that Doreen was probably already beyond help. She was tempted to call back and cancel the ambulance. It seemed a pity to take up their time when they could be attending to an urgent medical emergency. But it was too late now. She had made the call, and the ambulance was on its way. She would just have to wait and see it through. There was even a chance she might have saved her neighbour's life, but somehow she didn't believe that for an instant, and she was shocked to realise that she didn't really care. She sat down on her own doorstep to wait. She hoped the ambulance would arrive soon.

2

GERALDINE WAS PLEASED TO see her colleague and friend, Detective Sergeant Ariadne Moralis, who had just returned from her honeymoon. Geraldine greeted her, and was disappointed when Ariadne seemed reluctant to talk.

'Not now,' she said, when Geraldine suggested they take a break together. 'I've got so much to catch up on.' That was probably true, but somehow it felt like a rebuff.

By half past four, when they still hadn't spoken, Geraldine went over to try and start a conversation with her friend.

'Must be a bit of a downer coming back to work after two weeks on a Greek island. I can see you had good weather.'

Usually sociable, Ariadne just grunted.

'Is everything all right?' Geraldine asked quietly, moving closer and leaning over her friend.

Before Ariadne had time to reply, they were summoned to an unscheduled briefing. Working on a murder investigation team, they both knew what that might mean. Their detective chief inspector, Eileen Duncan, glared severely around a small group of assembled officers as she instructed them to make enquiries into a woman who had died under suspicious circumstances. Little was known about the victim so far, and the team were set to work gathering as much information about her as possible, while the crime scene was being examined.

'I see the DCI's her usual positive self,' Ariadne grumbled as she accompanied Geraldine from the incident room.

Geraldine was tempted to retort that Ariadne herself was

hardly cheerful. She asked her friend once more if everything was all right and received a snappy reply, after which they made their way to the crime scene together in silence. Geraldine resolved to find out what was troubling her friend, but first they had work to do. However many crime scenes Geraldine viewed, she never failed to experience a frisson of excitement when she was about to visit another one. Once she arrived, her professional fascination would kick in and her own feelings would be swept aside by a fierce determination to discover the truth. In that moment, nothing else would matter to her. Geraldine used to wonder if she had fallen into the habit of using her work as a distraction from her own loneliness while she had been single. At least her preoccupation was easy to justify. No one could deny that murder investigations were important.

As they drove to the house, which was located in a side street off Gillygate, Geraldine did a mental recap of what little was known about the case. After being killed in suspicious circumstances at home, the woman had been discovered by her next-door neighbour. In spite of Ariadne's taciturnity, Geraldine was pleased to be working alongside her. Ariadne was usually sociable, and would no doubt return to her normal congeniality before long. But Geraldine had no time to worry about her colleague appearing downhearted when they had a possible murder to investigate. Unlike several of her colleagues, Geraldine had never been disturbed by the sight of a dead body. On the contrary, the sight of a corpse could engross her without touching her emotions. In the urgency of a crime scene, all that interested her was that a dead body held clues that might lead them to a killer. Distress and pity, which might cloud her judgement, had no place at a crime scene. She occasionally questioned whether she was callous for experiencing so little emotion in the presence of death, but at the same time she knew that her ability to shut herself off from her feelings made her a good detective, and she was secretly thankful for her ability to remain detached.

Reaching the address in Portland Street, they drew up outside a well maintained row of imposing Victorian terraced houses. The elegant brick-built property had a large bay ground floor window at the front, and a narrow front yard was fenced off from the street by low wrought iron railings. A scene of crime officer was busy checking the front step of the house where the victim, Doreen Lewis, had lived, not far from the centre of York. Another officer was scrutinising the yard, checking for footprints and any other sign of disturbance. Geraldine and Ariadne pulled on their protective coverings and overshoes, before following the established approach path along the hall, walking carefully along plastic stepping stones and manoeuvring their way past a folded wheelchair leaning against the wall. Entering the front room they saw the dead woman lying flat on her back. Nothing in the room suggested there had been a struggle. Magazines lay in a tidy pile on a low wooden coffee table beside the dead woman, and two armchairs and a small sofa were neatly arranged around the room, as though forming a protective wall around their dead owner. A basket of different coloured wools lay on the floor beside one chair. In the centre of the wall facing the door was a Victorian fireplace, which was probably original although it had an obviously fake log fire, with a row of ornamental cats displayed on the mantelpiece.

Geraldine turned her attention to the dead body. Had her skin not been grey, Doreen Lewis might have looked as though she was resting. Dark hair threaded with grey fanned out untidily around her head, and her gaunt face appeared to gleam, pale against the patterned red carpet.

Ariadne glanced at the dead woman, before she turned and left.

'Are you coming?' she asked, looking back as she reached the door to the hall. 'We've seen her. We need to leave SOCOs to get on. We're only going to be in the way.'

Geraldine grunted. 'Just give me a minute,' she called out. 'I want to look around here for a bit longer.'

Once Ariadne had gone, Geraldine stood perfectly still for a moment, taking in the orderliness of the room in which the only jarring note was struck by the dead body stretched out on the carpet. Geraldine closed her eyes. The silence was broken by the scratching and shuffling of scene of crime officers as they moved softly around the room, slipping samples into evidence bags, and their occasional muttered exchanges. The stench from the body almost masked a faint, musty smell. Slowly opening her eyes, she gazed around. Everything from the shabby curtains to the heavy, dark wooden furniture was covered in a film of dust, and there was a sense of abandonment in the room, as though it had once been carefully looked after but had been neglected for a long time. The explanation for this air of deterioration was evident on a closer examination of the scene. The woman's legs looked withered, and ruts worn in the carpet suggested that a wheelchair had frequently moved across the floor. The dead woman had clearly not been physically capable of taking care of the house herself, even if she had managed to keep it tidy.

'How did she die?' she asked the nearest scene of crime officer.

He turned to face her and his youth surprised her. He barely looked out of his teens.

He frowned anxiously. 'We haven't established the exact cause of death yet. But it looks as though someone else was involved. That is, the medical officer doesn't think it looks as though she could have walked here unaided, and what we've found so far confirms that.'

'What have you found?'

The scene of crime officer spoke rapidly, with an air of

suppressed excitement. 'There are marks on the carpet where her feet may have pushed against the pile when she was dragged in here.' He indicated two almost parallel furrows across the floor which could have been made, as he said, by a person's heels being dragged across the room. 'The width of the grooves matches the back of her heels. Plus her wheelchair's in the hall. So how could she have got here if she couldn't walk?'

'Very well,' Geraldine said, hiding her impatience with the young officer. 'The reason for those tracks has not yet been established so your theory is mere speculation at this point. She might have been able to walk around indoors, holding on for support.' She pointed out a handrail that had been installed along one wall. 'So let's gather some more evidence and see what can be proved beyond any doubt.'

She spoke more sharply than she had intended. She was not yet too jaded to remember the wildness of her own enthusiasm when she had been a young detective working on her first cases. Every possibility had seemed thrilling to her in those days. She still had not lost her visceral sense of excitement when viewing a crime scene. She had just grown more careful to hide her feelings beneath a mask of detachment. On closer examination, she tended to agree that the body had been dragged to its final position. The dead woman could probably move around the house, supporting herself on furniture and clinging to rails on the walls, but the marks on the carpet did not appear to have been made by wheels. With a sigh, she turned away, unable to interpret the signs on the carpet with any certainty.

'The medical officer thinks she may have been strangled,' the SOCO went on. 'But that's not been officially confirmed.'

Geraldine looked down at the body again, but the woman's neck was concealed by her clothing and couldn't be disturbed. There was nothing more Geraldine could learn for now. As Ariadne had said, it was time for SOCOs to gather evidence, after which a post mortem would establish the cause of death.

'We'll get to the truth of what happened,' she muttered to the dead woman as she turned away.

'What was that?' the scene of crime officer enquired. 'I didn't catch what you said.'

'I wasn't talking to you,' Geraldine replied.

Ignoring his baffled expression, she left.

3

Doreen's body had been discovered by her next door neighbour, Julie West. Leaving the dead woman's house, Geraldine removed her protective clothing and dropped it in the disposal bin before going to question the neighbour. A small, skinny woman opened the door straight away, as though she had observed Geraldine's approach and had been waiting for her to knock on the door. Geraldine held up her warrant card but before she had a chance to explain the reason for her visit, the other woman darted backwards, beckoning to her.

'I know why you're here,' the neighbour called out, sounding eager and excited, her speech as rapid as her movements. 'Come in, come in. This way, this way. Give the door a good slam behind you.'

Still gesturing to her visitor to follow her, she led the way down her narrow hall, with Geraldine at her heels. Julie ushered Geraldine into a front room. Similar in size to Doreen's, it was very differently furnished, with two upright wooden chairs, a black and chrome chair that would have been more suitable for an office, and a small green leather sofa. Instead of a fireplace, the room boasted a gigantic television screen on the far wall, which looked out of place in the small square living room. No one piece of furniture was unattractive by itself, but everything in the room clashed.

'You've come about Doreen next door,' Julie said, her voice rising in agitation. It wasn't a question, but Geraldine nodded. 'It was me found her,' the woman went on, with a nervous cough.

25

'I saw her through the window and I thought to myself straight away, something isn't right here. That's what I thought, and I was right.' She coughed again, gazing anxiously at Geraldine.

Quietly Geraldine invited her to relate exactly what had happened. Julie launched into an account of how she had gone next door to deliver a parcel that had been left lying on the front doorstep.

'I mean,' she went on, suddenly animated, 'anyone could have come along and taken it. Whoever delivered it just left it lying there, in full view of anyone passing by. Surely there must be laws about this? And if there aren't, there should be. It's just asking for thieves to steal parcels if they're left lying around like that, in full daylight. Doreen's in a wheelchair. How is she supposed to pick up something left lying on the ground?'

She seemed to be more exercised by the negligence of delivery men than by her discovery of a dead body.

'What if it was something valuable being delivered?' she continued her rant. 'Or it could've been something poor Doreen had been waiting for, and really needed. And even if it wasn't valuable or urgent, that was someone's property left lying around in the street. What if it was stolen from the doorstep? What then? Who was going to pay for it?'

Manoeuvring the neighbour past her indignation, Geraldine heard how Julie had discovered Doreen lying flat on her back on the floor. More time was wasted in hearing her insist that she hadn't been prying, but had just chanced to glance through the window next door.

'I mean, I'm not one to go snooping,' she said. 'I respect other people's right to privacy.'

Gradually Geraldine set about pumping Julie for information about Doreen. She learned that Julie had been living next door to Doreen for nearly twenty years. Doreen rarely left the house and then only in a wheelchair.

'She used to be spry as anything,' she added mournfully. 'But then it got to her.'

'What did?'

Julie shrugged. 'It was the stroke put her in a wheelchair, must be five or six years ago. I couldn't say for certain. The time just goes, doesn't it? But I've seen her on her feet, shuffling around the bins,' she added in a whisper, as though she was afraid someone might be listening. 'She could walk all right. I watched her one day, moving around their scrapheap of a garden, and she wasn't even using a stick. She told me she had good days and bad days, but I don't know about that. And Eddy's a strange one,' she added, shaking her head. 'Very strange.'

Geraldine waited to see if she would elaborate and, sure enough, Julie explained herself without any prompting. Geraldine learned that Doreen had lived with a son who made Julie feel uneasy.

'He always struck me as odd,' she explained.

'Odd in what way?' Geraldine prompted her.

'Odd, you know, odd. There was something not quite right about him, if you follow my meaning.'

'Did he say something that made you feel uncomfortable?'

'No, not as such, but he did it all right. Eddy killed her, you take my word for it. I wouldn't tell tales about something like that if I didn't know what I was talking about.' She nodded sagely.

'What is it that makes you so sure he's guilty?' Geraldine asked. 'If you're keeping any information to yourself, now is the time to share it.'

'I just know he did it,' Julie replied. 'It seems obvious, doesn't it, when you think about it? I live next door to them. I know what he was capable of.'

'Did he ever threaten you, or did you witness him being violent?'

'No, but that's not the point. I'm not the one he attacked.'

'Did you ever hear him threatening his mother?'

'No, but that doesn't mean he didn't kill her.'

'I'll be making a note of what you've said, and everything you told me will be taken very seriously by the team investigating Doreen's death. In the meantime, can you recall seeing anyone else visiting the house recently?'

Julie sighed. 'Yes, yes, people come and go a bit. She has health workers and social workers or carers, who visit the house. Probably Eddy's probation officer, I wouldn't be surprised.'

'Do you know why Eddy's on probation?' Geraldine enquired.

'Well, I'm not saying he is, necessarily, but if he isn't he bloody well ought to be. He shouldn't be allowed out by himself. I'm telling you, he's a danger to us all,' Julie retorted, seeming irritated.

'But he's never attacked you?'

Julie hesitated. 'Not as such, no,' she replied. 'Not yet.'

'And has he ever attacked anyone else, to your knowledge? I need you to be honest, Julie.'

'Not exactly, but he used to follow my sister before she moved away. I know that for a fact. Every time she went out, he'd be there, shuffling along behind her. I saw him with my own eyes, following her on the pavement, scurrying after her like a dog. It freaked me out. I'm telling you, he isn't normal.'

Geraldine asked where they could find Julie's sister.

'Don't waste your time,' Julie said, shaking her head. 'She didn't believe me when I told her he was stalking her. She thought I was imagining it. She was convinced he was harmless, but you can never be sure, can you? I've only spoken to him a couple of times. I avoid him, to be honest. He never said anything particular to me. He was never rude, nothing like that. But I wouldn't want to meet him alone on the street at night, if you know what I mean. He's strange and, well, he's not all there.'

Geraldine wasn't sure she knew exactly what Julie meant, her comments were so vague, but she nodded encouragingly all the same, and waited to hear what else Julie would say. Sometimes people were more forthcoming when they didn't feel as though they were being questioned.

'Not that there's necessarily anything wrong with a grown man living with his mother,' Julie went on. 'And Doreen idolised him. In her eyes he could do no wrong.' She snorted. 'But I'm telling you, there's something not right about Eddy. I don't want to speak out of turn, but you'll see for yourself when you meet him and then you can make up your own mind.'

She fell silent, and Geraldine made one further attempt to discover what she meant.

'I can't explain, but there's something not right about him. There's nothing more I can say about him really,' was all Julie said.

'What about Doreen?' Geraldine asked.

She was more interested in hearing about the dead woman's son, but Julie seemed to have nothing further to say about him, beyond her rambling allegations.

'What about Doreen?' Geraldine repeated. 'Can you tell me anything about her?'

'Other than that she's dead, you mean?'

Suppressing a sigh of impatience, Geraldine forced a smile. To her surprise, Julie launched into a lengthy character assassination of her neighbour, claiming that Doreen had only two topics of conversation.

'I don't like to speak ill of the dead,' she began, and Geraldine settled down to listen carefully. 'But Doreen was only interested in herself. She was forever banging on about her aches and pains, as though she was the only person in the world who had problems.'

Julie digressed into talking about her own back problems, and it was only with difficulty that Geraldine steered her back to talking about her neighbour.

'You try not to think about getting old and death and all that,'

Julie said, almost angrily, 'and then something like this happens, right on your doorstep, and you can't not think about it, can you? And then there's her son,' Julie concluded, sitting back in her chair as though she had finished her recitation.

'What else can you tell me about Eddy?' Geraldine prompted her.

But Julie appeared to have said everything she was prepared to say.

'Speak to him yourself,' she replied. 'You'll see what I mean.'

There was nothing more for Geraldine to do but thank Julie for her information, and take her leave.

'You catch that bastard who did her in,' Julie called out as Geraldine walked back to the street. 'You catch him and lock him up! We want to be able to sleep soundly at night.'

The weather had been mild all day, but a light breeze was blowing as she returned to the car where Ariadne was waiting for her. A stray leaf left over from the winter scudded across the pavement, dry and curling at the edges. Before she could step on it, the leaf was whisked away in a gust of wind.

4

DRIVING AWAY, GERALDINE THOUGHT about what Julie had said about trying not to think about death. Geraldine had never been unduly bothered by the awareness that people she cared about would one day cease to be. She had attributed her insouciance to the fact that she was more focused on trying to live a useful life than to any mental robustness of her own. Now she wondered if her feelings had actually stemmed from the fact that she had never before been emotionally dependent on anyone else. Until now. She had always had friends and family, people she would miss were they to die. Those were people she loved. But they had never been pivotal to her existence. Her thoughts drifted to her parents, and to the first detective chief inspector she had worked for, a woman who had taught her so much but had died of cancer not long after her retirement. Geraldine still regretted never having thanked her properly. She would have liked to have told her about her own promotion to inspector, only it was too late now. But while these were people whose death left a sadness in her life, their loss did not alter her existence.

Now that she was living with her colleague, Ian, it frightened her to think how her whole life would change if he were to die. Every minute of every day, waking and sleeping, her world would be filled with the anguish of her loss. She experienced a visceral fear that had never gripped her until she and Ian started living together. For the first time in her life she had given a hostage to fortune, and she had never felt so vulnerable. Maybe that was the real reason she had once been able to deal so dispassionately with death. Terror of its power over life had not really touched her before now. Casting such morbid thoughts aside with an effort, she turned her attention to Julie's comments on Doreen's son. He was most definitely a person of interest. The sooner they questioned him the better.

Back at the police station, Geraldine typed up her report, happy to stay late and read whatever else had been recorded by her colleagues about Doreen Lewis. She had nothing to rush home for since Ian wasn't there waiting for her. His brother was visiting from overseas, and Ian had arranged to meet him in London. He wasn't going away for long, but the time had begun to drag miserably after just two days, so Geraldine was pleased to find herself allocated to an investigation. Doing her best to ignore the fact that she was happy a dead woman had come along to occupy her, she reread her own notes. In retrospect, she realised her interview with Julie had been unsatisfactory. Julie's comments about Doreen's son had been speculative, riddled with innuendos but lacking any real substance.

The next morning, resolving to ignore her friend's surly behaviour on the previous day, Geraldine approached Ariadne and invited her over for supper one evening that week.

'There's no need to do that,' Ariadne snapped. 'I can live without your pity, thank you very much.'

Geraldine was taken aback. 'Ariadne, what are you talking about? What pity? If anything, you should be feeling sorry for me. Ian's only been away for two days and I'm already missing him.'

'What? Oh, okay. Sorry, I didn't know he wasn't around at the moment.'

'So what was that about?' Geraldine enquired, really concerned about her friend.

Ariadne merely shook her head, muttering that it was nothing, and abruptly left her desk. Geraldine determined to find out what was going on. She kept an eye on Ariadne and at lunchtime she followed her to the canteen and sat down at her table.

'I knew you'd be along,' Ariadne said ungraciously. 'What do you want now?'

'I want to know why you're so miserable.'

'I'm not miserable.'

'You refused to talk to me yesterday.'

'I didn't refuse to talk to you.'

'And you snapped at me this morning,' Geraldine went on, 'and you're being hostile now. And what was that about being pitied? What's happened? I think you owe me an explanation.'

Ariadne scowled. 'I don't owe you anything –' she began, and sighed. 'Oh, all right, it's true I've been behaving like a spoilt child, I know. But I can't talk about it here.' She glanced around as though afraid someone might be listening.

'Why don't you come over this evening and we can talk over a glass of wine and a takeaway?' Geraldine suggested. 'You'd be doing me a favour, really. Like I said, I'm lonely without Ian.'

'Love's young dream,' Ariadne muttered sourly.

Geraldine said nothing. Evidently Ariadne's honeymoon had not gone well after all. They finished their lunch in silence. Only a month had passed since Geraldine had watched Ariadne celebrating her wedding as a joyful bride. It was hard to believe she was the same woman who now sat wretchedly picking at her food. Her curly hair had lost its sheen, she was reluctant to meet Geraldine's gaze, and she seemed to be gripped by abject misery. Geraldine didn't want to press Ariadne to talk at work, but she resolved to do her best to persuade her friend to share her concerns. Late that afternoon, Geraldine was about to call by Ariadne's desk and arrange for her to come over, when she was summoned by the detective chief inspector. Doreen's son had been located but was refusing to answer questions.

'Where was he?' Geraldine asked.

Eileen nodded briskly. 'I say he was found, but he wasn't

exactly hiding. A neighbour called us to say he had returned home.'

Geraldine didn't need to be told the identity of the neighbour who had called the police. She drove straight to Doreen's house which now belonged to her son, Eddy, and found him sitting at a small table in the kitchen. There was a faint smell of burnt toast, and the sink was filled with dirty plates. He looked at Geraldine apprehensively, perhaps because a uniformed constable was stationed in his hall. With plump wrists emerging from his sleeves and a chubby face, he might have resembled a Renaissance cherub, were it not for his scowl. Small deep-set black eyes glared at her from his round face, so that he resembled a sullen oversized child rather than an angelic being. Scratching at his unevenly shaven chin with stubby fingers, he spoke in a curiously high-pitched voice, complaining that he hadn't invited any police officers into the house and he wanted them to go away and leave him alone. When he stopped talking, his bottom lip hung slackly, giving him a foolish air.

'Eddy, you're not under suspicion,' Geraldine replied.

That wasn't strictly true. She was aware of the irony in her trying to gain his trust with lies, but she suspected he was frightened. Eddy continued to glare at her from under lowered brows.

'We don't think you've done anything wrong,' she explained slowly and carefully, unsure how much he understood. 'We just want to ask you a few questions about your mother.' She wondered how far she ought to question him on his own.

'Where is she?' he asked unexpectedly. 'Why isn't she here? She's always here.'

Geraldine spoke as gently as she could. 'I'm afraid your mother's not coming home,' she said, instinctively talking to him as though he was a child. 'I'm sorry to tell you your mother is dead.'

Eddy's response was so surprising, Geraldine wondered whether it might actually be a calculated attempt to appear childishly innocent.

'What about my supper? Who's going to make my supper now? She always makes my supper.'

He seemed more put out that his mother wasn't at home to cook for him, than that she was dead.

'We're looking into the circumstances surrounding her death,' Geraldine said softly.

'What do you want with me?' he demanded. 'If she's not here, I'm going to be busy enough, aren't I? I'll have to make my own supper. I'm going to have beans.'

He seemed incapable of looking at Geraldine directly, and scarcely acknowledged what she had told him. It wasn't just that he was shy, or socially awkward. There was something almost sly about his reaction to hearing about Doreen's death. Geraldine recalled what Julie had said about him. She tried not to be influenced by other people's opinions, but she found herself agreeing with Julie. There was something decidedly odd about Eddy. When she asked him where he had been for the past twenty-four hours, he shook his head and refused to answer the question.

'I don't have to tell you anything,' he replied. 'You're a stranger. I'm not even supposed to be talking to you. Did my mother let you in? If she's dead, I never killed her. Go away and leave me alone. I don't have to answer any questions.'

Geraldine hid her astonishment. Perhaps he wasn't as capable of cunning as she had first suspected. But even if he was pretending to be vacuous, it wouldn't help his case. Stupidity was no guarantee of innocence. She spoke more firmly.

'Eddy, you do understand that we need you to account for your movements? You have to tell us where you were yesterday evening, and where you have been ever since.'

'No,' he replied, his eyes flicking around the room and

looking everywhere but at his interlocutor, 'I don't have to tell you anything. I don't know you.'

'You realise that refusing to talk to the police is bound to attract suspicion,' she said. 'We can continue this at the police station if you won't co-operate here. And we can ask someone you know to come with you.'

Eddy merely shook his head. 'I don't want anyone to come with me anywhere. I want you to leave me alone,' he said. 'This is my house now,' he added proudly.

Even though he was sitting down, Geraldine could see he was a short man. From that angle, his torso appeared almost stunted. When he rose to his feet, she found herself looking down on him.

'You know you will need to account for your movements on the day of your mother's death,' she said. 'It would be better for you if you did so straight away.'

Eddy didn't answer and Geraldine left.

'He'll have to accept sooner or later that he can't go on refusing to speak to us,' Eileen said irritably when Geraldine reported on her lack of success with Eddy. 'Let's bring him in and question him here. Perhaps the duty brief will talk some sense into him. And if that fails, I dare say a night in a cell will persuade him to talk.'

Everyone agreed with Eileen that Eddy was the most likely suspect. Doreen had owned her house, along with some savings, and her son was her sole beneficiary, so he had a motive of sorts, as well as ample opportunity, and as far as they knew he had no alibi. It was almost an open and shut case.

'We still can't be sure it was him,' Geraldine pointed out. 'This is all circumstantial.'

'He had motive, access to the house – there's no sign of any break-in, remember – and so far he's refused to account for his movements at the time of Doreen's death,' Eileen said with an air of finality. 'She was attacked at home, and he's the only one who stands to benefit from her death. It's obvious he's guilty. He must have thought we wouldn't be able to put two and two together and come up with the right answer, and now he doesn't know how to get out of it. The whole thing is completely stupid, of course, but we know he's not the sharpest tool in the toolbox. Only someone really stupid would have imagined they could pull it off. He seems to think if he doesn't say anything, he won't be apprehended.'

Geraldine agreed it was possible Eddy was guilty, but something didn't seem quite right.

'Surely if he had killed his mother he would be making some attempt to deny it,' she said. 'He doesn't seem to realise he's a suspect. At first he didn't even seem to know she was dead. He asked me where she was. And wouldn't he have arranged an alibi of some sort, if he's guilty?'

'Unless it wasn't planned,' Eileen replied.

'Perhaps he and his mother didn't get on and he snapped,' Ariadne suggested. 'You don't always know what other people are capable of,' she added in a low voice.

Geraldine resolved to speak to Ariadne again, but in the meantime she had to think about Eddy.

'I think we need to treat him carefully,' she said. 'He has a learning disability.'

'That could be an act,' a constable said.

Geraldine hesitated. She had contacted social services but the only response she had received was that Eddy's mother had been responsible for him, and he had been able to work and support himself. They had not been aware of any problems.

'We do have real issues to deal with,' the social worker had barked, when Geraldine had persisted.

'This is all speculation,' Eileen replied grimly. 'I dare say it won't be long before his lawyer claims he can't be held responsible for his actions. But even if he has a learning disability, if he killed his mother, we need to get him behind bars so he can't be a danger to anyone else he happens to fall out with. So let's start finding some more evidence. SOCOs found traces of DNA in her hair. And in the meantime, we'll bring him in and question him about his mother's death.'

Geraldine nodded uncertainly.

'If he continues to refuse to divulge his whereabouts at the time of his mother's death, we have no other choice,' Eileen added. 'Arrest him for obstructing our enquiry if we don't have anything else to hold him on. Once we have him locked up, it will just be a matter of time before he accepts it's all over and confesses. So come on, let's get this one wrapped up.'

Geraldine was taken aback by Eileen's pronouncement. Always brusque, the detective chief inspector appeared to be condemning Eddy just because he was Doreen's son and stood to gain materially by her death. Certainly people had been killed for less than a house, but it seemed peremptory to suggest that Eddy was guilty without any physical proof. Geraldine sighed. Already concerned about Ariadne, she now had another colleague to worry about, a colleague who was in charge of a murder investigation.

5

LOUISA'S PARENTS RAN A small but thriving tea shop in Whitby. Both her mother and father had done their best to persuade Louisa to stay with them. It wasn't that she didn't like Whitby, although in the summer it became quite claustrophobic, every street packed with chattering tourists. Her parents' tea shop was busy then. Sometimes there were queues outside in the street. Indoors, there was always one woman with a penetrating voice, shrill tones ringing out nonstop above the general hum of conversation. It was a different woman each day, but there was always one, and sometimes a crying baby as well. And when the tea shop was closed, and they could have enjoyed a quiet evening, her mother would be there, yacking away. The constant jabbering irritated Louisa and she longed for some peace and privacy. Her favourite season was autumn, before the weather turned bitterly cold, when she could walk along the deserted seafront, lost in her own thoughts.

If the holiday season was busy, it was not really much better working in the tea shop through the winter, sitting at a table, waiting for an occasional customer to turn up and give her something to do.

Whitby was her home, and she loved all its little winding streets, and shops with their displays of polished jet-black ornaments and jewellery. She had done her best to explain to her parents that it was the very familiarity of the place that made her so keen to get away. More than keen, she was desperate. Sometimes she had felt like screaming with longing to move away and experience something different in her life. Her mother, who had lived all her life in Whitby, seemed incapable of understanding Louisa's desire to leave. Her father, who had once lived in London, ought to have understood. He knew there was a world to explore outside Whitby. People from elsewhere visited Whitby all the time, bringing with them an air of adventure and excitement. Her father grew animated, discussing places he had visited before he married Beattie. He, of all people, should have understood his daughter's hunger for adventure.

Eventually Louisa stopped trying to explain her wishes to her parents. After searching for a few months, she found a job in York. Her mother flatly refused to accept that Louisa was choosing to leave home to go and work in a hotel elsewhere, when she already had a perfectly good job right there in Whitby.

'What can you possibly hope to find in York that you can't find here in Whitby?' she had asked. 'What's wrong with us? With the town? Isn't it picturesque enough for you? Aren't the people here friendly enough? You're a fool if you think life will be any better in a big city. You couldn't be more wrong.'

'How would you know?' Louisa had countered, stung into retorting. 'You've never lived anywhere but Whitby, and that's made you narrow-minded. There's a whole world out there. You might be happy to live your entire life ignorant of anywhere but this one small town, but I'm not.'

Somehow the more her mother nagged, the more determined Louisa had been to leave Whitby and embark on a life of her own.

'I just want to be independent,' she said. 'It's my life.'

'You can't go,' her mother had insisted, resorting to tears in her attempt to persuade Louisa to change her mind. 'You can't leave Whitby. How will we manage without you?'

'I'm sorry, but you're going to have to. You managed all right before I was born, didn't you?' Louisa replied, guilt making her cruel. 'You have to let me live my life. I can't always be here as your skivvy. I'm only talking about going to York,' she added, relenting a little. 'It's not like I'm moving to the other side of the world. York's only fifty miles away.'

As things turned out, the move had not proved as thrilling as Louisa had anticipated. The job itself was fine. The hotel manager was friendly and efficient. With her blonde ponytail swinging behind her, and her steely blue eyes, she had quickly put Louisa to work in the housekeeping department. Although it took Louisa a few weeks to understand what was expected of her, it was really quite easy once she faced up to the challenge of familiarising herself with the system. Her fellow chamber maids were all foreign, and most of them spoke limited English. The one exception was Shona. She was dark-haired and came from Edinburgh. She seemed very friendly, but Louisa soon learned that her colleague's sociability only lasted during the working day. Louisa's tentative suggestion that they go out for a drink together was quickly dismissed. Louisa didn't ask again. She had left her old friends behind in Whitby without a second thought. If the price of her independence was to face unaccustomed loneliness, she would just have to get used to it. She could hardly return home to Whitby so soon, after fighting so hard to leave. And she was never going to crawl back to her mother. After passing her day trundling her trolley along the corridors, straightening bed covers, emptying bins, and replacing towels and sachets of tea and coffee, she didn't really mind the novelty of being alone in the evenings. But something was bothering her, and it was far more disturbing than spending time in her own company.

It started one day when she was on her way home from work. Her rented flat in Dale Street was only about half a mile away from the hotel, and although it was basic it was certainly convenient because she could walk to work and back, passing Micklegate Bar, one of the city's huge medieval stone gateways. The turreted grey monolith once guarded the entrance to the city, and was redolent of ancient conflicts. Weeks after her arrival in York it still gave her a thrill to walk past it. Seeing it towering over her, she felt as though she was reaching out and touching history. At first she paid no attention to any of the people walking behind her along Nunnery Lane when she went back to her digs at the end of her shift. Against the hum of traffic and the drone of voices, she barely noticed footsteps behind her. She was walking along a busy street, so there were often other people around in the evening, on their way home from work, or going out for the evening. But when she turned off the busy main road she was vaguely aware of someone walking behind her. All at once, she had a strange feeling that she was being followed.

Dismissing her suspicion as nonsense, she continued on her way home, involuntarily increasing her speed. Behind her, the footsteps seemed to quicken their pace as she drew close to her lodgings. Feeling in her bag for her keys, she forced herself to resist the temptation to look round as she dashed up to the front door, opened it and flung herself inside. Standing in her own studio flat with the door closed, she stared at the locked door, trembling. She half expected someone to come crashing through it, but no one did. No one even knocked on her door. She hadn't realised how fast she had been running but she was panting now, her breath coming in hoarse gasps. Slowly she sank into a chair, shaking with delayed shock. Gradually her breath slowed, her heart stopped racing, and she sat back to take stock of what had just happened. Nothing. Her terror was her own fault, a product of her overactive imagination. She had been spending too much time alone.

On Sunday she had the day off, with nothing to do but wander around the centre of town where even the allure of the extensive shopping centre had palled. After three months in the city, she was suddenly overwhelmed by homesickness and was tempted to visit her parents only that would have felt like she was retreating home, defeated. So she resolved to stick it out in York. It was a beautiful city and she hadn't yet spent time exploring the streets and sights. She had the whole day free, and decided to visit the cathedral precinct. Finding she could walk all the way round it, she made her way through the crowds by the entrance to a small café, where she sat outside and watched the people passing by an ancient house that stood in the shadow of the Minster. Centuries ago, a small girl suspected of having the plague had allegedly been imprisoned there. People said that her ghost still haunted the house, and a small child could often be seen waving desperately through the window, begging to be set free.

After about half an hour Louisa became aware of a lone figure who, like her, was completely still in all the bustle of people walking by. He was perched on a low fence pillar opposite the café where she was seated. The man didn't appear to be moving a muscle, although it must have been difficult to balance there, not to mention uncomfortable. It was his stillness that first caught her attention. There seemed to be something almost other-worldly about it.

When she was preparing to leave, at the periphery of her vision she noticed him stir. As though they were connected by an invisible cord, he stood up at just the same moment as her. She spotted him again on Lendal Bridge, walking a few feet behind her. He wasn't looking at her but she had an uneasy feeling he was watching her. It was alarming, but she did her best to dismiss the idea that the stranger was stalking her. There was nothing remarkable about a man sitting in Minster Yard looking at the cathedral, and then leaving at the same time as her. He just happened to be walking in the same direction as her. She walked hurriedly. It was only about a mile to Dale Street, but it seemed to take her a long time. Reaching her front door and glancing around, she was relieved to see that the stranger had not followed her home. She didn't mention the incident when her mother phoned her that evening, nor did she mention it to anyone else. After all, nothing had happened, and she had no intention of showing herself up as a hysterical fool in front of her colleagues at work. But she was unnerved all the same and found it difficult not to dwell on her mother's warnings against life in the city.

'As a single woman, you're vulnerable to all sorts of strange men,' her mother had told her. 'You won't be safe, and you'll never feel safe.'

6

'No Ian again?' Jonah greeted Geraldine. 'What is going on with you two?'

Waving a scalpel at her across the table, the ginger-haired pathologist looked like a character out of a horror film, his ugly pug-like face grinning at her above gloved hands smeared with blood.

'You can't keep visiting me without a chaperone like this. People will start to talk,' he went on, chiding her with pretend severity. 'We don't want to start a scandal at the police station.' He rolled his eyes in mock horror.

Geraldine had worked with Jonah Hetherington on a number of cases, and she laughed at his teasing. His cheery banter was a welcome contrast to Ariadne's sullenness.

'You're such a flirt,' she scolded in return. 'Now come on, let's talk about her.'

'Ah yes, a woman who can't answer back,' Jonah said. 'You can see why I love my job.'

Geraldine laughed again and nodded at the body. 'What can you tell me about her?'

'Always harping on about work,' Jonah grumbled sullenly. 'And I thought you'd come here to see me. Oh, very well, let's talk about work if you insist.'

They both looked down at the body of a woman, lying on her back, her face twisted in a fixed grimace. She had very pale eyes, and her mottled skin looked dry as parchment. At odds with her withered legs and misshapen frame, there was an air of haughty determination in her expression that seemed to intimate she had once been a forceful character.

'For such a frail woman, there's something determined about her expression, don't you think?' Geraldine murmured, although she could not have said why, exactly. 'It's just a feeling,' she added, seeing Jonah's eyebrows rise at her words.

'I didn't think you had feelings,' he replied with a wry smile. 'Does this mean there's hope for me yet?'

Ignoring his teasing, Geraldine stared at the dead woman's face. 'Don't you think there's something unyielding in her expression? She doesn't look very gentle, does she?'

Jonah shrugged. 'I don't know about that. She looks very dead to me.'

Silently, Geraldine wondered whether the dead woman had been difficult to live with, and if her son had indeed killed her. He was due to inherit his mother's house and her modest savings. People had been killed for less. Perhaps his mother had aggravated him beyond endurance, and in desperation he had decided to get rid of her, and cash in. He might have been driven by a sudden fit of anger. Shaking off her speculation, she asked Jonah what he could gather from the corpse. She knew it was crucial for a detective to focus on evidence, and not be distracted by stray possibilities. It was easy to be led by a theory, misinterpreting evidence to fit a particular assumption which might turn out to be false. Clearing her mind of all suspicion, she listened carefully to the pathologist.

'She was strangled,' Jonah said, suddenly serious. He indicated dark bruising on the dead woman's neck. 'As you know, it's impossible to pin down an exact time of death, even in known and stable conditions, but I'd say she was still alive at midday, and probably for a couple of hours after that, because the medical examiner at the scene reported rigor had set in only in the smaller muscles of her face and neck by four o'clock. It hadn't yet reached any of the larger muscles. Her assailant attacked her from behind, strangling her with what was in all probability a length of rope. You can see the pattern of contusions, and we found minute threads lodged in the stratum corneum, the top layer of the epidermis, or skin,' he added, seeing Geraldine's perplexed expression. 'I think he may have been wearing woollen gloves, or perhaps a jumper. It's difficult to be sure, but we found a few threads of dark fibre adhering to her fingers. They've all gone off for examination, so we should know more about them soon.'

'Is there anything you can tell us about the killer? Height? Anything at all? Was he right or left handed?'

Jonah grunted. 'There's nothing I can tell you that would confirm beyond any doubt that the killer was a man, but it would take some physical strength to kill like this, so I'm guessing the killer was probably male, but it could have been a powerful woman. I don't think this poor victim would have had the strength to put up much resistance. You can see how frail she was.'

'At least physically,' Geraldine added.

Jonah looked up sharply but didn't respond to her comment.

'So, to summarise, she was strangled – almost garrotted – most probably with a piece of rope,' Jonah said. 'We found fibres which have gone off for forensic examination but I'm not sure they'll be able to identify the source.'

'SOCOs found traces of DNA in the woman's hair, so we'll know more very soon,' she said. 'In the meantime, can you hazard a guess at the height of the killer?'

Jonah shook his head. 'She was significantly shorter than her attacker but that really doesn't help us because she was probably sitting down when she was killed. DNA was found in her hair, so someone might have been leaning over her when she was killed. I take it there was no evidence of anyone else having been present?'

'As far as we know, only the victim and her son lived there, and he doesn't appear to have an alibi.'

'There was one odd thing,' Jonah added.

Geraldine waited, hardly daring to hope that Jonah had found something helpful.

'We can't be sure of the reason, but a clump of her hair is missing.'

He indicated a small bald area on the back of the victim's scalp. Her hair was generally thick and coarse, apart from the one bare patch. Geraldine stared at it, slightly surprised. She had noticed it but had assumed Jonah had cut away a section of hair on the dead woman's head in the course of his examination.

'Could the hair have been torn out during the attack?'

Jonah shook his head. 'No, it wasn't pulled out. It was cut off, very close to the roots. Look.'

Geraldine bent forward. 'And that wasn't your handiwork?'

'I think I'd remember if it was. But it must have been cut off very recently, not necessarily when she was killed, although that seems likely. There was no disturbance of the skin, and –' He paused, frowning. 'It looks as though the hair was cut post mortem. SOCOs found a few stray hairs that are the right length. They were found on the carpet near the body. But there was no sign of the rest of the cut-off section of hair. It seems the killer took it away with him, perhaps as a kind of macabre trophy.'

'Or to dispose of it,' Geraldine said, 'if he'd sneezed on it, perhaps.'

'Yes, very true. The killer may have realised he had let fall a drop of saliva or nasal mucus on her hair, and was concerned to remove any trace of his identity. If so, he failed,' he added with grim satisfaction.

'Well, it's a charming image,' Geraldine said. 'Would he have had scissors to hand?'

As she asked the question, she recalled seeing a knitting basket on the table which might have contained a pair of scissors. A careful killer could have taken some with him and disposed of them after using them.

'But you still need to check out the DNA in Doreen's hair, which ties in with her being attacked from behind. He seems to have left a few droplets of saliva behind.'

Geraldine felt the tautness of the muscles in her face as she smiled. 'Let's hope that's enough.'

But she knew it wouldn't be enough to secure a conviction. All they might possibly use the DNA for would be to establish that someone had been in contact with the victim; what with her son and her carers, and anyone else who might have visited her shortly before she died, it might not be an indication of anything suspicious. Even the hair that had been cut might turn out to have an innocent explanation.

'Careful, but not careful enough,' Eileen said, when Geraldine told her about the results of the post mortem. 'He couldn't prevent us from finding traces of his DNA. That will confirm her son's guilt.'

Once again, it struck Geraldine that the detective chief inspector seemed unusually ready to jump to conclusions. Finding Eddy's DNA on his mother's body would only confirm that he had been in close contact with her on the day she died. It could hardly be taken as confirmation that he had killed her.

7

A CONSTABLE DISPATCHED TO collect Eddy had not yet been able to locate him. He was not at home and had quit his job not long before his mother's death.

Eileen assembled the team to discuss this development. 'We have to find him,' she snapped. 'This is a priority. According to the manager of the café where he was briefly employed, he walked out for no reason on Friday, the day before his mother was killed. His disappearance seems to give a further indication the murder was premeditated.'

'Doreen and Eddy might have disagreed about his quitting his job,' Ariadne suggested. 'He could have lost his temper while they were arguing, and strangled her.'

'We can't make any assumptions without questioning him further,' Geraldine said.

'And in the meantime he's scarpered, which definitely makes him look suspicious,' Ariadne replied.

Eileen didn't seem to be unduly worried about finding Eddy, who had now been confirmed as a suspect. 'He can't have gone far.'

Geraldine was tasked with setting up surveillance at the local stations and bus terminals.

'If he is planning to do a runner, we'll find him,' Eileen said grimly.

Geraldine hoped she was right about that. Eddy's disappearance certainly seemed to confirm his guilt. She thought about the strange, almost childlike man she had questioned, and wondered whether he was capable of planning anything like this.

Meanwhile, there was a flurry of excitement at the police station when results of DNA tests on samples found in Doreen's house were reported. As expected, Doreen and Eddy's DNA and fingerprints were evident everywhere in the house. But other DNA was found on the body belonging to a man who was no relation to Doreen, and there were other prints that had not yet been identified once Doreen's carers had been eliminated from the enquiry. Unidentified DNA had been detected on the back of the victim's neck and hair, as well as on a chair in the living room. While Eddy remained a suspect, and had to be found, it was imperative they discover the identity of Doreen's unknown visitor.

Ariadne organised a team of constables to question all the residents in Portland Street to find out whether anyone had been spotted entering Doreen's house that day. Geraldine herself went to question Julie, who might have noticed what was going on next door.

'A stranger?' Julie repeated, her eyes alight with excitement. 'You're looking for a man who went next door to Doreen's on Saturday?'

Geraldine nodded, afraid she had already led Julie too much. She could almost see the other woman's mind working, piecing the clues together, and unintentionally fabricating details to fill any gaps.

'You think a stranger went there and killed her?' Julie asked at last.

'We are exploring every possibility.'

Julie shook her head. 'It was him,' she replied. 'Doreen's son, Eddy. I told you, he's strange. I hope you're not thinking of letting him go. I don't want to be living next door to a murderer. I'm telling you, there's something about him that gives me the creeps.'

'Eddy will be helping us with our enquiries,' Geraldine replied carefully. 'We have no evidence to suggest he's killed anyone.'

'Of course he killed her,' Julie replied impatiently. 'It's obvious it was him.'

Julie was unlikely to be hiding anything that might point to Eddy's guilt, as she seemed convinced he had killed Doreen and was desperate to see him convicted. But Geraldine had to be sure no one else could have been at the house on Saturday morning.

Refraining from mentioning that they didn't know where Eddy was, she reassured Julie that Eddy would be thoroughly investigated.

'We also need to know about anyone else who might have visited Doreen's house on Saturday morning. They might have useful information for us,' she added, implying that another witness might be able to help them convict Eddy.

Returning to her original question, she asked whether Julie had noticed anyone entering Doreen's house on the day she was murdered. Julie hesitated, and appeared to be thinking.

'There was a man,' she admitted at last, as though reluctant to acknowledge Doreen might have been killed by someone other than Eddy. 'He went there – oh, I don't know what time it was exactly, but it was sometime in the morning. I was cleaning my front windows or I would have missed him. I just happened to be looking out of the window and I saw a man going up Doreen's path. He was walking very quickly, and he was wearing a hood so I didn't see his face,' she added. 'I remember being puzzled because she doesn't have many visitors and all her carers are women. I nearly went and rang the bell, just to make sure everything was all right. Well, we have to look out for each other, don't we?'

Geraldine suspected Julie was making up her story as she went along.

'And this was definitely a man?'

Julie nodded.

'You would have recognised him if it was Eddy, though?' she said.

Julie nodded again. 'Yes,' she admitted with seeming reluctance. 'Whoever it was, he was taller than Eddy and not as fat, and Eddy has a funny way of walking. He sort of rolls from side to side as he walks, a bit like a duck.'

Suppressing her frustration that Julie hadn't mentioned this before, Geraldine focused on the stranger Julie had noticed going next door on the day of the murder, if such a person even existed.

'I didn't actually see him go in,' Julie said. 'I just saw him going through the gate.'

'Did you see him leave?' Geraldine asked, hoping Julie had caught a glimpse of the man's face.

But Julie shook her head. 'No, I wasn't looking out for long and I didn't see him leave. All I saw was the side of his head as he walked up the path, and his face was completely hidden. But it was definitely a man. I could tell from his clothes.'

It wasn't much to go on, but if Julie's account was true, someone else had visited Doreen on the day she died, a report that seemed to be confirmed by the DNA found at the scene. As she drove back to the police station, Geraldine wondered how trustworthy Julie's account was. If her account was accurate, she hadn't even been home all morning and she claimed to have seen a package on Doreen's doorstep on her way home from the shops. It was just as well Eddy had a clumsy way of walking, or Julie might have been convinced the unknown visitor was Doreen's son, and claimed to have seen him enter his mother's house at the time of her death. Geraldine wasn't convinced Julie was reliable, yet on reflection she was inclined to believe what Julie had said about an unidentified man going to her neighbour's house. If Julie had fabricated the story, she would have imagined seeing Eddy entering his mother's house the day she was killed. She seemed very keen for him to be convicted, yet she had been clear that it was not Eddy she had seen going to the house the day Doreen died.

Julie's story seemed to confirm that an unidentified man had gone to Doreen's house on the day she was killed. All they had was his DNA and a neighbour's unhelpful description of a shadowy figure who might be guilty of murder, or could be an innocent passerby. Meanwhile, constables were going door to door speaking to residents of Portland Street, and a team was tasked with scrutinising any CCTV in the area, searching for a man, possibly wearing a hood, walking towards or away from Doreen's road the previous Saturday. They quickly established that no one had been selling anything door to door that afternoon, and no one had knocked on any other door in Portland Street that day. In addition, none of Doreen's carers had been to see her at that time, the morning one having left at nine.

It was frustrating, knowing that Julie might have spotted Doreen's killer, yet was unable to tell them anything that could help them to find him. Eileen prowled around the police station with a long face, as was customary when an investigation was going slowly, and members of the team avoided her as far as possible. They were all waiting for the results of the visual images and identifications detection officers' search of CCTV, and checking comments from Doreen's neighbours. Both avenues had so far led nowhere. Apart from Julie's sighting of a hooded man next door, no one in Doreen's street seemed to have seen or heard anything unusual that day, or to have noticed a stranger in Portland Street. And they still hadn't found Eddy.

8

THAT EVENING, ARIADNE ACCEPTED Geraldine's invitation to supper. They agreed to get a takeaway and settled on Chinese. After a little discussion, during which Ariadne appeared distracted, they phoned for their order. As they settled down to wait, Geraldine opened a bottle of wine.

'This is good,' Ariadne said appreciatively as she took a sip of wine.

'Yes, I'm glad you like it,' Geraldine smiled. 'It's one Ian bought.'

'He won't mind, will he?'

Geraldine smiled again. 'He's not here, is he? And no, he wouldn't mind. He'd be pleased. And in any case, it's only wine. It's replaceable. Now, enough about the wine. What's going on with you? Ever since you came back from your honeymoon you've been like a bear with a sore head. I know it's a downer having to come back to work, but did something happen while you were away?'

Ariadne heaved a sigh and took several gulps of her wine. Geraldine was tempted to tell her to slow down. This was a wine to sip and savour, not to knock back, but she kept quiet. In her experience, it was best to remain silent when she wanted someone else to speak and, as Geraldine had hoped, Ariadne began to talk. Hesitant at first, she spoke with growing conviction as the alcohol started to take effect. Ariadne's hair was black, like Geraldine's, and fell to her shoulders in long loose curls. Brushing it back from her face, she described her honeymoon without once mentioning her husband. Geraldine listened patiently to descriptions of the hotel, and the location, and the food.

'And how was it with Nico? Did you get on?' Geraldine prompted her eventually. 'What happened between you?'

'The thing is, there's something wrong,' Ariadne finally admitted, her dark eyes filling with tears.

'Wrong? You mean in bed?' Geraldine asked, shocked to think that Nico might have married her friend concealing his sexual orientation.

Ariadne hastened to reassure her there had been no such duplicity.

'No, no, nothing like that. I'd have known before we got married, wouldn't I?'

Geraldine shrugged. 'It's not unknown for people to come out after the wedding. He might have felt under pressure to get married. Things like that happen, even now.'

'No, no, I told you, it's nothing like that. It's just that he's – well, he's secretive. And he says he can't stand me being a police officer. But the thing is, he knew all about my work before we even got engaged. He's always known what I do, and he's never minded before, not really. I mean, he's never liked what I do but he's accepted it. Only now that we're married, he seems different.'

'Does he want you to give it up?'

Ariadne shook her head. 'It's not that. I don't know what he wants, but there's something wrong.'

Geraldine nodded. She knew from her own experience how difficult it was to pursue a career on the force and maintain a relationship. When she was in her twenties, her boyfriend had struggled to cope with her irregular working hours and eventually they had split up. He had accused her of putting her career before him, and he had been right. Young and ambitious, she had been unable to cope with so many conflicting demands on her time. When her boyfriend had issued her with an ultimatum, she had refused to give up her career, and he had left her. She still stood by her decision. If he had really loved her, he would never have forced such a choice on her. Her partner, Ian, had experienced similar problems with his wife. She and Ian both hoped they would be able to deal with their relationship better, with the benefit of maturity and hindsight. Although they both knew only too well that many relationships between police officers failed due to the stresses and demands of the job, they still hoped their relationship would survive. It wasn't unheard of for police officers to be happily settled in relationships. All of this flashed through her mind, while Ariadne continued talking.

'Nico's changed. I think something happened and he's worried I'll find out.' She paused. 'I think he's met someone else.'

There was a ring at the bell and Geraldine went to fetch their food delivery. A brief hiatus in their conversation followed while they sorted out the different dishes, but at last they were seated at the table, with all the cartons open in front of them. Geraldine brought out a second bottle of wine.

'I shouldn't,' Ariadne said. 'I'm already over the limit as it is.'

'You can stay here tonight, or get a cab home,' Geraldine replied promptly. 'Now come on, eat up and hand over your glass. Good. Now, you were telling me about Nico.'

'There's nothing to tell, really,' Ariadne replied, but she looked close to tears. 'I'm probably just imagining things. You know how it is, newly-weds and all that. It's a big change and it's easy to get the wrong end of the stick.'

Geraldine didn't point out that since Ariadne and Nico had been living together before the wedding, being married couldn't have made a significant difference to their lives.

'You said you thought Nico's changed,' Geraldine reminded her gently.

Ariadne gave an awkward laugh. 'No, no, that was the drink

talking. Everything's fine.' She laughed again, very loudly.

'Ariadne, you're pissed.'

They both giggled, but beneath her façade of camaraderie, Geraldine was concerned, and she knew Ariadne was too. After another glass of wine, Ariadne unexpectedly burst into tears.

'He says he can't stay with me. He says he's no good for me and it can't work but he can't say why. Oh, Geraldine, he's moved out and I don't know where he is.' Ariadne broke off, unable to speak for sobbing.

Geraldine fetched a box of tissues and brewed some coffee and after a while her friend grew calm.

'I'm sorry, I'm sorry,' she mumbled, 'I don't know what came over me.'

'A combination of pent-up stress and too much booze, I'd say,' Geraldine replied, smiling anxiously. 'Did Nico give any indication as to why he was moving out?'

'No, and we haven't told anyone. I don't want my family to find out. Please don't say anything to anyone, Geraldine. My mother would be devastated and I'd never hear the end of it. I'm finding it hard enough to cope with what's happened as it is.'

'Don't worry, I won't say a word to anyone. But what about you and Nico? Don't you think you need to talk about this?'

'That's just the problem. We can't talk about it now he's gone, disappeared. Before he left, he refused to explain what had happened to make him change. It was like he became a stranger overnight.'

Haltingly, Ariadne explained that everything had been fine on their honeymoon. Nico had behaved completely normally. He had been his usual calm and cheerful self, and had shown her every consideration.

'We were happy,' she hiccupped. 'We were really happy. I knew I'd made the right decision, marrying him. We got home on Friday and everything was fine. He went out to see someone yesterday, and I know it sounds crazy, but when he came home, he was like a different person. I hardly recognised him. And he wouldn't tell me where he'd been or who he'd been with. He said it was something to do with his work, but that's not true. I know he's not due back at work until tomorrow.'

She paused. Geraldine tried to think of something reassuring to say. It was impossible to believe he had met someone else so soon after his marriage. If he was with another woman, it must be someone he knew before he married Ariadne, which made it even worse. It was hard to see how his strange behaviour could be due to another reason altogether. If he was gay, for example, Ariadne would surely have known.

'What exactly did he say?' she asked.

'Only that he was no good for me and it was never going to work. Why did he marry me?' she wailed.

'I think it's not uncommon for newly-weds to get the collywobbles,' Geraldine said gently, pouring Ariadne a cup of coffee. 'I'm sure this will sort itself out and he'll come to his senses. You know he loves you. It was all fine before you were married, wasn't it? I'm sure he'll come to his senses.'

Ariadne nodded, sniffing. 'I hope you're right,' she muttered. 'Just when everything seemed to be going so well… and now he won't even talk to me. I just want to know what's going on. Why won't he talk to me? I'm his wife.'

9

THE NEXT MORNING, EDDY was brought to the police station, protesting at the top of his voice. He was easily pacified with a cup of tea, and a plate of biscuits, while his mother's social worker was contacted. Eileen had issued instructions that Eddy be left alone for a while to calm down and consider his position. Geraldine refrained from remonstrating, although she doubted that Eddy was going to consider anything beyond whether or not he was going to be given any more biscuits, and when he would be allowed to go home. While they were waiting for a duty brief to arrive, he was left alone, as the detective chief inspector had suggested.

Finally the social worker and the duty brief both arrived and the interview could proceed. The social worker seemed flustered, insisting that she had supervised care for Doreen, not for Eddy himself, and she knew nothing about his mother's death. Once she had been reassured that social services were not implicated in the investigation into Doreen's death, she explained that she had not been involved with Eddy, whose mother had accepted full responsibility for him. She had, however, met Eddy on several occasions and he said he was happy for her to accompany him to his interview.

After a few hours in a cell, Eddy entered the interview room looking even more dishevelled than when Geraldine last saw him. His T-shirt was creased and sweat-stained, his jeans were loose, and his shoes were scuffed. Watching him from across the table, Geraldine could see that he was probably only a little over five feet tall. Beside the constable who accompanied him, he looked like a disgruntled gnome. He dropped down on to a chair and sat wriggling awkwardly, like a man uncomfortable in his own skin. Geraldine wondered if he suffered from piles, he seemed to find it so difficult to sit still. Close up, his cheeks looked oddly sunken, like a deflated balloon, his skin was slightly greyish, and he appeared dazed, perhaps from lack of sleep. He rubbed his bloodshot eyes with the back of a dirty hand and yawned, making no attempt to hide his uneven teeth. At his side, a shabby-looking lawyer lowered himself into a chair and gazed incuriously at the two detectives, while the social worker kept looking pointedly at her watch and sighing loudly.

'Eddy, you understand your mother's dead?' Geraldine began. 'We're very sorry for your loss, but we do need to know where you were between midday and three o'clock on Saturday afternoon.'

Eddy folded his arms and pressed his normally slack lips together, refusing to reply.

Glancing at Eddy, the lawyer requested a moment alone with his client, and the two men left the room, with the social worker trailing after them. Geraldine and Ariadne waited impatiently for them to return. When they reconvened, the lawyer shook his head at Geraldine, clearly nonplussed.

'My client has nothing to say,' he announced, almost furtively. 'Unless you are in a position to formally charge him with having committed a crime, it is time for him to go home.'

Eddy's broad face broke into a grin. 'Can I go home?'

His expression darkened immediately, as though he had just remembered that his mother would not be at home to give him dinner. Geraldine glanced at the poker-faced lawyer, before leaning towards Eddy with a smile of encouragement.

'Eddy,' she said, 'tell us about yourself.'

He shrugged one sloping shoulder, and his eyes met her gaze and darted away again, like nervous flies.

'What about me?' he asked gruffly. 'There's nothing about me. I don't have to say anything.'

Realising how frightened he was, Geraldine spoke gently.

'Do you have a job?'

'Had one,' he replied tersely.

'Tell us about your job,' Geraldine urged him, as though she was genuinely interested.

'I was serving customers,' he said, unexpectedly expansive. 'Taking their orders. It was a good job and I'm a good worker.'

'So you liked your job?'

'Was all right.'

'Why did you leave?'

'Because of Kylie, of course.'

Geraldine hesitated. Now that Eddy was prepared to start talking, it seemed there was a lot to unravel. She decided to begin by asking for more details about his job. There might be other people working there who could tell her about him. At the moment, the only people the police knew about who had come into contact with Eddy were his dead mother, and an inquisitive neighbour who had observed him from a distance but had never really spoken to him.

'Where was your job?'

Eddy answered readily enough, giving the name of a small café in town.

Geraldine nodded. 'And what exactly was your role there?'

Eddy spoke as though he had learned the answer by rote. 'I ask customers very politely what they want, write down their orders carefully, and pass the information on to Daryl who works the till.'

Geraldine was about to ask another question but Eddy continued, barely pausing for breath.

'As soon as the customer pays, I pass the order to whoever is making the drinks. I was learning to work the coffee machine,' he added wistfully. 'It's not as easy as it looks and it's really noisy and you have to be careful to put the right amount of coffee grounds in and push down hard. We don't want to waste coffee or make any mess. It's my job to take the drinks over to the waiting area, and sometimes there's a tray with cups and milk and everything on it, as well as food if the customer orders food. It isn't an easy job, because we aren't allowed to spill anything, not even a drop. Not ever. If we do, we have to pay for it out of our wages. I never did spill anything, not one drop,' he concluded, with evident pride.

Geraldine gave another nod. 'It sounds as though you were very conscientious. Tell me again why you left the job. Didn't you like it there?'

Eddy's eyes darted skittishly around the room. 'It's a good job,' he repeated. 'I'm a good worker.'

'So tell me why you left. Was that your idea, or did they ask you to leave?'

'It was because of Kylie, of course,' he repeated.

'What do you mean? Was she working in the café with you? Did you fall out?'

'No, no, no, she doesn't work there. That was me. I worked there, but I had to leave, because of Kylie,' he repeated with exaggerated patience. 'I can't carry on working there and devote myself to her, can I? There isn't enough time for everything. You know that. You're not stupid.'

'I see. And who is Kylie?'

'She's my girlfriend.'

'Why do you need to devote all your time to her?'

'Because I love her,' Eddy answered simply.

'I'm not sure I follow you, so help me understand why seeing your girlfriend meant leaving your job.'

'I want to spend as much time as possible with her,' Eddy repeated, rolling his eyes as though Geraldine was being really slow. 'I can always find another job.'

'Tell me more about Kylie. Does she have any special

requirements that mean she needs you to be with her all day?'

Eddy shook his head, frowning. 'Kylie's perfect.'

'I see,' Geraldine said again, although she didn't. 'And now tell us where you were on Saturday afternoon. Start at the beginning, from when you woke up, and tell us where you went and everything you did that day. Think carefully before you answer.'

Eddy frowned. 'I was at home and then I went out.'

'What time did you go out?'

'I went out at eight to wait for Kylie to go to work. She was working on Saturday so I knew what time she was going out. There was no point in getting there too early, because I would only have waited longer to see her.'

He lowered his eyes and his cheeks flushed slightly, whether with embarrassment or apprehension was impossible to determine.

'I don't understand,' Geraldine said. 'Why did you want to wait for Kylie if she was going to work?'

'To see her,' he replied simply. 'I love her.'

'What happened between you and your mother before you went out?' Geraldine asked softly.

'Nothing happened.'

'You'll have to do better than that,' Geraldine said. 'What did you say to each other? Tell us what happened.'

'Nothing happened. I didn't see her, that's all. She was asleep when I went out.'

'Are you sure you didn't see her?'

'I'm sure.'

'How do you know she was asleep?'

Eddy sighed. 'I don't know. But she's never up that early.'

'How did you know she was asleep?' Ariadne asked, taking over the questioning.

The shabby lawyer cleared his throat. 'My client has already told you he didn't see his mother before he went out.'

'Didn't you say goodbye to your mother when you went out?'

Eddy shook his head. 'No, I just went out.'

'You didn't even call out to say goodbye?'

He shook his head again. 'No. I thought she was asleep. So there was no point in saying goodbye. She wouldn't have heard me and, if she did, she would have been cross with me for waking her up.'

Geraldine leaned forward. 'Eddy, it's very important you tell us the truth now. Think very carefully. Did you see your mother before you went out?'

Eddy shook his head. 'No, I just told her.' He glanced at Ariadne. 'I went out to see Kylie. What I did and where I went was nothing to do with my mother,' he added, with a burst of irritation. 'It was none of her business.'

At Eddy's side, the lawyer stirred in his crumpled suit.

'My client's girlfriend is not the issue here,' he said. 'He has not come here to be questioned about his private life.'

'Oh please,' Geraldine replied impatiently. 'You know as well as I do that nothing is private in a murder investigation. Eddy,' she went on, turning back to the suspect, 'did your mother get on well with your girlfriend?'

'What do you mean?'

'Were they on good terms? Did they like each other?'

'I don't know. They never met.'

'But your mother didn't like you seeing Kylie, did she? Was she angry about you giving up your job, was that it?'

Eddy nodded, his face reddening with temper. 'She said we needed the money,' he replied. 'That was all she ever thought about. "How are we going to manage if you're not earning, Eddy? You can't expect me to support you forever. How are you going to manage when I'm gone, Eddy?" on and on and on. She wouldn't shut up about it.'

'So you shut her up?'

'That's not what he said at all,' the social worker muttered.

65

'I went out, and I stayed out all day.' Eddy sniggered. 'She didn't like that. And it served her right.'

'Where were you on Saturday night? Were you with Kylie?'

Eddy looked down. 'When I tried to go home, there were police cars everywhere and I couldn't get past them, so I went away again.'

'Did you stay with Kylie?'

'I went back to her house, yes.'

Geraldine put the next question without any preamble. 'Why did you cut your mother's hair?'

Eddy looked surprised. 'I never cut her hair. The carer who came, she did everything like that. She cut my hair as well,' he added with a wistful smile.

The lawyer requested a break, insisting he needed to speak to his client.

'Just as he was about to tell us how much he hated his mother,' Ariadne fumed.

'That doesn't mean he killed her,' Geraldine said. 'He doesn't strike me as particularly bright, but there's no evidence to suggest he's a killer. A lot of people get angry with their parents but not everyone resorts to murder to shut them up.'

Ariadne glared at Geraldine for a second, then laughed. 'I suppose I asked for that,' she said.

'No,' Geraldine lied, 'I wasn't thinking about what you told me about your mother. It's well known that a lot of people find their mothers intrusive.'

'But not you,' Ariadne replied, with a hint of reproof in her tone. 'I suppose you were always the perfect daughter.'

Geraldine's relationship with her mother was complicated and she didn't feel inclined to discuss it with Ariadne, at least not while they were involved in a murder investigation. The truth was that she had been given away at birth, only discovering her adopted status by accident when she was an adult, after her adoptive mother's death. As for her birth mother, she had died shortly after her first meeting with Geraldine.

'No, I wouldn't say I was perfect,' she replied. 'But it's complicated.'

'Mothers and daughters always are,' Ariadne sighed.

'So if Eddy didn't cut a patch of hair from his mother, I wonder who did.'

They checked with the carers who visited Doreen's house, all of whom denied having left her with a small bald patch on the top of her head. None of them had seen it, and most were certain they would have noticed it.

Eileen wasted no time in instructing Geraldine to arrest Eddy. 'Of course he's committed a crime,' she fumed when she heard what the lawyer had said. 'At the very least we can hold him on the grounds of obstructing our enquiries,' she said. 'As for killing his mother, I can't see him holding out on us for very long once he knows he's our only suspect.'

'Apart from the unknown person who left a trace of DNA in Doreen's hair,' Geraldine muttered, but in the absence of any definite evidence to the contrary, she held back from openly challenging her senior officer's conviction that Eddy was guilty.

They agreed to hold Eddy overnight and speak to him again in the morning. Eileen was confident a night in a cell would persuade him to finally start telling the truth but Geraldine was uneasy, not only about the way Eddy was being treated, but about the grounds for holding him at all.

10

EDDY HAD BEEN HELD in custody overnight but, without evidence on which to hold him, they would have to release him before the end of the day. Eileen sent Geraldine to question him again, with instructions to push harder for a confession.

'I can't get him to admit to something he didn't do,' Geraldine grumbled but Eileen sniffed dismissively.

'He's the only person with an obvious motive to kill her, and he had the opportunity to do it. He's admitted he was in the house with her on Saturday when she was killed, for goodness sake. How much more proof do we need?'

Muttering that the detective chief inspector's evidence was all circumstantial, Geraldine went to question Eddy again.

'Eddy,' she began,' when you went out on Saturday, did you go anywhere on a bus or a train? If you did, we can trace your journey and confirm your story.'

Eddy looked surprised. 'What story?' he asked, in genuine perplexity.

Geraldine repeated her question but Eddy told her he had walked to see Kylie.

Eddy's lawyer was sounding frustrated. 'Charge my client or release him,' he said, glaring at the recording device. 'You can't hold him for obstruction when he's answered all your questions to the best of his ability. He's held nothing back. Not giving you the answers you're looking for is not obstruction, it's telling the truth. He refutes your accusation of any wrongdoing and demands to be released immediately.'

Geraldine thanked him for his remarks before turning her attention to the suspect. 'Eddy, you do realise that unless you tell us where you were on Saturday, you are going to be a suspect in your mother's murder investigation?'

The social worker turned to Eddy. 'You remember what we talked about, Eddy? You need to tell the police the truth about what happened between you and your mother.'

'Nothing happened,' he cried out, an expression of alarm stamped on his face. 'Why do they think I killed my mother? Why would I do that? Who's going to look after me now?'

Geraldine wondered if he was really as helpless as he claimed. He was twenty-six, an adult who had allegedly held down a job, yet he wanted them to believe he had been completely dependent on his mother for everything.

'Look after you how?' she asked. 'What did your mother do for you, exactly?'

Eddy shrugged. 'I don't know, do I? Cooking, washing my clothes, you know, all the things women do. I can't do any of that, can I? Who's going to wash my clothes now? Who's going to give me a shopping list I can read, and make my dinner?'

Geraldine decided not to pursue that line of questioning, which didn't seem to be leading anywhere. Instead she tackled the relationship between Eddy and his mother directly, asking Eddy whether he and his mother had got on well.

'She's my mother,' he replied.

'Answer the question,' Geraldine said sharply.

She was beginning to feel trapped between Eddy's vagueness and Eileen's determination to pin him down with a confession.

'Eddy, you really need to start answering my questions directly. You're not helping yourself. Now, tell me about your mother.'

'She was my mother.'

Somehow the more Geraldine pressed Eddy for answers, the more he equivocated, while seeming to attempt to answer her questions. She wondered if he was actually more cunning than she had given him credit for, and was being deliberately disingenuous in his ambivalence.

'Eddy,' she said, leaning forward in her chair and staring at him. 'If you don't give me straight answers to all of my questions – every single one of them – you will give us no choice but to arrest you for murdering your mother. I know you understand what I'm saying. So, let's start again, shall we? And this time you really do need to answer my questions. Tell me about your mother. Was she an easy person to get along with?'

Eddy didn't answer. The social worker murmured to him that he needed to talk to the police if he didn't want them suspecting the worst of him. He blinked, but appeared to take no notice of her.

'I know you must have an opinion on this,' Geraldine went on. 'Was it easy living with your mother? I imagine she must have been quite a difficult woman in some ways.'

She paused, waiting, while Eddy sat fidgeting with the edge of his sleeve, and refused to look at her.

'What was she like?'

'I don't want to talk about my mother,' Eddy replied at last. 'I don't want to speak to you ever again.'

'We need you to answer our questions,' Ariadne said. 'My colleague is already growing very impatient with you, so you see, you really must start to co-operate, if you don't want to make trouble for yourself, that is.'

The lawyer stirred, leaned over to his client, and murmured into his ear. Eddy shook his head and repeated that he didn't want to talk about his mother.

'I'm afraid that's not your decision to make,' Geraldine said. 'Eddy, you've already told us you were at home with your mother on the day she was killed. Give me one reason why we shouldn't arrest you right now for murdering her.'

For the first time, Eddy looked at her. His eyes were dark and he looked frightened. But when he spoke, his voice was firm.

'I went out on Saturday morning. When I got up, I got ready and then I went out. I never even saw my mother.'

'What were you getting ready for?'

'To see Kylie, of course.'

'Your girlfriend?'

He nodded.

'What is her full name?'

'She's just Kylie.'

'Where were you meeting her?'

Eddy willingly recited his girlfriend's address in Dale Street, and told them where she worked.

'And you say you were with her on Saturday?'

Eddy confirmed that he had not seen his mother on the day of her death, and that he had gone out at about eight o'clock to see his girlfriend.

'Tell me what your mother said about Kylie.'

Eddy scowled. 'She laughed at me when I told her I had a girlfriend. But that just shows how little she knows. She says I'm stupid –'

The lawyer interrupted to insist that Eddy's private life was no concern of the police.

'A man is entitled to privacy,' Eddy added, as though parroting what he had heard.

'So are you telling us your mother didn't respect your privacy?' Geraldine asked.

Eddy's frown deepened. 'She doesn't respect me,' he said.

'Did that make you very angry?'

The lawyer interjected to complain that Geraldine was putting words in his client's mouth.

'I'm simply asking a question,' Geraldine retorted. 'That's what we're here for, isn't it? Eddy, how did you feel when your mother laughed at you?'

Eddy shrugged and glanced nervously at his lawyer. 'All

right,' he muttered. 'I felt all right. She's my mother. She's always laughing at me. It's because she loves me.'

They continued for a while, going over the same questions, while Eddy mumbled and his lawyer quibbled, and the social worker tried to encourage Eddy to speak freely. In the end, Geraldine gave up. She wasn't getting anywhere.

'The only good thing to say about it all is that he won't be treated so gently in court,' Eileen said.

It sounded like a criticism of Geraldine's interrogation technique.

'But honestly,' she complained to Ian later that evening on the phone, 'there was nothing else I could do. I couldn't get a thing out of him. All he kept saying was that he'd been with his girlfriend. So tomorrow we'll talk to Kylie, and she'll back him up, and that'll be that, until we come up with something more concrete. Eileen's keen to arrest him, but all we have is circumstantial. He's the only beneficiary of Doreen's will, and he had plenty of opportunity. That's all we have against him. And someone else's DNA's been found at the scene.'

Ian chuckled. 'If we arrested everyone who stood to gain from someone else's suspicious death, we'd need a bigger custody suite.'

Geraldine agreed. 'We couldn't hold him, so he's gone home for now, but I don't think Eileen's finished with him yet. But enough about me, how's things with your brother?'

She knew Ian had not seen his brother for a few years and hoped their meeting was going well.

'I hardly recognised him,' Ian replied. 'Seriously, if I hadn't known it was him, I wouldn't have believed it. He's even speaking with an American accent. I'm telling you, it was bizarre at first, until I got used to it, like he was my brother and he wasn't. He's so different. He thinks I've changed too,' he added thoughtfully.

'Changed how?'

'He said I've put on weight, which is nonsense, and he thinks

I look happy, which is certainly true. But it's nearly four years since we last met, and people do change.'

His words reminded Geraldine of Ariadne's words: 'when he came home that evening he seemed like a different person'. If that was true, Nico had undergone an unusually rapid transformation.

Geraldine trotted out a sympathetic response, but she was still thinking about her friend's husband and how he had altered within the space of a few hours. People didn't change that quickly. And then there was the mother who had evidently been unable to come to terms with her son finding a girlfriend. Geraldine wondered if Doreen had been killed as a result of her possessive attitude towards her son. Until he met Kylie, he had always been dependent on her alone.

'Perhaps she just couldn't let go,' she murmured.

'What? What's that?' Ian replied. 'You're still thinking about your case, aren't you?'

Geraldine apologised, surprised that she had spoken aloud, but Ian didn't mind.

'If you can't talk to me without watching what you say, who can you talk freely to?' he asked.

Geraldine thanked him although, really, there was no need.

'It's like you're here in the room with me,' she said. 'Only I can't reach out and touch you.'

'I'll be home soon,' he promised her. 'And then you can talk about your case as much as you like.'

'I'm sorry,' she said. 'Tell me about your brother. I want to hear all about him.'

Ian laughed. 'It's fine, I don't expect you to be interested in my relationship with my brother, not while you've got a murder on your mind.'

Geraldine sighed, aware that her job obliged her to let the dead take precedence over the living.

11

ANALYSIS OF THE DNA samples found on the victim indicated the unidentified suspect was related to a known criminal who had once spent time in York before returning to his native Greece. Like his wife, Ariadne's husband was of Greek descent, and Geraldine found herself avoiding looking at Ariadne after she read the report. She couldn't imagine what Ariadne must be thinking, knowing that the evidence pointed to someone who might conceivably be related to her husband. The criminal in question was out of the country and couldn't be easily contacted, and a sergeant was tasked with tracking down all his male relatives currently living in the UK. Other than Geraldine and Ariadne herself, no one yet seemed aware that one of those relatives might be married to a member of the team investigating the murder.

Uncertain what she herself would have done in Ariadne's situation, Geraldine wondered whether her friend was planning to speak to Eileen about it. Glancing up, she saw Ariadne staring at her screen. Observing her rigid expression, Geraldine suspected her friend had also read the report and concluded the killer might be related to Nico, who might know more than he had disclosed. Concealing information from a murder enquiry was ill-advised for many reasons, not least because it was a criminal offence. Geraldine hesitated and decided not to broach the subject in case Ariadne felt awkward, even though it was hardly her fault if her husband happened to be related to a criminal. But then Geraldine recalled Ariadne's words, 'when he came home that evening he seemed like a different person', and she shuddered to think what might have happened to Nico the day after he returned home from his honeymoon, on the day that Doreen had been murdered.

Geraldine lowered her head and pretended to be busy, but she glanced up surreptitiously from time to time, to see how Ariadne was doing. Ariadne meanwhile said nothing and when she took a break, Geraldine followed her to the canteen. Feeling like a stalker, she lurked in a corner waiting for her friend to sit down before taking a seat at her table. Ariadne barely looked at her.

'Are you okay?' Geraldine asked.

'Yes. Why wouldn't I be?'

Given that Ariadne's husband had recently left her, it was no wonder her smile looked forced.

'No reason.'

Neither of them spoke for a few minutes, while Ariadne sipped her tea and Geraldine sat opposite her feeling awkward.

'Ariadne –' she began at last, when the silence between them became oppressive.

Ariadne spoke at the same time. 'Well, I'd better get back to work,' she said.

'Ariadne, don't shut me out like this,' Geraldine blurted out.

Perhaps if Ian had not been away, she wouldn't have felt so strongly impelled to reach out to her friend. As it was, Ariadne just shook her head and stood up.

'I don't know what you're talking about,' she replied coldly. 'I'm not shutting anyone out. I told you everything's okay and it is, so you can stop speculating about my life. Save your theories for your work.' With that, she turned away.

Geraldine watched her friend stride across the room and out of the canteen, before she too rose to her feet. With a sigh, she bought a coffee and took it back to her desk. It crossed her mind that she might perhaps speak to Nico and ask him what was wrong, but the likelihood was that Geraldine's interference would only make matters worse. In any case, even Ariadne didn't know where Nico was. When Geraldine was upset, she found her best response was to bury herself in her work. There was nothing she could do if Ariadne chose not to share any further details of her troubles. Geraldine could only hope she sorted things out with Nico soon, because a break-up so soon after a honeymoon couldn't be good news.

Later that afternoon, three men were brought into the police station for questioning. Each of them was of Greek descent, and they all shared some DNA characteristics with the traces found in Doreen's hair by a man who had left a trace of saliva in her hair.

Geraldine saw one of them seated in a waiting area, a black-haired man who stared at his feet as she passed by, as though he was afraid to look up and see where he was. Two others were also waiting inside the police station to be questioned about their whereabouts between midday and three in the afternoon on the day of the murder. They sat, shuffling their feet and fidgeting, but whether they were feeling scared or impatient was impossible to determine.

'There is a fourth relative of Milos Moralis who hasn't yet been questioned,' Eileen said. 'His name is Nico Moralis, first cousin of Milos.'

The detective chief inspector looked straight ahead as she uttered the name of the missing Greek man, as though determined not to catch anyone's eye, but by now everyone present knew that she was referring to Ariadne's husband.

'Now, we know that Milos was in Athens on Saturday,' Eileen continued, without a pause, 'and in any case, his DNA isn't an exact match to that found on the victim. But we do want to interview all of his male relatives who were, or may have been, in York on Saturday. So if anyone knows the whereabouts of Nico Moralis, the one man who has not yet been questioned, that information needs to be passed on promptly. I hardly need to point out,' she continued heavily, 'that failure to disclose information in a murder enquiry is always a serious matter, regardless of who you may be.'

It was obvious she was addressing Ariadne who stood with her eyes lowered, staring at her feet. When the meeting closed, Geraldine followed her friend out of the room and caught up with her in the corridor.

'Ariadne,' she said. 'We need to talk.'

Ariadne shook her head. 'There's nothing to talk about.'

'Listen, there's no point in Nico trying to avoid all this –'

'Nico's not trying to avoid anything. Do you really think he'd be that stupid? Please don't go spreading unhelpful rumours about him.'

'I'm hardly spreading rumours by talking to you. But you know as well as I do that this isn't going to go away. He needs to come forward, Ariadne, and get this sorted out. If he's innocent, as I'm sure he is,' she added hurriedly, seeing Ariadne's expression darken, 'he's holding us up by not giving us a sample of his DNA. Why would he do that? Doesn't he know we're looking for him?'

Ariadne lowered her voice. 'What if he was there, visiting Doreen, but had nothing to do with the murder?'

'Wrong place wrong time, you mean?'

Ariadne nodded. But there was no need for Geraldine to answer. With a stifled sob, Ariadne hurried away.

'She as good as confessed to me he was there,' Geraldine told Ian that evening when he called her. 'What am I supposed to do with that? Should I keep her confidence, or do you think she told me because she wants me to pass it on to Eileen?'

Ian listened silently to her outpouring.

'I mean, she's my friend, and I don't want to betray her trust. But why would she tell me if she didn't want Eileen to know? She must know I'd be obliged to share the information.'

'If you are really asking for my opinion,' Ian said at last, 'you shouldn't do anything. If Ariadne wants this information to be known, she can speak to Eileen herself. She didn't tell you in any official capacity. She spoke to you as a friend. And don't forget it's just hearsay, after all. Ariadne wasn't there in the victim's house, and I thought Nico had refused to tell her what happened. So if I were you, I'd keep quiet. If you have to do anything, then at least speak to Ariadne before you say anything to Eileen.'

'Yes, you're right. I'll speak to Ariadne. I'm sorry, Ian, I can't seem to stop myself talking about the investigation and now Nico Moralis has gone AWOL and things aren't looking good for Ariadne. How's your visit going?'

She sighed. Lately whenever Ian called she ended up feeling guilty, although he was the one who had taken time off to see his brother, while she was at home, working.

12

THE NEXT MORNING GERALDINE drove to Toft Green. It was a blustery day, and daffodils were jiggling about on the slopes below the ancient city wall as she drove past. The hotel where Eddy had told them Kylie worked was part of a well-known chain. It was a smart redbrick building with large picture windows and a separate annexe that had been added at some point. A rectangular flower bed had been laid beside the car park, an apology for a garden. A few daffodils and bright red tulips made a splash of colour which Geraldine scarcely registered as she hurried past.

Inside the hotel the drone of traffic was reduced to a barely audible hum. A receptionist summoned the duty manager, a brisk young woman with sharp blue eyes and a blonde ponytail.

'Yes, Inspector, how can I help you?' she enquired, as she ushered Geraldine into her office.

A smile curled her lips but failed to reach her eyes, as she gazed anxiously at her visitor.

'We'd like to have a word with one of your staff, a woman called Kylie,' Geraldine said as she took a seat. 'I'm afraid we don't know her surname.'

'Kylie?' The manager frowned, sitting down behind her desk. 'That name doesn't ring any bells, but give me a minute to check. We do employ a lot of people here.'

Geraldine waited patiently while the manager tapped at her keyboard and studied her screen for some time, a perplexed expression on her face.

'No, I'm sorry,' she said, looking up at last, a fake smile once more plastered on her face. 'I can't find anyone called Kylie anywhere on our staff. Do you know anything else about her, like the nature of the work she does for us? We do have a record of anyone who has submitted an invoice for freelance work on the premises as well as details of our permanent staff on the pay roll. Basically anyone who has received any payment from us is on record, but I've searched and can't find any reference to anyone with the name Kylie. I've looked for females who have an initial K, in case she uses an unusual spelling, but nothing's come up. This woman must have invoiced us under another name, or else there's been some mistake, because there's no trace of anyone called Kylie on our system. We don't employ volunteers in any capacity, so I'm afraid you've got the wrong name, or else you've come to the wrong hotel. I'm so sorry I can't help you.' She stood up with an air of finality.

There was nothing more for Geraldine to do but thank the manager for her time and leave. If Kylie wasn't her official name registered with her place of work, there was not much Geraldine could do to trace Eddy's girlfriend through her job. A few minutes later she drew up outside the house in Dale Street where Kylie was alleged to be living. This visit was also a little puzzling, as there was no record of anyone by the name of Kylie living in the property, which contained several flats. She studied the list on her phone, and checked the names written by each of the bells. There was one K. Stanton, living in Flat 3, so she tried that bell. A man's voice spoke through a crackly intercom.

'Yes?' He sounded impatient.

Quickly Geraldine introduced herself and asked to speak to Kylie.

'What?' came the reply. 'Kylie who? There's no Kylie here.'

'Kylie could be a nickname or a name she doesn't generally use.'

'No. No Kylie here.'

The intercom clicked off into silence. There were three other bells. Geraldine tried them all, but could find no one called Kylie living on the premises. 'Kylie could be a nickname or a second name, or a name she doesn't generally use,' she explained each time, and each time she received the same response. There was no one called Kylie living in the block. She must have moved. The lettings agent might know her new address, so Geraldine went to a tiny but smartly furnished lettings agency in the centre of the city, along Walmgate. It seemed strange that Eddy would be unaware his girlfriend had changed her address. Remembering what Julie had said about her sister, Geraldine wondered if she had moved to avoid him.

Sinking into a comfortable office chair, Geraldine smiled across the desk at a smartly turned out young woman. Her ginger hair was neatly curled, her make-up was immaculate and rather overdone, and her nails were so perfectly manicured Geraldine suspected they were false, like her eyelashes.

'How can I help you today?' the agent asked, as though Geraldine was in the habit of dropping in to enquire about properties.

'I'm looking for a tenant,' Geraldine began.

The agent's smile didn't falter. 'Did you say you're looking for a property to rent?'

'No, I'm not looking for a property.' Displaying her warrant card, Geraldine introduced herself. 'We understand there's a tenant by the name of Kylie living in one of your properties in York. We're keen to trace her.' She mentioned the address Eddy had given the police.

The agent nodded uncertainly. Her curls jiggled every time she dipped her head and raised it again. 'Kylie,' she repeated thoughtfully. 'Do you have anything more for me? A surname would be helpful.'

'No. That's the trouble. If we knew more about her we'd be able to trace her without too much difficulty. The problem is, we know only that she was living at that address, and that her first name's Kylie.'

The agent was not as incompetent as her confusion had suggested. 'I see,' she said. 'I see your problem. Wait a minute, let me pull up our list and we can see exactly who has been a resident there recently. We're looking for a woman, I take it? Are you sure of that? I mean, a name isn't necessarily conclusive. What I mean is, names can be misleading.'

'Definitely a woman. She might not always go under the name of Kylie.' Geraldine paused. 'I'd say we're looking for a woman of around late twenties to late thirties, and she works in a hotel in York.'

She mentioned the name of the hotel, although she was beginning to think the woman Eddy had spoken of didn't use the name Kylie at all. Meanwhile the agent did a search on her computer, and shook her head.

'I'm sorry,' she said, 'but I can't find any trace of anyone called Kylie on our database. I'm afraid we'll need more to go on than that. And,' she added, her frown deepening, 'no one has moved in or out of that block in the past three months.'

Back at the police station, Geraldine reported her findings to Eileen. The only conclusion they could reach was that Eddy had given them a false name for his girlfriend, or a false address. Possibly both. Geraldine went to question him once more.

'Eddy, we've been unable to trace Kylie,' she said.

He didn't answer.

'You do realise how important this is?' she pressed on. 'You're relying on Kylie for your alibi.'

Eddy shook his head, looking puzzled. 'What do you mean?'

Geraldine suppressed a sigh of exasperation. 'You told us you were with Kylie at the time of your mother's murder. We need to speak to Kylie so she can confirm your statement. Without her confirmation, you have no alibi for the time of the murder, and automatically become a suspect.'

Eddy looked puzzled. 'You can't suspect me. I haven't told you anything,' he said.

'You need to tell us where we can find Kylie. She wasn't at the address you gave us for her, or at the hotel where you claimed she works. In fact, there was no record of anyone called Kylie living or working at either of the addresses you gave us. Eddy,' she leaned forward, 'does Kylie really exist?'

Eddy burst out laughing. 'Of course she exists. You must have got her name wrong, That is, she told me she was called Kylie, but she might have given me a name she doesn't use anywhere else.'

'Why would she do that?' Geraldine asked.

Eddy shook his head. 'You can ask her, can't you, when you speak to her? I think she wanted to give me a name that would be a secret between us. I probably shouldn't have told you about it. She might be cross with me.'

Frustrated, Geraldine was determined to find Kylie, but it seemed an impossible task.

Eileen was sceptical Kylie even existed. 'Even if you find this woman, it seems clear Eddy's a liar or a fantasist. I'm not sure we can trust anything he tells us.'

Geraldine instructed a constable to check the names of all the staff working at the hotel against the tenants of the lettings agent, and she found a match at once. A woman called Louisa Thomas worked in the housekeeping department at the hotel and lived at the exact address Eddy had given them. Geraldine called the lettings agent who confirmed there was a tenant named Louisa Thomas currently living at that address. Armed with that knowledge, Geraldine returned to the hotel to speak to Louisa.

13

LOUISA WAS A SHORT, dumpy young woman. Doe-eyed, with mousy hair and rabbit teeth, each of her features seemed reminiscent of a different woodland creature. She perched on the edge of a chair, chubby knees pressed tightly together, delicate fingers entwined, staring anxiously at Geraldine.

'Thank you for agreeing to talk to me, Louisa. We are hoping you might be able to help us with an enquiry.' Geraldine smiled encouragingly at the young woman. 'We'd like to know where you were last Saturday, from around midday until three.'

Louisa gazed back, her wide eyes making her look startled. It appeared to be her habitual expression.

'Where I was last Saturday?' she repeated. Her eyes darted around the room as though searching for an answer. 'You want to know where I was last Saturday?'

'Were you at work?' Geraldine prompted her.

'At work?' Louisa repeated. 'Last Saturday? No, I only work one weekend in two and I wasn't on last weekend.'

'So did you spend the day with your boyfriend?'

Louisa looked down, blushing, as she muttered that she didn't have a boyfriend.

'Who were you with on Saturday then?'

'No one,' Louisa mumbled. 'I went to the shops. I've not been here long enough to have made any friends,' she added awkwardly, as though being alone required an excuse.

Recalling the years she had spent living by herself, often friend-less, Geraldine suppressed an urge to say something comforting.

Instead, she asked, 'What about Eddy?'

Louisa looked puzzled. 'Who's Eddy?'

Geraldine drew in a deep breath, careful to maintain her outward composure, although Louisa's answer was frustrating. It had taken Geraldine so long to track Louisa down, and now it seemed she was unlikely to confirm Eddy's alibi. But perhaps, like Louisa, Eddy had used an alias in their relationship.

'Do you know anyone called Kylie?' she asked.

'Kylie? No.' Louisa shook her head, as though to emphasise her reply.

'Does anyone call you Kylie?'

At this question, Louisa giggled. 'No,' she said, her voice rising slightly. 'Why would anyone call me Kylie? My name's Louisa.' She giggled again.

Geraldine decided against elaborating. She was almost sure Louisa was telling the truth, but all the same there was something very peculiar about the whole situation. She tried again.

'Do you know anyone called Eddy?'

'No, and you already asked me that.' Louisa pouted slightly which made her look very young. 'Who is he anyway? And why are you asking me all these questions?'

Geraldine smiled, trying to put the girl at her ease. 'Well, it looks like this may well be a case of mistaken identity, and the man we're interested in has nothing to do with you. But he could have introduced himself to you under a different name. If I show you a picture of this man, would you take a look please, and just let me know whether you recognise him.'

Louisa shrugged. 'Okay.'

'Thank you.'

Geraldine found a head shot of Eddy on her phone and held it up for Louisa to see. Expecting Louisa to shake her head and confirm that she didn't know him, Geraldine was surprised when she leaned forward and studied the picture carefully, with a slightly puzzled expression.

'I don't know,' Louisa admitted at last. 'I definitely don't know him, or anything like that, but he does look vaguely familiar. What I mean is, I think I might have seen him before but I can't think where. Was he on the telly or something?' She looked up. 'He looks weird. Who is he anyway? I might have seen him on the street, just out and about, you know. Does he live near me? Or maybe he stayed here?'

Geraldine put her phone away. 'It's not important any more. Thank you, Louisa, you've been very helpful.'

'Is that it then? Can I go back to work? Only if I'm away too long, they'll dock my pay.'

'Yes, you can go now, and thank you again.'

Geraldine dismissed a stray temptation to suggest Louisa meet her for a drink after work. Feeling sorry for a potential witness was hardly professional, and there was still a chance Louisa was lying through her prominent teeth. Besides, the two of them were never actually going to be friends. Geraldine couldn't fill the void in Louisa's life, nor would it be appropriate for her to try. Louisa was lonely, but she was young, and she would make friends in time.

'You're new to the area,' Geraldine began and stopped herself from offering an encouraging platitude.

'Yes,' Louisa replied.

'I – I hope you like it here in York,' Geraldine concluded lamely. 'I'm sure you're going to settle down and find friends.'

Louisa looked surprised and stammered her thanks, but the moment was awkward. Geraldine hoped Louisa didn't realise the detective who had questioned her actually felt sorry for her and her solitary status.

If Geraldine was disappointed by the outcome of her meeting with Louisa, Eileen was pleased.

'So there it is,' she crowed. 'It was obvious all along, really, wasn't it? His alibi seemed weak at the best of times, and now it's been exposed as a complete lie. He just made up having seen a girl, to try and get himself off the hook. How stupid does he think we are? For goodness sake, I think that must be the most pathetic attempt to invent a false alibi I've ever come across. The man's an idiot, a complete idiot. Obviously he's guilty. This confirms it.'

'It confirms he lied about having a girlfriend,' Geraldine replied. 'It doesn't prove he killed his mother.'

'Why else would he make up a story to try and give himself an alibi?'

'Because he was scared? Because he can't prove he's innocent?' Geraldine hazarded.

But she knew her protestations alone could not save Eddy from facing prosecution. She wasn't even sure why she was so keen to exonerate Eddy. Ariadne was even more pleased than Eileen when she heard that Eddy's alibi had collapsed.

'Obviously he did it,' she told Geraldine when she heard the news. 'Why else would he lie about where he was?'

Geraldine sighed. The whole situation had become too complicated for her to penetrate the confusion. Like Eileen, she couldn't understand why anyone would fabricate a relationship with a stranger to create an alibi that could so easily be destroyed.

'Perhaps there's a real Kylie,' she suggested. 'Louisa was just a mistake.'

But she knew she was beaten, even before she spoke.

'There's no Kylie working at the hotel or living in the block of flats where Eddy told us she worked and lived,' Ariadne pointed out. 'Instead, there's Louisa who's never even heard of him, let alone spent Saturday with him. His lies are just desperate. Pathetic. Either he's completely stupid, or he panicked and blurted out the first thing he could think of, and then having said it he had to stick to his story. But at least we know it was him.' She beamed, and Geraldine smiled.

Like Ariadne, Geraldine had been worried about the suspected connection between Nico and Doreen and although she was not yet convinced about Eddy's guilt, she was relieved for her friend.

Discussing the development with Ian that evening on the phone, he was guarded in his response. 'It certainly sounds as though this Eddy character is a plausible suspect,' he said.

'He had means and opportunity and, most importantly, motivation,' Geraldine agreed.

'Yet you don't sound very sure he's guilty.'

'Oh, I don't know, it just seems like such a dreadful crime.'

'That's a surprising statement from you, of all people. I mean, when is murder not a dreadful crime? I thought you'd be hardened to it by now.'

'But to kill his mother... It's so horrible.'

'It certainly is, but we both know that's no reason to think he's innocent.'

'I know. He just seems such a harmless person. I mean, he's weird and creepy, but he doesn't seem vicious or aggressive, and he doesn't seem to have a temper. And I really don't think he's capable of planning something like this.'

'Well, if he did plan it, he didn't do a very good job of getting away with it. And as for weird and creepy, that's hardly a recommendation.' Ian laughed. 'I can't say you're doing a very good job of defending him if you really think he's innocent.'

14

'I SEE NICO'S HANDED himself in,' Naomi said to Geraldine when they arrived at the police station at the same time the following morning.

Geraldine smiled. Naomi was a bright young constable, keen to progress in her career, and Geraldine had taken an interest in her.

'He hasn't "handed himself in", as you put it,' Ariadne snapped, overhearing Naomi's comment. 'You make it sound as though he's committed a crime. He's only come in to give a DNA swab, that's all. I don't know why you would go around making insinuations like that. He's not even a suspect. We all know who killed Doreen Lewis.'

Ariadne moved away, and another sergeant told Geraldine that Nico had been picked up by a passing patrol car as the driver had recognised him from an image being circulated. It was disappointing that he hadn't come forward voluntarily, which only served to increase the suspicion against him. It wasn't long before a rumour spread around the team that Nico's DNA matched the sample found on Doreen's body. Geraldine glanced over at Ariadne who was keeping her eyes fixed on her screen.

'It's hardly a surprise,' Naomi pointed out, as she stood in a huddle with Geraldine and a few other officers. She lowered her voice. 'The other relatives have all been eliminated, so it had to be Nico Moralis who visited Doreen.'

Naomi was right. Nico had three cousins living in York. Not only did they all have alibis for the time of Doreen's murder, but their DNA had not matched the unidentified sample found on the body. In the light of the new evidence which appeared to implicate Nico in the murder, Eileen summoned the team to a briefing.

'Ariadne's gone home for a few days,' she announced. 'She's been given compassionate leave.'

'How terrible to discover you've married a murderer,' a constable murmured.

'Especially for one of us,' another colleague agreed.

'It would be dreadful for anyone,' the first constable said.

Geraldine bridled. 'What happened to innocent until proven guilty? All we can say for certain is that Nico Moralis was in Doreen's house at some time, probably on the day she died. That doesn't make him guilty, and it doesn't even make him a suspect.'

Eileen nodded. 'Ariadne will be back next week. Be careful what you say in front of her. This is a very difficult time for her.'

'I'd say it's difficult, discovering her newly-wed husband is a murderer,' Naomi said.

'No one should be jumping to conclusions before all the facts are established,' Geraldine interrupted angrily. 'We don't yet know what Nico was doing, visiting Doreen. We certainly don't know that he was in any way involved in her murder.'

'Yes,' Eileen agreed solemnly, 'we all know that evidence can be misleading. There could be a perfectly innocent explanation for the trace of his DNA found at the scene of the murder.'

There was a murmur of sceptical responses to this statement.

'Is there seriously any doubt that he's guilty?' Naomi asked. 'He didn't come forward voluntarily and he must have known we wanted to see him. If nothing else, Ariadne would have told him.'

'It looks like she warned him in advance,' another constable muttered.

'All the evidence proves is that Nico was in Doreen's house,'

Geraldine insisted. 'It doesn't necessarily follow that he killed her. And if it turns out that Nico's innocent, we don't want to cause Ariadne unnecessary stress for nothing. This must be difficult enough for her. We need to support her in any way we can.'

Eileen nodded her agreement. 'So next week, we all treat Ariadne as though nothing has happened. She'll be removed from the team, of course, and assigned to a different case, but we should all remember she's a good officer and deserves to be allowed to get on with her job. There are to be no adverse comments made in her hearing. So be careful. And if I hear that anyone's been upsetting her with careless chatter, you'll be dealing with me. So keep your idle speculation away from her, please.'

With Nico under suspicion, Geraldine determined to do everything she could to discover the truth, and hopefully clear Nico's name in the process. When Ariadne called her and asked her to visit Nico in his cell and pass on a message for her, Geraldine agreed at once, and made her way slowly to the cells. The custody sergeant greeted her with his cheerful smile. A well-built man, whose bulk was turning to fat, she rarely saw him without a genial smile on his face.

'To what do I owe this very great pleasure?' he beamed, with a mock bow.

Geraldine couldn't help returning his smile.

'How are you keeping?' she asked.

'All the better for seeing you,' he replied. 'Nothing like a pretty face to cheer a man up when he's stuck down here with the prisoners.'

'Watch it, or I'll have you up for sexual harassment,' she laughed. 'I'm here to have a word with Nico Moralis.'

The sergeant gave her a shrewd look, but made no comment. It was no secret that Geraldine and Ariadne were good friends.

It was quite surprising that Nico had been identified by a

passing officer, he looked so different to the man Geraldine had last seen when they were celebrating his wedding to Ariadne. She hardly recognised him, and she felt a pang of guilt at having offered so little support to Ariadne, who must have been suffering terribly. Nico's hair looked shaggy, and he was unshaven. His jacket was creased and even his shoes looked old and scuffed. It was shocking to see that a man could deteriorate so rapidly. His eyes were slightly bloodshot and he looked as though he had been drinking, although Geraldine knew he never touched alcohol. At least, that was what Ariadne had told her. Geraldine wondered whether Ariadne had really known her new husband at all. She shivered, fearing for her friend's happiness, and did her best to hide her shock.

'Nico,' she greeted him, 'how are you?'

He raised his eyes to meet hers but didn't answer.

'I hope you're being looked after in here,' she pressed on.

Nico raised his hands and opened his arms, gesturing at the walls that hemmed him in, as if to say, you see how it is.

'It all happened so quickly,' he said, breaking off to sneeze.

His voice was hoarse and Geraldine had to strain to make out that he was muttering about suffering from hay fever. She wondered if that was how his spittle had reached Doreen's hair. She watched him closely as she put her next question.

'Did you cut Doreen's hair at all?'

Before he uttered a word, she knew Nico's answer from the bewildered expression on his face. He shook his head.

'This is completely surreal. One day you're on top of the world, marrying the woman you love, off on a wonderful honeymoon, and then, before you know what's happening, you're thrust into a nightmare from which there seems to be no escape. I didn't do it, Geraldine. You have to believe me. You have to help me. To help Ariadne –' He was interrupted by another sneeze, after which he fell silent.

Sinking down on his bunk he sat, staring at the floor.

'I didn't come here to offer help, although I'll do what I can, you know that. I've come here to bring you a message from Ariadne.'

Nico looked up, his expression anguished at hearing his wife's name, but he didn't speak.

'She said not to worry,' Geraldine concluded feebly.

Nico let out a bark of laughter, but his expression was bitter and he didn't speak.

'She said you're not to worry,' Geraldine repeated firmly. 'She's going to discover who killed Doreen, and before long you'll both be at home and together again. She wanted me to tell you that whatever happens, she's always there for you.'

Nico's shoulders dropped. 'She thinks I did it.'

'No, no, she told me you couldn't possibly have killed someone. She never believed it for a moment.'

'But she thinks I'll be found guilty. Why else would she say she'll be there for me, whatever happens?'

'No, you mustn't think like that. She only meant it might take a little while for us to uncover the truth. In the meantime, she wants you to know that she'll wait for you, however long it takes for us to sort this out.'

'Why didn't she come and see me herself?'

Geraldine shook her head. 'I don't know,' she admitted. 'I think she's finding this difficult.'

She didn't elaborate on how painful Ariadne would find it to contemplate visiting Nico in a prison cell. She hoped it wasn't something her friend was going to have to get used to. Geraldine's relationship with Ariadne made it difficult for her to view the case objectively. She longed to surrender to her own bias and destroy the case against Nico, but the reported change in him seemed to confirm his guilt. She wondered whether Ariadne regretted having told anyone about it, and imagined Ariadne's expression if Geraldine could only tell her that Nico's name had been cleared. At the same time, Geraldine remained sceptical about Eddy's guilt. The only satisfactory solution for her would be if a third suspect turned up, but that was a vain hope. Either a man whose innocence she hoped for, or a man whose innocence she believed in, was going to be convicted. Powerless to halt the inexorable advance of justice, she was shocked that it would even occur to her to balk at the system to which she had dedicated her life. Whatever happened, regardless of Geraldine's personal feelings about Ariadne's happiness, Doreen's killer had to be apprehended. She had to cling to that belief, or surrender to chaos.

15

WHILE SUSPICION APPEARED TO be falling on Nico Moralis, the evidence against him was as yet circumstantial. Geraldine had been at pains to point out that they could prove only that Nico had visited Doreen at some time before her death. Traces of his DNA at the scene failed to reveal exactly when he had visited her, nor did they indicate how long he had stayed. There could be an irreproachable reason for his presence in her home. Not only that, but Geraldine had discovered a credible explanation for droplets of his saliva having reached her hair. Nothing they had so far discovered indicated that he was guilty of murder. Geraldine had a horrible feeling she had encouraged Eileen to condemn Nico. Distraught, she slipped out of the police station.

A light rain was falling as she walked slowly across the police compound, and she shivered. But she had to speak to someone and couldn't risk being overheard. She was relieved when Ian answered his phone straight away.

'People visit other people all the time. It doesn't mean they kill them,' she blurted out when she had explained the situation.

'This is hard, I know,' Ian replied softly. 'Ariadne's a good friend.'

'But why didn't Nico come forward sooner, if he has nothing to hide?' Geraldine asked.

It was true that Nico hadn't helped himself by delaying coming forward. So far he had only been in custody for a few hours, but Eileen was agitating to find a reason to keep him there.

'He behaved like an idiot, but perhaps he was scared,' Ian replied. 'It doesn't mean he's done anything wrong.'

'Only now that's given Eileen the idea that he must be guilty.' Geraldine frowned. 'One minute she's convinced it was Eddy, now she's stuck on Nico being guilty. Honestly, Ian, I can't work out what she's doing. She doesn't seem to be acting rationally.'

'I'm sure she knows what she's doing,' Ian replied.

'And the worst of it is, I want to support Ariadne, but I think I've gone and done just the opposite.'

'What do you mean?'

Geraldine hesitated. 'Ariadne told me that Nico had changed suddenly, and –' she paused. 'She thought he was seeing someone else. But the point is, she said he seemed different on Saturday, after he'd gone out to see someone. I mentioned it to Eileen and I think that's what's convinced her Nico killed Doreen.' Geraldine bit her lip, struggling to keep her voice steady. 'I shouldn't have told Eileen, should I? Ariadne spoke to me in confidence. If she thought it was anything significant, she would have told Eileen herself. I should have kept my mouth shut. Oh God, I hope it doesn't turn out to be him.'

Ian sighed. They both liked Ariadne, who was Geraldine's closest friend at work.

'You can't blame yourself,' he said. 'You only did what any responsible officer would have done. You couldn't keep something like that to yourself.'

'Ariadne did.'

'No, she didn't. She shared the information with you. She must have known you wouldn't keep it to yourself.'

Geraldine knew Ian was trying to be kind, but it didn't help that only two days earlier he had advised her to keep quiet when Ariadne had shared her suspicion that Nico had visited Doreen. Now that Geraldine had told Eileen that Ariadne thought Nico had changed, Ian was telling her she had done the right thing in breaking her friend's confidence.

'What if the change in Nico had nothing to do with Doreen at all? What if he really is just seeing someone else, and I've persuaded the DCI he's guilty?'

'That's not for you to determine all by yourself, is it? Anyway, I don't suppose Eileen paid that much attention to what you told her.'

Geraldine sighed. 'I think she did. She had that gleam in her eye, you know, like she does when we find a lead. Like a predator spotting its prey.'

Ian laughed but Geraldine shook her head.

'It's not funny, Ian. It's really hard. I really want to support Ariadne and now I don't even know how to talk to her. I feel so bad about all this. I'm sure she suspects I spoke to Eileen.'

Nico claimed he had been to see Doreen to advise her over her tax affairs. That made sense, as he was an accountant, and it could possibly explain why traces of his DNA had been present in Doreen's hair. A constable was following up Nico's statement with Doreen's tax office to check the story before they questioned him further. But if his reason for visiting her stacked up, that didn't prove whether or not he was guilty of murder. In the meantime, Eddy's alibi appeared to have fallen apart.

'So we now have two suspects,' Naomi complained. 'Why do they have to turn up in pairs, like buses?'

Geraldine sent a car to bring Eddy back so she could question him again about his movements on Saturday. He looked exhausted, and his voice was taut with anxiety.

'They said you'd leave me alone,' he complained to Geraldine as soon as she entered the interview room.

Eddy sat shaking his head, morose and silent, as his lawyer objected to his being questioned again.

'You can question me and question me as much as you like, but I've already told you where I was on Saturday and I'm not telling you again,' Eddy added when his lawyer had finished.

'You have no grounds for questioning my client any more,' the lawyer insisted, sounding bored.

'Yes, you've told us where you were on Saturday,' Geraldine agreed pleasantly. 'Tell me again.'

'Why do I have to say it all over again? Weren't you listening the first time?'

'I was listening, and I remember what you said, and we even recorded it so I can listen to you as many times as I like. What I'm asking you to do now is confirm what you told us. We don't want any misunderstanding.'

'There isn't a misunderstanding. I was with Kylie all day.'

'Ah yes, Kylie,' Geraldine nodded.

Rifling through a folder, she drew out a picture of Louisa. Taken from a social media website, the image was grainy and slightly blurred, but still recognisable. She placed it on the table in front of Eddy who looked surprised.

'Is this Kylie?' Geraldine asked.

Eddy's expression softened but he looked wary and said nothing.

'This is a picture of a young woman who works at the hotel where you told us Kylie works, and lives at the address you gave us for Kylie,' Geraldine said.

Eddy remained silent. At his side the solicitor appeared to have woken up and sat listening intently, probably wondering where the conversation was heading.

'So we have a woman who looks like Kylie, lives at Kylie's address, and works at the same hotel as Kylie.'

Eddy nodded uneasily.

'Our problem is that this is a picture of a woman called Louisa Thomas.' Geraldine tapped the edge of the photo. 'Louisa lives at the address you gave us for Kylie, and she works at the hotel where you told us Kylie works.'

The lawyer shifted in his seat and glanced askance at his client as Geraldine carried on talking.

'What's more, there's no one called Kylie living at the address you gave us, and there's no Kylie working at the hotel where you told us she works. In fact there's no one at either of those locations who knows anything about anyone called Kylie.' She paused. 'Kylie doesn't exist, does she? You invented her to give you an alibi.' She sat back in her chair. 'I'm sorry, Eddy, but you can't simply invent a story to give yourself an alibi. You need to tell us the truth. You can't protect yourself by lying. We always learn the truth in the end. So start talking, and this time tell me the truth. Who is Kylie?'

'That's Kylie,' Eddy muttered, pointing at the picture of Louisa. 'That's her. That's Kylie.'

'This isn't Kylie. It can't be, because Kylie doesn't exist, does she?' Geraldine tapped the picture again. 'And this is a picture of Louisa Thomas.'

'That's Kylie,' Eddy repeated stubbornly.

'If this woman, Louisa Thomas, gave my client a false name, he cannot be held responsible for her actions,' the lawyer said. 'I suggest you stop harassing him –'

Geraldine interrupted him, but she was looking at Eddy. 'We've spoken to Louisa. She doesn't know you. She told us she's never met you. So,' she leaned forward, staring at Eddy, who dropped his eyes. 'Why don't you tell us the truth? Because we know you didn't spend Saturday with this woman.' She tapped the photo again. 'We know you've given us false addresses for Kylie's home and place of work. What's going on, Eddy? And what made you pick her?'

Eddy sat staring at his hands clasped together in his lap.

'This is clearly a case of mistaken identity,' the lawyer blustered, animated for the first time now that he understood the threat to his client. 'You've stumbled on an image of a woman who resembles my client's girlfriend, that's all. It means nothing,' he added, turning to Eddy. 'They're clutching at straws here. Don't worry, you'll soon be going home. This means nothing.'

'But this isn't a case of mistaken identity, and she isn't just any random woman,' Geraldine replied. 'This is a woman who not only looks like Kylie, but lives at the address Eddy gave us for Kylie, and allegedly works at the same hotel as Kylie. Only she doesn't, because we can find no trace of anyone called Kylie at either location. We've questioned staff at the hotel, and the lettings agent for the block of flats where Eddy told us Kylie lives. No one knows anyone called Kylie. So this is far from a simple case of mistaken identity, isn't it?' She stared at Eddy. 'Kylie doesn't live where you told us she lives, does she? And she doesn't work at the hotel. You invented those details for her, didn't you? Why? Did you think we would give up looking for her, when we couldn't trace her straight away, and just take your word for your alibi, without attempting to see if your story checked out?'

'I was with Kylie all day,' Eddy said doggedly, still staring at his hands.

Even the lawyer could see that they were heading down a blind alley. With a sigh, he requested a break so he could talk to his client.

'I think that's a good idea,' Geraldine agreed. 'Please make it clear to Eddy that he needs to start telling us the truth. We need to speak to Kylie. The more you lie, Eddy,' she added, turning to him, 'the less we're going to trust anything you say. You may think you're protecting Kylie, or that you'll succeed in hiding your own situation from her, but believe me, you're not helping yourself by concealing Kylie's whereabouts. We need to talk to her and, one way or another, we'll find her, with or without your co-operation. All you'll achieve is to make life more difficult for yourself if you persist in concealing her details.'

'I was with Kylie all day,' Eddy repeated stubbornly.

'There's only one reason for him to lie,' Eileen said, when Geraldine told her how the interview had gone.

Geraldine shook her head. 'There's any number of reasons

why he might lie to keep his girlfriend out of this. He might have some peculiar old-fashioned notion that he's protecting her from being questioned by us or, more likely, he might not want her to find out he's been accused of killing his mother. It's a pretty grim charge. Even if it turns out he's innocent, he still might not want anyone else to know he was ever a suspect.'

Eileen gave Geraldine a shrewd look. 'So you really think it's possible he's innocent?'

'I don't know,' Geraldine admitted. 'But isn't that the point of our job? To establish what's true, or at least likely, not just what's possible? We're not meant to act as judge and jury.'

'Don't lecture me on our responsibilities,' Eileen snapped, suddenly irate. 'I suggest you get going and find Kylie, and in the meantime, let's put some pressure on Nico Moralis and see if we can get him to talk. We have two suspects. At least one of them must have something to tell us.'

'Unless they're both innocent and someone else killed Doreen,' Geraldine said quietly.

Eileen grunted and turned her attention to her computer screen, muttering about negativity and obstinacy. Assuming Eileen was referring to her, Geraldine didn't linger to hear any more.

16

Having reached an impasse with Eddy, Geraldine instructed Naomi to organise a search for all women called Kylie living in or around York. It was a mammoth task, but they had to track her down, if she really existed, and they couldn't rely on Eddy's testimony. A team of constables were tasked with contacting every woman called Kylie between the ages of seventeen and fifty, who looked even vaguely similar to Louisa Thomas.

'This is assuming he wasn't lying when he described Kylie, or when he told us Louisa's picture was her,' Naomi said.

'We have to start somewhere,' Geraldine replied despondently.

While the search was being set up, Geraldine went to question Nico. He shuffled into the interview room with an understandable air of dejection. Geraldine had expected him to be angry, but he seemed resigned to his situation.

'When can I see my wife?' he asked as he sat down.

Geraldine hesitated. Ariadne had gone home in a state of extreme distress, and was not due back at work until after the weekend. As her friend, Geraldine should have called her, but she had been preoccupied with work. She resolved to call Ariadne that evening to ask how she was.

'Where is she?' Nico asked. 'Why hasn't she been to see me? Why isn't she here?'

'You'll see her soon,' Geraldine fibbed.

The answer to Nico's question depended on Ariadne. It was possible she wouldn't want to see him.

'Tell her I didn't do it,' Nico burst out, momentarily losing his self-control and raising his voice. 'Tell her I've done nothing wrong! Tell her!'

'I think she knows that,' Geraldine replied.

If Nico was innocent, those words might console him. If he had murdered Doreen, his wife's blind trust in him might prompt him to feel guilty enough to confess. Either way, Geraldine wanted Nico to stay calm.

'Now, this isn't about Ariadne, Nico. You know why you're here.'

He nodded miserably. His lawyer was a black-haired young man, possibly a relation of his. They exchanged a brief glance and the lawyer nodded almost imperceptibly.

'I have no idea why I'm here,' Nico replied in what sounded like a prepared speech. 'I've done nothing wrong and you're hounding an innocent man for no reason.'

'Nico,' Geraldine interrupted him. 'Do you recognise this woman?'

She showed him a picture of Doreen, taken in what appeared to be a back garden on a sunny day. She was smiling, squinting in the bright sunshine, and apparently talking to whoever was taking the photo.

'That's Doreen Lewis,' Nico replied without any hesitation.

'What is your relationship with her?'

'I look after – that is, I help her – with her financial affairs. Just unofficially. I mean, I don't charge her for my time, but it doesn't take very long and she's on her own.'

'How do you know her?'

'She was married to my uncle's friend. Her husband died a few years back and she asked me to help her sort out her affairs. She knows I'm an accountant. She didn't take up much of my time, and it was no trouble. She's a widow. I was happy to help her. It wasn't anything, really.'

Geraldine nodded. 'So you knew her,' she said.

Nico looked perplexed. 'I just said that,' he replied. 'She was never what you might call a client, because there was no formal arrangement. I just helped her out.'

'Were you close?'

'Close? No. I hardly knew her. But like I said, her husband was a friend of my uncle, Yiannis. When Doreen went to him for help, he sent her to me. I met her three or four times to talk about her financial position. Now the probate's settled, there's very little for me to do. That is, there *was* very little to do, I should say, because I heard what happened.'

'What did you hear?'

'It was on the news, and Ariadne told me she was working on the case. But she didn't say anything that wasn't already in the public domain,' he added quickly. 'We never talk about her work other than in the most general terms. How was your day, and all that, you know. She doesn't talk about what goes on here any more than I'd tell her about my clients' confidential financial affairs. But Doreen's murder has been in the news, and I can assure you I know nothing about it other than what's been reported by the media, and Ariadne told me to pay no attention to that. She was sure you'll soon find out who's responsible and that will be the end of it.'

Geraldine grilled Nico about his movements on the day of Doreen's death and he admitted he had visited her on Saturday morning to finalise her accounts. He claimed he had arrived at eleven, as arranged, and had left her at home, alive and well, at about midday. Although she had probably been killed a couple of hours later, it was possible the murder had been committed as early as midday.

'Where did you go when you left her?' Geraldine asked.

'I went for a walk,' Nico replied.

'A walk?'

'Yes, to clear my head. The sun was shining.'

'Where did you walk?'

'Just around, along the river.'

'Did anyone see you?'

Nico shrugged. 'I don't know. That is, I don't remember seeing anyone.'

There were now two suspects in custody, independent of each other, neither of whom had an alibi for the time of Doreen's murder. They couldn't both be guilty. The difference was that Nico appeared to have no motive for wanting Doreen dead, whereas Eddy had inherited her house. Having completed her initial interview with Nico, Geraldine went to see Eileen and was surprised to find the detective chief inspector confused over what to do. It was unlike her to be indecisive.

'You've spoken to both of them, Geraldine,' she said. 'What do you think?' She looked anxious and Geraldine hesitated.

'Obviously we know they were both there in the house, with Doreen, at some point. Neither of them has an alibi for the time of death. Nico says he went for a walk on his own, and he doesn't know whether anyone saw him or not. As far as we can tell, Eddy made a bizarre attempt to fabricate an alibi which fell apart as soon as we started to investigate his story.'

'So they both lied about where they were when Doreen was killed,' Eileen said.

Surprised at Eileen's poor grasp of the situation, Geraldine replied that Nico hadn't lied, as far as they knew, but he had been unable to give a verifiable account of his movements at the time of Doreen's death. That was not the same as lying. In fact, if anything, he had almost been too honest in making no attempt to offer an alibi.

Eileen frowned. 'What about Eddy, who said he was with his girlfriend. Have you spoken to her yet?'

Geraldine carefully summarised the two suspects' statements again and waited for Eileen's decision, but the detective chief inspector just waved her hand in a dismissive gesture.

'We can't have two suspects in custody,' she said. 'Release one.'

'Are you saying we release Eddy, even though he has a

clear motive for killing Doreen, and Nico doesn't?'

'What motive?' Eileen asked.

'Apart from any personal animosities, he was heir to her estate. That's enough to give him a motive.'

'Then he must be guilty,' Eileen said.

'I'm not convinced. He doesn't seem like a killer.'

'I don't know what that means,' Eileen snapped.

Geraldine shrugged unhappily. 'I don't see that he could have done it. I mean, in practical terms yes, it's possible, but what really did he stand to gain by her death? It seems to me that he lost a lot more than he stood to gain.'

'What are you doing keeping him here, then?' Eileen replied irritably. 'Release him. I don't believe he killed his mother either. Why would he? She was in a wheelchair, and he was free to do whatever he wanted, so what reason could he have for killing her? The house was already his, to all intents and purposes, and we have no reason to disbelieve him when he said he was with his girlfriend.'

'We only have his word that he was with her,' Geraldine said, thinking that Eddy seemed confused about who Kylie actually was.

'Well, you need to ask her where he was when his mother was murdered, and get to the bottom of this.'

'We're trying to trace her, but we haven't had any luck with that yet.'

'Luck? Luck? What's luck got to do with anything? What we need is graft and more application. So start trying harder, and meanwhile you can release Eddy. You can't keep punishing him for your failure. That's all for now.'

Puzzled by Eileen's seemingly peremptory decision-making, Geraldine left, feeling unnerved by the conversation. Something was not quite right with Eileen. No one else appeared to have noticed anything amiss, and Ian was away so she couldn't solicit his opinion.

'I can't wait for you to come home,' she told him that evening and he agreed.

She decided against sharing her concerns about Eileen with him. There was no point in worrying him when there was nothing he could do to help. It would have to wait until he returned to York.

17

WHEN EDDY REQUESTED A soft pillow the uniformed officer chuckled, his fleshy face criss-crossed by tiny wrinkles, his eyes all but concealed in creases of skin.

'Shall I run you a bath?' he asked.

Eddy explained that he preferred to shower. His mother had told him it was cleaner than lying in a tub of water, washing his hair in the water where he was soaking his feet and his backside.

'It's not hygienic,' he explained earnestly.

The officer left, laughing. Eddy sat down on the hard bunk and gazed miserably around his cell, which was small and stank of piss and pungent cleaning fluids. The meal he was given reminded him of school, where he had been forced to eat slimy food or go hungry. Often he had chosen hunger. Disagreeable as the physical privations were, the worst aspect of his imprisonment was not knowing how long it would last. No one said anything about when they would let him go. Whenever he tried to ask, his query was batted away with a vague muttering about having to 'wait and see', and an exhortation to 'be patient'. They didn't seem to understand that it was difficult for him to remain calm when he didn't know what was going on. He tried pleading and complaining, but it was futile. No one cared, and that frightened him. Without his mother, he was helpless. She would never have let this happen.

When the black-haired detective came to see him, he was afraid she was bringing more bad news, although it was hard to imagine anything worse than being shut up in a cramped and stinking cell. Instead, she smiled briskly and told him he was free to go. At first he didn't grasp where she wanted him to go, but once he understood the situation he felt giddy with relief. The lawyer had been right after all in assuring him he would be going home soon. It felt like good news until Eddy remembered what awaited him at home. Without his mother waiting to welcome him, he wasn't sure he wanted to go home. At least in police custody he was fed and looked after, even if his bed was uncomfortable and the food was tasteless. At home, he would have to fend for himself. So when the detective announced that he was free to go, he greeted the news with mixed feelings.

'Go where?' he stammered at first. 'Where am I going?'

'Go home,' she replied, 'you're free to go home. Collect your things from the custody sergeant. Come along.'

He could hardly say he wasn't ready to leave just yet. So he followed the detective to the desk where a stocky officer handed over his wallet and keys, after which he took the bus back to an empty house. He hesitated on the front doorstep, half expecting to hear his mother's shrill voice calling to him.

'Eddy?' he imagined her irritated tone. 'Is that you, Eddy? Where the hell have you been all this time? You can't keep disappearing like this. Don't you know I worry about you when you don't tell me where you're going?'

Only his mother didn't call out his name, because she was dead. She would never call his name again. For the first time since her murder, a wave of grief washed over him and he felt dizzy as the finality of her death hit him for the first time. This was no game. His mother had gone and she would never come back. He had to reach out and grab on to the door frame for support. At the same time, out of the corner of his eye he thought he noticed the next-door curtain twitch, and he had the uneasy feeling he was being watched. He went inside, slamming the front door firmly behind him. The nosy cow from next door could just mind her own business. He had often caught sight of her spying on him as he went out and when he returned home, as though where he went was any of her business. Even his mother didn't know how he had been spending his time.

He leaned back against the wall and slithered down until he was sitting on the floor with his legs stretched out in front of him. He was going to have to manage on his own. Gazing around in despair, his eyes fell on a scuffed brown envelope lying on the doormat. He stared at it in dismay. His mother had always dealt with household affairs. Now a letter had been posted through his door, and he had no idea what he was supposed to do with it. He knew bills had to be paid, but he had never gone through that process himself. Leaving the envelope where it was, he clambered to his feet. Kylie would help him with his bills. She would know what to do. Resolving to speak to her as soon as he could, he shuffled into the living room, sat down comfortably in an armchair, and switched on the television. This was better than being in prison after all. He knew where his mother kept her money. Soon he would go out and get himself some chips, and then he would go and see Kylie.

Staring at the flickering screen, he felt his eyelids begin to close and muted the television. Although he had been alone in his cell, he had been disturbed by a background noise of footsteps, doors banging and voices calling out, muffled through the walls but irritating, nonetheless. It was a relief to hear nothing but the distant hum of traffic and the intermittent purr of cars driving past. As he was relishing the quiet, his doze was interrupted by the bell. Startled out of his pleasant stupor, he stared in the direction of the front door, even though he couldn't see it from where he was sitting. Hardly daring to breathe, he waited for the caller to go away. The bell rang again, and then again. Trembling, he staggered out into the hall. Through the frosted glass panel he could make out a figure on the other side of the front door.

'Go away,' he called out. 'Leave me alone. I don't want to see you. I don't want to see anyone.'

The bell rang again and someone shouted his name.

'Eddy, open the door. I know you're in there. I can hear you. Stop being a dick and open the door.'

For an instant, he thought he recognised the voice.

'Mother? Is that you?'

He flung open the door and was dismayed to see his cousin standing on the doorstep.

'Eddy,' Alec said, putting down the bags he was holding and stooping to grab hold of Eddy's hand and shake it vigorously. 'Eddy. I came to offer my condolences and to see if there's anything I can do to help.' His brown eyes seemed to pierce right through Eddy's skull.

'I don't need any help,' Eddy lied, snatching his hand from the warm grasp.

Alec smiled. 'Don't tell me you don't want any company right now,' he said, seemingly oblivious to Eddy's unease. 'We're family, after all. I'm your cousin.'

'I know who you are,' Eddy mumbled, uncomfortable under the intensity of his cousin's gaze.

He desperately wanted his cousin to go away, but didn't know how to persuade him to leave. Lately Alec had begun pestering him, although they hadn't seen much of each other for years. When Eddy was about ten, his mother had fallen out with Alec's mother and there had been what Eddy's mother called a 'rift' in the family. Eddy never understood what it was about, but they hadn't seen Aunty Mary and Alec again after that for a very long time. His mother had been angry about the estrangement, but Eddy had been secretly jubilant on learning he wouldn't be seeing his cousin any more. Alec used to bully him, calling him horrible names, deliberately tripping him up, thumping him, and nicking his toys when their mothers weren't looking. He had threatened to break Eddy's arm if he told anyone, and Eddy had been too scared to complain.

'Well, I just want to know if there's anything I can do,' Alec said now. 'I'm still your cousin, in spite of everything.'

'Yes, I know who you are,' Eddy said. 'But I don't know what you want with me.'

Alec smiled. 'There's no reason for you to shut me out. I'm not thirteen any more, and you're not ten. I told you, we've both changed. And we're still cousins.'

Eddy wished Alec would stop going on and on about them being cousins. While they were talking, Alec stood on the doorstep, looking at him expectantly.

'What are you doing here?' Eddy asked bluntly. 'What do you want?'

He wished Alec would go away, but was scared to say so aloud.

'I don't want anything,' Alec replied.

But he wouldn't be standing on Eddy's doorstep if that was true.

'Why are you here then?'

'I thought it would be a good idea to come and see if you need anything,' Alec said, spreading his hands in an expansive gesture.

'No. I don't want anything,' Eddy replied. 'Only Kylie,' he thought to himself.

'That's good then.' Alec smiled, but he made no move to leave.

'You can go away then,' Eddy said. He didn't care if he sounded rude. 'I don't know what you're doing here.'

'I came to see you're okay.'

'Yes, well, I'm okay so you can go away. It's none of your business anyway. I hardly know you and I want you to leave me alone. I'm busy.'

For answer, Alec picked up his bags and took a step towards Eddy. 'At least you can invite me in for a beer after I've come all this way to see you. We are still cousins.'

While he was talking, Alec edged forwards until he had one foot over the threshold. Eddy would have to physically push him away to stop him entering the house. Alec obviously didn't mind Eddy being so unwelcoming. In fact, he didn't even seem to have noticed. Eddy wondered what was wrong with his cousin.

'Well, all right, you can come in, but you'll have to look after yourself. I'm going out. And there isn't any beer.'

'No problem,' Alec replied, smiling. 'You can pick some up while you're out.'

He pushed his way into the house, dropped his bags, grabbed Eddy by the arm and dragged him into the living room.

'I'm going out,' Eddy announced, pulling himself free from Alec's grasp. 'I'm going to see my girlfriend,' he added and then wished he hadn't. 'You can't come with me,' he added quickly.

He didn't want Alec bossing him around in front of Kylie.

'Before you go, you need to sign this contract. It's a legal requirement, now the house is yours.'

With an elegant flourish, Alec produced a paper from his jacket pocket. Eddy had never trusted his cousin. Alec kept assuring him that he only wanted to help, but Eddy knew he was up to something. All the same, the prospect of having to deal with an official document made him panic. He remembered the brown envelope in the hall and felt his throat constrict with panic.

'Why do I need to sign anything?' he croaked, struggling to conceal his alarm. 'What is it anyway?'

'It's nothing to worry about,' Alec assured him, 'but you need to sign it. Here, where it says sign.'

'What is it?'

'It's for the insurance,' Alec explained.

'Insurance?' Eddy repeated anxiously.

'I told you I'd be around to help you until you sort yourself out, didn't I?' Alec said. 'Aunty Doreen once said to me that if anything happened to her, she wanted me to look after you. She

113

made me promise. So that's why I'm here.' He smiled. 'Sign here, otherwise the house won't be insured and if anything goes wrong you'll have to pay for it.'

His mother had always taken care of everything, and Eddy had no idea what to do. With a sigh, he signed his name where Alec was pointing.

'Good,' said Alec. 'I'm going to look after everything for you, so there's no need to worry.'

'I'm going out,' Eddy repeated firmly.

Alec was always trying to take control, but Eddy could put his foot down when he wanted to, and there was nothing Alec or anyone else could do to stop him seeing Kylie.

18

It had been a gruelling day. Louisa's colleague, Shona, had warned her that guests could be vexatious. Sometimes the carping was justified. Housekeeping could be slapdash, and problems arose with faulty light bulbs and kettles, or missing or stained towels. But, according to Louisa's colleague, the most common reason behind complaints was money.

'Some people are a right pain in the neck. They make a fuss just for the sake of it,' Shona explained. 'Some are just attention seekers, but mostly they're angling for a reduction on their bill. They think they're getting their money's worth if they find fault with something and kick up enough of a stink to make us offer a discount.'

'Can we do that?' Louisa asked, surprised. 'Take something off the bill if they ask?'

She wondered why everyone didn't make the request if it was so easily granted.

Shona laughed. 'No, we're not authorised to offer discounts. All we can do is give out extra sachets of coffee or shampoo, although it's supposed to be no more than one a night for each guest. We're just chamber maids, the lowest of the low. If you have what seems to be a genuine complaint, or a seriously disgruntled guest, you need to refer it to management to deal with. They judge whether or not to take anything off the bill and how much. We don't have anything to do with money. That's way above our pay grade.'

That morning, Louisa had been harangued by a guest who

claimed she was unhappy at being interrupted while she was on the phone. It wasn't as if Louisa had knocked on the door early, and the guest hadn't turned her sign around on the door to indicate she didn't wish to be disturbed.

'And I booked a room on the ground floor,' the woman snapped. 'What if the lift breaks down? I can't go up and down stairs in my condition. Look at me!' She raised a walking stick and brandished it in the air. 'I insist on being moved to the ground floor.'

Louisa was tempted to point out that the woman had spent a night in a room on the first floor. Instead, she called the manager, who didn't answer her phone. Duly apologetic, Louisa assured the guest that the manager must have been unaware of her disability when she booked the room.

'I don't have a disability,' the woman retorted, almost spitting in her indignation. 'I have a strained Achilles tendon and walking any distance at all is extremely painful. I shouldn't have to justify myself to you. I'm paying a lot of money to stay here, and if I request a ground-floor room, that's what I expect to be given.'

She raised her voice, banging her stick on the floor, and another guest knocked on the door to complain about the noise. Flustered by all the commotion, Louisa struggled to assure the injured woman that the manager would find her a room on the ground floor. She called the manager again but there was still no response.

'What if the lift breaks down, or there's a fire?' the guest ranted. 'I could be stranded here on the first floor. Do you want to put your guests' lives in danger? I told you, I can't go up or down stairs in my condition and I shouldn't be expected to. You'll have to pay for me to stay somewhere else if you don't have a spare room on the ground floor. I specifically stated that I wanted a ground-floor room when I made the booking.'

Louisa would have liked to say they had no rooms available

on the ground floor and the woman was welcome to find somewhere else to stay, because she was no longer welcome in that hotel, but she knew she would lose her job if she was rude to a guest. Finally, the manager arrived to deal with the situation and Louisa left her with the angry guest. But that wasn't the end of it. At the end of her shift, Louisa was summoned to the office where the manager asked her to give an account of herself.

'The guest was really upset,' she said sternly.

Louisa explained she had knocked on the door before attempting to enter, and the guest hadn't displayed the 'Do Not Disturb' sign.

'You can stand there defending yourself until you're blue in the face, but that's absolutely missing the point,' the manager said. 'Our job is to make sure guests enjoy their stay here. If they're dissatisfied, they can post scathing reviews about us and too many of those can damage our business. We expect our staff to show more sense. You haven't even been here for three months, and already you've started upsetting guests.'

'No, no, that is, I'm sorry,' Louisa mumbled, filled with dismay at having landed in trouble so soon after her move to York.

'I'm giving you a verbal warning,' the manager said. 'I hope you treat this as an opportunity to learn how to conduct yourself when you're speaking to guests. But bear in mind this is a warning. Any further trouble from you and I won't hesitate to send you packing.'

It was really unfair. Someone in Louisa's position ought never to have been left to deal with an irate customer. If the manager had answered her phone when Louisa had first called her, Louisa would never have become involved, but she was too rattled to protest. Not that it would have done her any good to argue. The manager already had the impression she was confrontational, thanks to one belligerent guest. If she claimed the manager was at fault, Louisa would almost certainly lose her job.

LEIGH RUSSELL

'What were you thinking of, Louisa?' the manager went on. 'You've only just started here and already you're taking it on yourself to deal with complaints. Unbelievable.'

There was a lot more along those lines, but after a few minutes Louisa stopped listening. All she could do was bleat an apology and promise it would never happen again.

'You're damn sure it won't happen again,' the manager spluttered. 'Didn't Shona tell you to send complaints straight to me?'

Eventually the manager sent her back to work, and Louisa ran to the toilet to sob to herself in a locked cubicle. She emerged red-eyed, and returned to her chores. Thankfully the rest of the day passed without any further problems. By the time her shift ended, she no longer looked as though she had been crying, but she left hurriedly all the same.

'How was your day?' a colleague enquired as she passed the front desk.

'Everything's fine. Got to rush, I'm meeting a friend,' Louisa fibbed, scurrying away before the receptionist could question her further.

More than anything, she was afraid of breaking down in tears in full view of the front desk, where she knew security cameras would capture her humiliation for everyone to see.

All in all, she was not in the best of moods, and as soon as she left the hotel she realised she was hungry. Usually she ate a huge lunch – a welcome perk of her job – but in her agitation she had missed her midday meal altogether. She had no food at home to speak of, so she went to the supermarket on her way back. Carrying her shopping along Nunnery Lane, she noticed a hooded figure walking on the opposite pavement, keeping pace with her. Shaking off an uneasy suspicion that she had seen that same figure before, she hurried home. After eating a huge bowl of pasta, she felt much better. Probably everyone made the same mistake as her when they started the job, and she resolved to forget about it. By the next day, the manager would have had so many other issues to sort out she wouldn't even remember that she had issued Louisa with a warning.

On her way to bed she glanced out of the window, wondering what the weather would be like in the morning. A hooded figure was standing motionless across the street from her block. She couldn't see anything of his face, but was sure he was staring straight at her window. Pulling the curtain closed, she did her best to dismiss her anxiety, assuring herself angrily that no one could possibly be watching her. She didn't even know anyone in York apart from the few people she had met at work, and if they wanted to see her they could approach her at the hotel, not lurk outside her flat, looking out for her. There were any number of reasons why someone might happen to be standing outside her block of flats just when she glanced through the window. He was probably waiting for someone, or pausing to light a cigarette, or gazing up at the stars. She wasn't used to living alone, and that was making her jumpy. Her stressful day at work wasn't helping. Nevertheless, she was determined not to crawl back to her parents. Her mother wouldn't show her triumph openly, but she was bound to feel vindicated about warning Louisa against going to live in the city. If anything, that only made Louisa even more determined to stay exactly where she was. Everything was unfamiliar and intimidating, but she was sure the city would turn out to be a really exciting place to live. It was just going to take longer than she had expected to settle in and find her way around. But she was prepared to be patient. Things had to improve soon.

19

IT WAS A WEEK since Doreen's body had been discovered and the investigation was proceeding slowly. Everyone was disappointed to learn that the dark fibres discovered on Doreen's fingers had been too generic to trace. Somehow all the evidence in this case felt baffling, as though they were trying to peer into the distance through a heavy mist.

Nico had been in custody overnight, kicking his heels in a cell. With Ariadne due back at work after the weekend, Geraldine was desperately hoping he would confess before her colleague returned. Even though they had enough evidence to charge him, he continued to insist he was innocent. The problem was, he appeared to have no motive for killing Doreen. Of course Ariadne being a sergeant had no bearing on the case, and it certainly didn't mean Nico was innocent. Nevertheless, Ariadne's presence at the police station was likely to prove uncomfortable, especially for Geraldine, who was her friend. Eileen had arranged to transfer Ariadne to another case, but she was still working in the same building, and it would be impossible for her to ignore what was happening with Nico. Geraldine was very fond of Ariadne, and it wasn't as though she had many other friends, so she hated the thought of falling out with her. But it was difficult to see how their friendship could weather this, especially if it turned out that Nico had been wrongly arrested. She wasn't sure Eileen fully appreciated how tricky the situation was. Nico's arrest had been ordered in quite a cavalier fashion.

'I can't make any exceptions,' the detective chief inspector said firmly, when Geraldine raised the issue with her. 'I have to treat Nico the same as everyone else.'

'But we have no evidence,' Geraldine protested. 'There's no reason to hold him, and certainly not on such a serious charge.'

'He was there in Doreen's house,' Eileen said dogmatically. 'That's enough. We can't go letting every suspect off just because they refuse to confess.'

Geraldine did her best to conceal her shock at Eileen's words. 'What if he's innocent?' she asked.

'Why was he there then?'

'He explained why he was visiting her. He knew her. He was looking after her financial affairs.'

But Eileen didn't want to listen. Geraldine went to question Nico again. She was pleased to see he had shaved and was looking slightly less dishevelled than the last time she had seen him. His dark-haired lawyer was muttering to him in a foreign language, presumably Greek, when Geraldine joined them. The lawyer flashed a smile at Geraldine as she took her seat. She had an impression of gleaming teeth and bright eyes, as she turned her attention to Nico.

'Tell me about your relationship with Doreen Lewis,' she said.

'What do you mean by relationship?' Nico asked, looking slightly alarmed. He glanced at his lawyer, before adding, 'I don't admit to anything.'

'You seem to be implying there was some kind of relationship between my client and the murdered woman,' the lawyer interrupted smoothly. 'He is clear that was not the case.'

'But you knew her?'

'Yes, she was married to a friend of my uncle. But I've already told you everything there is to know about my meetings with her. We were introduced by my uncle, and I met her half a dozen times, at most.'

'That seems rather inexact for an accountant,' Geraldine murmured. She did not add that the last time she had questioned him, Nico had told her he had only met Doreen three or four times.

'Are you making a joke of this?' the lawyer demanded, suddenly animated.

'A man's freedom is not something I would ever joke about,' Geraldine replied calmly. 'But I am asking your client about his relationship with a woman who was murdered on a day when we know he visited her at home.'

'Which he has never denied,' the lawyer said quickly. 'We both know this is merely circumstantial evidence. You yourself visited her house on the day she died. Your DNA will be detectable in the room where she was killed, but no one has accused you of murdering her.'

Geraldine smiled at his equivocation. 'I was never alone with her, and only set eyes on her after her death. This is very different, as you are well aware. Nico visited Doreen on the day she died, shortly before her death, and he went there alone. Surely you agree it is in his own interest that he share with us what happened that day?'

'I already told you I went to see Doreen to help her with her tax affairs,' Nico said. 'There really isn't anything else to say.'

'My client was acting in good faith, helping an old woman for no personal gain,' the lawyer added. 'This is not how such a good deed should be rewarded.'

Geraldine noticed how they both placed particular emphasis on the word 'help'. It almost made her suspect Nico had something to hide, although it was probably just nerves that made him so eager to create a good impression for the tape.

'What did you do after you spoke to her about her tax affairs?' Geraldine asked.

'I've already answered that question. I went for a walk,' Nico said.

'Alone,' Geraldine pointed out softly.

'It's not a crime to take a walk by yourself,' the lawyer said. He was beginning to sound irritated.

Geraldine wondered whether his frustration was sincere, or if he was putting on an act for her benefit. Turning to Nico, she went over the times of his arrival and departure. According to his testimony, he had been in Doreen's house for less than an hour.

'So you left at midday?'

'Yes.'

'Are you sure of that?'

Nico sighed. 'I didn't make a note of the time, but yes, I'm pretty sure. She asked me if I wanted to wait and stay for lunch but it was too early and besides, I'd arranged to meet Ariadne in town.'

'At what time?'

'We were meeting for lunch at one o'clock.'

'We can check that.'

'Go ahead, ask her. She'll tell you we met at one.'

'So there's a period of up to an hour when Nico's movements are unaccounted for,' Geraldine told Naomi that afternoon.

They had met by chance in the canteen, and were sitting down for a coffee together. Ian was still away, and Ariadne was no longer involved in the case. Geraldine was happy to work with any of her colleagues, but she felt slightly lost without her two best friends on the team. She appreciated having someone to chat to informally about the cases she was working on. Since she had recently saved Naomi's life, her young colleague had been keen to befriend her. Although she knew Naomi's friendliness was prompted by gratitude, rather than any particular affinity, Geraldine was pleased of the company.

'If we could find someone who saw him while he was out walking, we might be able to prove he's innocent,' Naomi suggested. 'We know he met Ariadne at one.'

'But he said he went out on his own and didn't notice anyone

123

else after he left Doreen. He hasn't even been able to tell us where he went exactly. He just said he wandered around the streets to stretch his legs and ended up down by the river. Could his account be more vague?'

Geraldine didn't share her anxieties about the detective chief inspector with Naomi, but on the phone to Ian later, she voiced her concerns freely.

'I'm worried about Eileen,' she admitted bluntly.

'What do you mean? Are you in trouble with her? What have you done this time?'

'No, it's not me, and this is no joke. I think she might be in trouble. I mean, she seems to be losing the plot. She had Nico arrested even though we don't really have a very strong case against him. It's all put together on circumstantial evidence.'

'Are you sure you're not being unduly influenced by your friendship with Ariadne?' Ian asked.

'Of course I'm not,' she snapped, but her vexed retort suggested he might be right.

'I am capable of thinking objectively,' she continued, and sighed. 'At least I think I am, but it's impossible to be absolutely sure, isn't it?'

'So your concern isn't really about Eileen at all, is it? You're worried about upsetting your friend.'

Geraldine hesitated before replying. 'No, no, that's not it at all. I'm telling you, I don't think Nico's guilty.' But she knew Ian had noticed her hesitation. 'But it's not just that.'

She went on to describe how muddled Eileen had seemed. 'At one point she seemed to be confusing Nico and Eddy.'

'Are you sure you're not overthinking this? Two suspects can be a bit confusing, and she probably wasn't paying attention to what you were saying. I'm sure she has a lot on her mind with this case, and she must be concerned about Ariadne.'

Geraldine didn't pursue the point, but she was worried.

'Well, let's see what you think when you get back,' she said.

'But I've got the impression something's not right about the DCI.'

'I don't like the sound of that,' Ian said, but Geraldine wasn't convinced he was taking her concern seriously.

20

ARIADNE GAZED DISCONSOLATELY AROUND her living room. Only a few weeks ago, she had been admiring it with Nico who had been standing at her side with his arm around her.

'Our home,' she had whispered, and he had leaned down to kiss her cheek.

It had taken them some time to arrange everything so they were both satisfied. Nico had insisted on bringing his own armchair to their house and it clashed with their new furniture. Ariadne recalled how irritated she had been that he hadn't mentioned his horrible chair to her before they ordered a sofa, but she was pleased with herself, remembering how accommodating she had been. Marriage was a matter of compromise, and a living room where the furniture didn't all match perfectly could only rankle with her as long as she focused on it. So she had kept quiet and, in the event, the chair didn't look too out of place. What was more important was that they had moved all their belongings in without exchanging a single cross word.

Now Ariadne had been at home on her own for almost a week. Unable to sleep, she had tidied the living room several times, shifting the chairs around and then returning them to their original positions, swapping the pictures hanging on the walls, and displaying photos of her husband before putting them away again, out of sight, as though they had never been married at all. Having finished in the living room she had cleaned the kitchen, gone up to the bedroom – their bedroom, hers and Nico's – taken all her clothes out of her wardrobe and returned them, in only slightly tidier piles. His clothes she left untouched. Moving his belongings felt like a betrayal, as though she believed he would never return to sort them out for himself.

Returning to the living room, she sat down in front of the television and stared around her. The house felt empty without Nico. All at once she broke down in tears. Telling herself she was angry, not upset, she forced herself to calm down and gradually her sobbing subsided until only faint hiccups persisted as a reminder of her crying fit. But she could not maintain the pretence that she wasn't scared. With her husband arrested for murder, she had good reason to be afraid. Being a police officer, she knew that suspects were not arrested without clear evidence of guilt. Such evidence could be misleading, but it was a necessary condition for an arrest. And if a suspect was arrested, that could only mean there was a chance they were guilty. That possibility scared her more than anything else.

The worst of it was that she had not seen Nico since the police had first shown interest in taking a sample of his DNA, so she had not had a chance to press him about what had happened. When his name had first been mentioned in connection with the murder of Doreen Lewis, Ariadne had laughed at the accusation, it had seemed so far-fetched. For days she had remained convinced of Nico's innocence. But as the days passed, she became increasingly anxious, until she realised it was possible she had not known her husband at all. He had always seemed so calm and measured, but perhaps that steady exterior masked a demon she had never even glimpsed. He had never so much as raised his voice in her presence. It scarcely seemed possible he had a dark side she had never suspected, but she knew only too well how duplicitous people could be. Intelligent criminals had a way of covering their tracks. It was even possible that she had shared information with Nico about how the police had caught other killers. She felt physically sick thinking that she might have unwittingly contributed to his decision to kill, confident that he knew how to evade conviction.

Suddenly she couldn't bear the uncertainty a moment longer. Picking up her phone, she called Geraldine.

'Hi, how's things?' Geraldine asked.

It was an inane question given the circumstances, but Ariadne accepted her friend was trying to speak normally, as though nothing dreadful had happened, and Nico would soon be home.

'I'm fine,' Ariadne lied. 'I just wondered how it's all going with the case?'

'One step forward, two steps back,' Geraldine replied vaguely. 'There's nothing more yet. We're still casting around in the dark. You know how it is at this stage of an investigation.'

'What about Nico?' Ariadne asked directly, when it seemed Geraldine was determined to avoid saying anything specific.

'He seems to be bearing up.'

'Yes, yes, I'm sure he is. What I meant was, what's happening? When will he be released, or is there actually a case against him?'

Geraldine didn't answer straight away, which was an answer in itself. 'There may be a case,' she admitted at last. 'It's difficult to say for sure. It's early days. How are you?'

'Geraldine, you know what I'm asking you,' Ariadne replied, ignoring Geraldine's question. 'Was Nico's DNA really found at the scene?'

Again Geraldine hesitated, but there was no point in trying to conceal the truth.

'Nico's DNA was found in the dead woman's hair, yes, consistent with his having breathed on her. He could have been exerting himself, but I think he might have just sneezed on her.'

'He gets hay fever,' Ariadne interjected urgently.

'He's been questioned and he admits he visited her on the morning of her death. He told us he was helping her with her finances. According to Nico's statement, Doreen's deceased husband was a friend of his uncle. We've checked that out and it's all been confirmed, and in any case the evidence against him is by no means conclusive. But –' she paused again.

The waiting was unbearable. 'What? But what?' Ariadne burst out. 'Surely evidence he was there only proves that he visited Doreen, and he's never denied that. He's given a perfectly sound reason for wanting to see her.'

'Yes, you're right.'

'So why hasn't he been released?'

Over the phone it sounded as though Geraldine stifled a sigh. 'Eileen seems to be convinced Nico killed Doreen.'

Ariadne took a few seconds to process that information. If there really was no evidence that Nico was guilty, it didn't make sense that he hadn't been released. At the same time, if Eileen was treating him as a suspect, then there must be more to it than Ariadne had been told.

'What is it you're not telling me?'

'Nothing.'

'I don't understand. What's going on?'

'Honestly, I'm not sure. Either Eileen knows something she hasn't told me, or she's losing her grip. I'm a bit worried about her.'

'Yes, well, I don't give a toss about Eileen,' Ariadne said, making no attempt to conceal her irritation. 'Nico's the one we should be worrying about. Have you even seen him?'

'Yes, I questioned him, and I assured him you're convinced he's innocent.'

'What did he say to that?'

'Not a lot, really, but he was probably too shocked by what's happening to say anything. And he was being careful not to say too much. I think his lawyer's advised him to keep his mouth shut, the way they do. But he's been insisting he's innocent all along, and I believe him.'

'Geraldine, what's going to happen to him?'

'If he's innocent, we'll find out and he'll come home and everything will be fine, you'll see.'

They both knew Geraldine was skirting around the issue, in an attempt to be reassuring.

'What if he's found guilty?' Ariadne asked. 'What do I do then?'

Geraldine didn't answer. There was nothing to say.

'Geraldine –' Ariadne began and broke off as her voice cracked. 'Geraldine, you have to help him,' she whispered. 'I know he didn't do it.'

But of course she didn't know, not really. No one really knew what anyone else had done. Ending the call, she ran to the bathroom and threw up. All she wanted was for this nightmare to end, and for Nico to come home.

21

THE NEXT DAY GERALDINE went to see the detective chief inspector in her office. Eileen's square face looked pale and drawn, and there were dark grey shadows under her eyes. She smiled with an uncharacteristically wary expression, and fired a series of repetitive questions at Geraldine.

'Yes? Yes? Come in, come in. What is it? What do you want with me? What are you doing here?'

'We've charged Nico Moralis,' Geraldine said heavily.

'Good, good.'

For a second, Geraldine thought Eileen was actually going to clap her hands. Instead, the detective chief inspector asked another question.

'So you're telling me he's decided to confess?'

'No, he hasn't, and I don't think he's going to. He's still insisting that he's innocent.'

Eileen tapped her fingers impatiently on her desk, with a curious pout. 'Well, he would say that, wouldn't he? But just because he tells us he's innocent doesn't mean he is. You know that as well as I do.'

'Of course it doesn't necessarily mean he's innocent, but I believe he's telling the truth.' Geraldine gazed anxiously at her senior officer, fearing an irate outburst.

'Believe? You believe? What's that supposed to mean? This isn't a question of what you or anyone else believes. Keep your opinions to yourself,' Eileen snapped. 'Right now your job is to get our suspect to confess so we can close the case with a minimum of fuss. That's all you need to focus on.' Her cheeks flushed and she glared and raised her voice. 'I suggest you get on with your job and do whatever it is you're paid to do. There is no room for dead wood on my team. If you think you can drag your heels on this because Ariadne is your friend, then you can hand in your resignation right now, before I send you packing. You've been demoted once, don't think it can't happen again.'

However vehemently Eileen had disagreed with Geraldine, she had never before lost her temper with her, or threatened her so unreasonably.

Geraldine hesitated, but she couldn't just walk away. 'Eileen,' she said gently, taking a step forward. 'Are you feeling all right? I mean, it seems a bit like we may be jumping to conclusions before we have all the evidence in place. And it's not like you to be so –' She hesitated, fumbling for the right word to express her reservations about her senior officer. 'It just all seems a bit rushed and – well, peremptory,' she concluded.

Eileen stared at Geraldine, but she spoke quietly. 'We have to guard against allowing bias to affect our judgement.'

'I'm not sure I understand what you mean.'

'I think you understand me perfectly, but let me spell it out for you. Ariadne is off the case, but I'm wondering if you feel able to keep the necessary distance from this case, given the nature of her relationship with the suspect. If I can't rely on you to behave professionally, there's no place for you here.'

Geraldine nodded. 'I appreciate the need to remain objective, but shouldn't we also be careful that our reluctance to be influenced in any way doesn't push us too far in the opposite direction?'

Eileen shook her head wearily. 'Quibbling won't achieve anything. Just get that confession, Geraldine.'

As she went to question Nico again, Geraldine wished she could speak to Ian. He had been working with Eileen for longer than she had, and he was the only person with whom she could safely discuss her suspicions about their senior officer. She would have valued his opinion, but he needed to see the detective chief inspector's erratic behaviour for himself.

Nico seemed dejected and scarcely looked up when Geraldine entered the interview room.

'Are you sure there's nothing else you want to tell me?' she enquired, when they were seated facing one another, with Nico's black-eyed lawyer at his side. 'You must know it will be far easier for you, and for Ariadne, if you're honest with us.'

'I am being honest,' Nico insisted. 'I've been honest right from the start. I have nothing to hide. Why won't you people believe me?'

'My client is telling you the truth,' the lawyer said.

'What I don't understand is why you left your wife,' Geraldine continued, ignoring the interruption. 'If you're innocent, as you claim, why did you walk out on your wife straight after Doreen was murdered?'

Nico shook his head. 'It was stupid of me,' he mumbled. 'I was afraid.'

'What were you afraid of? If you're innocent, as you claim, you must have realised it would be in your interests to co-operate fully with our investigation instead of running away?'

'I was afraid you'd find out I visited Doreen on the day she died,' Nico replied. He hesitated. 'I went back to Portland Street after lunch because I realised I'd forgotten to check on something. It wasn't really that important but I thought I'd deal with it straight away, but there were police cars and an undertaker's van outside Doreen's house. Then they brought a body out on a stretcher. A group of onlookers, neighbours I guess, were saying an old woman in a wheelchair had been killed. They all seemed to think she'd been murdered, and I thought – that is, I didn't really think at all. I was too frightened to think clearly. I just made myself scarce and I thought that would be the end of the matter. The next day Ariadne told me she was working on a murder case. I asked her about it, and as soon as she told me the victim was in a wheelchair, I knew who it was. I didn't want Ariadne to know I'd visited Doreen on the day she was killed. I didn't want to get in trouble with the law. I just wanted to disappear quietly and not cause Ariadne any embarrassment. There was no need for her to get caught up in all this.'

'How can she not be caught up in it? Did you really think you could just walk away? You're her husband, and you're a suspect in a murder investigation. By running away you made yourself look guilty. You must see that.'

'But I keep telling you, I've done nothing wrong. I just happened to visit an old woman on the day she was killed.' Nico leaned forward and fixed Geraldine with a penetrating gaze. 'Do you think I'd plan a murder without even attempting to set up an alibi? Do you really think I'm that stupid?'

'No, I don't believe you're stupid,' Geraldine replied softly. 'But intelligent people can act on impulse, just like anyone else. It's possible you panicked. Doreen might have been threatening you in some way. Perhaps she was blackmailing you. You're married to a detective. You must be aware that not all murders are carefully planned. More often than not they happen when someone loses their temper.'

She waited for a moment, but Nico didn't respond. He sat staring sullenly back at her without saying a word.

'Was that what happened?' she resumed. 'Did you lose your temper with Doreen? Talk to me Nico, tell me how she died. You know it will be easier for Ariadne if you just tell us the truth. She'll understand if you were pushed beyond the limits of your endurance and lost control.'

The lawyer answered for Nico. 'My client has already told you that he's innocent of the charges brought against him. You are going to have to look elsewhere for your killer.'

Geraldine studied the lawyer. Dressed in a dark grey jacket and black shirt, his black hair gleaming and oily, he looked like an old-fashioned Hollywood film star. Judging by his swagger as he walked into the room, and his air of easy nonchalance at the table, he was conscious of his good looks, and confident in his abilities. Geraldine suspected he was vain, and wondered whether she might turn that to her advantage by flattering him.

'Thank you for your clarity,' she ventured, 'and for your ready grasp of the situation. Not many people are as articulate and clear thinking as you. It is a relief, I can assure you.'

The lawyer looked sceptical, and she realised that he had seen through her clumsy ruse. They weren't making any progress, and Eileen had made it quite clear that she wanted Nico behind bars. Geraldine felt she was in an impossible situation. She could hardly confide in Ariadne, and when she tried to call Ian he didn't answer his phone. She tried to contact him again that evening. This time he picked up but before she had a chance to speak, he told her he was on his way out for dinner and he would speak to her the next day. There was something dismissive in his tone that upset her. She appreciated that he was busy, but she felt miserable all the same.

Although she had lived on her own for nearly twenty years, her flat now felt empty without Ian. She regretted her insistence on staying there. Ian had been keen to move but she had refused to even discuss the possibility. It had taken his absence to shake her into acknowledging that the four walls around her were unimportant in themselves. Much as she loved her flat, and thought of it as her home, it was just a hollow shell. When she went to bed, the sheets felt cold and unwelcoming. As she waited impatiently for Ian's return, she wondered how she would cope if he never came back. Her thoughts drifted to Ariadne, and the torment she must be experiencing, and she realised that Eileen was right. It was impossible to remain detached from the case, knowing her friend's husband was being held on a charge of murder.

22

LOUISA WAS REALLY PLEASED when her colleague, Shona, suggested they go out for a drink together that evening. At last she felt as though she was beginning to settle in. Having just one friend made all the difference. Shona seemed really nice, and she had grown up in York which meant she must have lots of local friends to introduce to Louisa. It became apparent in their conversations during their breaks that Shona had recently split up with her boyfriend and wanted another girl to go out with, 'on the pull,' as she put it. Louisa didn't mind that she had only been invited out when Shona was at a loose end and needed a companion to go out with. This was going to be a fun night out, and Louisa's first taste of night life in the city. She wondered if they would go clubbing, and was initially disappointed when Shona said they were going to a pub along Micklegate.

'It's where all the cool guys hang out,' Shona explained. 'We're going to have a blast. Trust me. It's the best place.'

Not knowing the area, Louisa was happy to fall in with Shona's plans, and agreed to meet her at Micklegate Bar. Keen to impress her new friend, Louisa wanted to know what Shona was going to wear.

'Jeans I guess,' Shona replied with a shrug.

'Okay then.'

Shona gave Louisa a curious glance. 'We're just going for a drink,' she said.

Louisa felt her face grow warm and she hoped she wasn't

blushing. 'Sure,' she said, trying to sound casual. 'It's just a drink. I know that.' She forced a laugh.

Despite her show of nonchalance, Louisa spent a long time agonising over her outfit for the evening. She had a new pair of jeans that fitted her snugly. She was what her mother called 'sturdily built' but her new jeans were navy and, being dark, were quite flattering. The problem was what to wear with them. Eventually she narrowed her choice down to a comfortable loose grey leopard print T-shirt, and a figure-hugging long sleeved navy T-shirt with sequins on one shoulder. In the end she opted for the sequins as more appropriate for the evening. Nervous about going out alone, she put on the long mac that she wore every day to work and set off.

Reaching Micklegate Bar early, she waited until her new friend arrived, and was surprised to see Shona in a tight black leather skirt that barely skimmed her backside, and a bright red tank top under a short denim jacket. She had painted her nails bright red to match her top, and was wearing heavy make-up. Louisa felt quite frumpy beside her and hurriedly removed her shapeless coat.

'You said you were wearing jeans,' she mumbled, and then felt like an idiot. 'I mean,' she stammered, 'I just thought…' She faltered and was silent.

Shona grunted. Louisa wasn't sure she had even been listening.

'You look great,' Louisa added quickly.

Shona smiled uncertainly. 'I thought I'd make a bit of an effort. I mean, Benjy might be there, you know. Show him what he's missing.' She wiggled her hips and grinned with forced bravado.

So Louisa learned the name of Shona's ex-boyfriend, and realised that her friend still liked him. In the pub, over a glass of wine, Louisa sat listening to Shona's account of why she and Benjy had split up. It wasn't exactly the fun evening Louisa had been hoping for, but at least she now had a friend in York. So she listened patiently while Shona talked and gazed over Louisa's shoulder, watching the entrance to the bar.

'I wasn't going to let him get away with snogging that slag, however pissed he was,' Shona was saying, when she froze suddenly. 'There he is,' she hissed.

Louisa saw a tall, skinny young man walk up to the bar. Despite a complexion scarred from acne, Louisa had to admit he was quite attractive, with a turned-up nose and slightly overhanging brow. While Louisa studied him covertly, Shona leaned back on her stool, laughed very loudly and downed the rest of her wine. Standing up, she strutted to the bar and stood sideways, leaning one elbow on the counter as she ordered another drink. As Louisa watched, the young man joined her and engaged her in conversation. It was difficult to be sure from a distance, but Louisa had the impression Shona was flirting with him. Once or twice she reached out and touched his chest with the flat of her hand in a blatantly possessive gesture. When he led her to a table on the far side of the bar, Shona followed him without a backward glance to where Louisa was sitting.

Abandoned, Louisa finished her glass of wine and was preparing to leave when a stranger approached and asked if Shona's place at the table was free. Louisa nodded. Expecting him to take the chair, she did her best to conceal her agitation when he sat down opposite her and introduced himself. He wasn't bad looking. About thirty, with a light brown fringe that brushed his eyebrows, and a direct gaze, he told her his name was Stan. Hesitantly, she gave him her name.

'I haven't seen you in here before,' he said and she explained that she had only recently arrived in York.

He smiled and offered to show her around. 'I can show you the best night clubs, if you like,' he added.

Louisa hesitated. 'I don't know,' she said at last. 'I'm not sure. That is, I don't think I can.' She glanced over towards the other side of the bar. 'I came here with a friend.' Shona was kissing Benjy.

'Sorry, I thought you were on your own.'

Before she had a chance to explain, Stan was on his feet and moving away, leaving her feeling relieved and disappointed. She had come to York looking for thrills, but at the first hint of adventure she had succumbed to a voice in her head warning her to be cautious. What made it worse was that it was her mother's voice she could hear.

'You don't know what goes on in big cities,' her mother had told her. 'You won't like it there all on your own. You're safer here at home with us.'

Resolved to follow Stan and tell him she had changed her mind, she clambered to her feet, ready to sample the night life in York. But Stan had vanished. Unsure whether to be thankful or not, Louisa made her way over to Shona.

'I'm going home.'

Shona barely glanced up from snogging Benjy. 'Okay,' she said. 'See you on Monday.'

Miserably, Louisa pulled her mac on and left, clutching her bag under her arm where it couldn't be easily slipped off her shoulder by a passing thief, her mother's warnings ringing inside her head. As she hurried along the street, she heard footsteps behind her. That was nothing unusual on a busy evening in the centre of town. Even so, she was afraid to look round and was aware that she was speeding up as she hurried along the street. No one met her gaze and she lowered her eyes, trying to be invisible. Several groups of rowdy revellers passed her, and it occurred to her that everyone she saw was probably on their way out, while she was going home.

As it turned out, she was pleased she had worn her mac, because it began to rain quite heavily. The walk seemed to take a long time, and at one point she had an uneasy feeling she was being followed. Cursing her mother for making her feel so paranoid, she hurried along the street. Everyone else seemed to be out enjoying themselves in spite of the wet weather. She wondered what might have happened if she had gone out with Stan, if that was even his real name. But he was just some creep who had accosted her in a pub, and she knew she was better off without him. She might be going home to an early night alone, but at least she was safe.

23

EDDY WAS FED UP. He had lost sight of Kylie in all the bustle of a Friday night out in York. The pavements had been thronged with people spilling out of pubs and milling about in the street. A group of women in skimpy outfits flocked around a stout woman in a veil, pale breasts spilling out of a white basque, her painted lips parted in a shriek of laughter. He very nearly got tangled up in an outlying net skirt. His heart pounded at the sight of so much exposed flesh and he scuttled away, head lowered and eyes averted, terrified by the screeching women. Equally daunting were the gangs of men who roamed the streets, shouting and gesticulating at him as he hurried by. Obviously tipsy, their rowdy exuberance was intimidating. He wondered why everyone was so noisy. It seemed as though they were afraid they would cease to exist if they stopped attracting attention with the racket they were making.

What made him even more fed up was that even without his mother he still didn't have the house to himself, because his cousin had turned up on Friday evening, and Eddy didn't know how to get rid of him. This would be the second night Alec would have slept in Eddy's house, and he was showing no sign of leaving. To Eddy's dismay, Alec had installed himself in Doreen's room.

'No,' Eddy had spluttered when Alec arrived. 'You can't stay here. There's no room for you. You'd have to sleep on the couch and you'd probably fall off. Or you'd have to sleep on the floor and that wouldn't be very nice for you. You'll have to leave,

141

go back to your own home. You'll be much more comfortable there.'

Alec had greeted this with a smile. 'Don't talk daft. Of course you've got room for me. There's a whole empty bedroom. Aunt Doreen won't be needing it any more, will she?' He laughed.

Eddy had been too shocked to remonstrate.

'Good. That's agreed then. And you won't be all by yourself with no one to talk to.'

It was true the house had felt oddly quiet without his mother calling out to him to come and help her every time he sat down. He almost missed hearing her nagging voice, telling him to go out and find a job because they needed the money, she wouldn't put up with him sitting around doing nothing all day, and he could wipe that silly smile off his face. She had been so maddening before death finally silenced her. It served her right. Her complaints had been unfair, because it wasn't as though he had ever been idle. He was always busy enough, just not with the things she wanted him to do. All she was interested in was money, but he had other things to do in life than earn a measly wage doing a menial job.

Apart from taking care of Kylie, there was the back yard to look after. He trimmed the grass verge behind the house regularly, but it was impossible to eradicate the moss that bedevilled the tiny plot, while weeds of all kinds proliferated in the gaps between the stone slabs of the yard. As fast as he removed them, they returned. He was sure they came from his neighbour's yard. Several times he had been tempted to knock on his neighbour's door and tell her exactly what he thought of the disgraceful strip of waste ground that edged her property. But since his cousin had arrived, everything was different. If his mother had been annoying, bossing him around all the time, his cousin was worse.

What made Eddy's life especially complicated was that Kylie didn't seem to have a regular work schedule at the weekends.

Sometimes she worked on Saturdays and Sundays, but other weeks she stayed at home or went shopping. He hadn't discovered her routine yet, so he wasn't sure if she would be at work that Saturday. She could be anywhere and he was too tired to trudge around the streets in hopes of finding her. Instead, he decided to have a lie-in and spend the day shopping and mowing his little strip of grass. He could be patient. On Monday he would definitely see her again, and this time he wouldn't lose sight of her. From now on, he determined to keep a close eye on her, wherever she went.

Having decided to sleep late, he was annoyed to be woken up on Saturday morning by someone tapping on his bedroom door. For a moment he hoped it was Kylie, paying him a visit to find out how he was. She must have heard by now that his mother was dead.

Hardly daring to breathe for excitement, he called out that he was on his way. He leapt out of bed and was reaching for his jeans when a voice replied. Instead of Kylie's gentle tones, he heard Alec asking him if he wanted fried eggs for breakfast.

'It's no trouble,' Alec assured him. 'Just pop out and get six eggs and I'll make us three each.'

'Go away,' Eddy shouted. 'Leave me alone.'

He was blowed if he was going to go out and get Alec's eggs for him. Knowing Alec, he probably had a whole list of things he wanted Eddy to buy for him. Disappointed that the caller wasn't Kylie, Eddy flopped back down on the bed. He had only just found a comfortable position when his phone rang.

'Hello? Hello? Eddy?'

'Who is it? Is that Kylie?'

Once again he was disappointed.

'Who's Kylie?' the woman on the line asked.

'Who are you?' he countered irritably.

'It's Mary. I thought you'd have been in touch by now.'

'In touch? With you? What for? Who are you?'

Eddy thought it must be his aunt, but he didn't remember ever speaking to her on the phone before. Now that his mother was dead, all his relatives seemed to be turning up. He didn't want to see them. He only wanted Kylie.

'About the funeral,' Mary was saying.

'What about it?'

'I'm calling you to find out the details.'

'What details?'

'The details of the funeral,' Mary replied in her curiously distant voice. 'As your aunt, your mother's sister, don't you think I'd want to attend her funeral? So, when is it?'

'It's not been arranged yet,' Eddy mumbled, annoyed.

'What are you talking about? It's been a week. What have you done about the funeral? You must have booked something. When is it? Just give me the date so I can put it on the calendar. We can agree on the details once I know when it is. I've got a few ideas but I can't do anything until I know the date.'

'I can't do anything either.'

'What do you mean? I'm calling about the funeral. Surely you've organised an undertaker? All you have to do is call and they'll guide you through the whole process. Do you want me to call them?'

'No,' he cried out, his temper rising. 'I told you, it can't be done yet.' He slammed the phone down.

His aunt called back straight away. 'Listen, Eddy,' she began in a syrupy voice he didn't recognise. 'I know you must be suffering terribly from the shock of losing your mother. Don't worry if it's all proving too much of a strain for you. There's no need for you to feel alone with everything that needs to be done. Of course you'll be paying for everything out of the estate, but I'm happy to help you with the funeral arrangements if you tell me who to contact. Alec and I have already talked about the wake and I'm happy to organise that. I just need you to send me the money and we'll give Doreen a send-off fit for royalty, not that she ever did anything to deserve it,' she concluded in a mutter.

'What money? I'm not sending you any money. Leave me alone.'

'Eddy, I just want to help –'

'You can't help me,' Eddy interrupted her. 'No one can.'

'Eddy, I know how hard this must be for you, but we have to see that Doreen has a decent send-off. You can't delay it indefinitely. Believe me, it's better to deal with it all straight away than keep putting it off.'

'I'm not putting anything off.'

'Don't be silly, Eddy. We have to make arrangements for your mother. It's not decent to leave it.'

'I keep telling you, I can't do anything about a funeral. No one can.'

'Why ever not?'

'Because the police haven't finished with her.'

'The police? Eddy, what are you talking about?'

'I don't know. Just go away and leave me alone and mind your own business.'

He hung up. This time she didn't call back. Disgruntled, Eddy went out to weed the garden. At least there he expected to find some peace, but his neighbour was outside her house, hanging out her washing. He nearly called out to her to do something about her weeds because they kept spreading into his garden, but she came right up to the fence and spoke to him before he had a chance to complain.

'I was sorry to hear about your mother,' she said. 'If there's anything I can do, just ask. You know I'm only next door.'

Without a word, he turned his back on her and hurried indoors. He had hoped to be free of interference without his mother's constant nagging, but first his cousin, then his aunt, and now even his neighbour was butting in, all wanting to poke their nose into his business and tell him what to do. He wished everyone would stop meddling in his affairs. He didn't need stupid people fussing over him. He didn't need anyone but Kylie in his life.

24

WITH IAN STILL AWAY and Nico in custody, Geraldine decided to invite Ariadne out for dinner. Somehow, she felt an explanation was necessary.

'We haven't gone out for a meal together for such a long time' she said. 'It would be lovely to see you and catch up. Ian's away and –' She hesitated to mention Nico's absence. 'And it's an ideal opportunity for us to have a good natter.'

Ariadne grunted at the reminder that she was on her own that weekend, but she accepted the invitation. Geraldine hoped to avoid talking about Nico but they had barely sat down when Ariadne challenged Geraldine about what she was doing to release him. As it happened, Geraldine was unhappy about Nico's arrest, but there was very little she could do about it. She was already regretting her promise to do her best to see Nico released. In the absence of any further evidence, it was difficult to know what more she could do, other than reassure Ariadne and counsel patience.

'How can I be patient, knowing he's locked up in a stinking cell when he's innocent?' Ariadne hissed angrily. 'You know he's not a cold blooded killer, Geraldine. You know he can't be. He's my husband. I'd know if he killed that old woman.'

'There's nothing we can do right now,' Geraldine said helplessly, hoping no one else could hear what they were saying. 'I don't know what you want me to say.'

As the silence grew oppressive, a waiter brought their menus to the table and began to recite details of the special of the day. His interruption broke the tense atmosphere and, having placed their order, they engaged in desultory conversation, both of them keen to avoid returning to disturbing or controversial issues. Despite their attempts to natter, it was an awkward evening, and they were both keen to leave as soon as they finished their hurried meal. It was not even nine o'clock, but they agreed to skip dessert, Ariadne claiming she was too full to eat another mouthful, and Geraldine responding that she was tired. Geraldine hid her distress about their estrangement. Ariadne had been a good friend, and it upset Geraldine to think they might never be close again.

'Did Nico say anything at all to you about where he went last Saturday?' Geraldine asked as they were leaving.

'I know Nico,' Ariadne blurted out. 'At least I thought I did,' she added almost under her breath. 'I don't have anything more to say to you.'

As Geraldine reached her car, Ariadne ran over to her. 'You have to do something,' she hissed. 'Nico didn't kill anyone. This is insane. Geraldine you have to keep me up to speed with what's happening.'

Geraldine promised to let her friend know if there were any developments.

'No,' Ariadne said, 'that's not enough. You have to promise to call me every single day and let me know what's going on, good or bad.'

Geraldine felt sorry for her friend but there was nothing she could say other than to mumble platitudes about everything being all right in the end. But although Geraldine could assure Ariadne that the justice system, if slow, was at least generally sure, they both knew there was no guarantee that Nico was innocent.

'Can you ever really know another person?' Ariadne asked.

It wasn't clear whether she was referring to Geraldine or Nico. Driving home, Geraldine wondered whether she really knew Ian as well as she thought. They had been friends for years before they started living together, but now Ian was away visiting his brother who had come over from America, and before that he had gone off to work under cover in London. Of course there was an obvious reason why he had felt unable to share details of his under-cover posting, but Geraldine had no absolute proof of where he had been or what he had been doing there. She had known Ian for years, but Ariadne had known Nico for years too, and it seemed he might have been hiding a terrible secret.

With a shudder, she shook off her fears. Nico was the one under suspicion, not Ian. Still, she was troubled by Ariadne's situation. Unable to sleep, she resolved to confront Eileen in the morning about Nico's arrest, and at least make the detective chief inspector listen to her reservations.

The next day Geraldine went to speak with Eileen, and was frustrated to find that her senior officer was convinced the case had been satisfactorily concluded.

'We don't yet have conclusive proof Nico's guilty –' Geraldine began to protest.

Eileen interrupted her with a bark of laughter. 'Cut out your daft ideas, Susan,' she said.

Geraldine glanced over her shoulder; she and Eileen were alone in the room.

'Are you talking to me?' she asked.

Eileen looked at her sharply. 'I don't see anyone else in here, do you?'

'No, well, as I was saying –'

'Do you remember when you had really long hair?' Eileen enquired inconsequentially.

When Geraldine was a child, her mother had kept her hair short. Later, when she was old enough to take responsibility for herself, she continued to keep her hair trimmed in a neat bob. It was a practical style, and it suited her.

'I've never had long hair,' she murmured.

Normally sharp almost to a fault, Eileen now seemed vague and easily satisfied with what was only half-baked evidence. A few days earlier, she had been positive that Eddy was guilty. Now she was equally convinced Nico was responsible for murdering Doreen. In neither case was there any sound proof. And now she didn't seem to recognise Geraldine. Geraldine prevaricated, concealing her apprehension and wondering how to proceed. The moment passed and Eileen addressed her as Geraldine again, apparently oblivious to her brief lapse.

'It's circumstantial evidence,' Geraldine said, when Eileen insisted that this time they had caught Doreen's killer. 'All we can say for certain is that Nico was with Doreen on the day she died. That doesn't prove he killed her.'

With Eileen remaining adamant that Nico was guilty, the investigation was effectively closed. Most of the extra officers who had been drafted in to help with the murder enquiry were sent back to their own police stations. Only the paperwork remained to be completed. Geraldine wasn't sure how she was going to face Ariadne.

As soon as she reached home, Geraldine called Ian but he didn't answer. She listened to his voicemail with a sinking feeling, but decided against leaving a message. She hoped he would call her back but he didn't. With Ian away until the following day, Geraldine decided to use her free time to pay a visit to her twin sister in London. Helena had been inviting her for weeks, but Geraldine had been too busy to travel to London to see her sister. Now she picked up the phone with some trepidation. Meetings with her twin didn't always go well. Even though they were identical twins, their lives had followed completely divergent trajectories.

Geraldine had been adopted at birth into a family who enjoyed financially comfortable circumstances. Growing up, she had wanted for nothing. Her twin, Helena, had been a sickly baby. No one had expected her to live, so she had remained with their dysfunctional birth mother. Against the odds, the puny baby had survived to become a heroin addict. As an adult, Geraldine had traced her birth mother and had been shocked to discover she had an identical twin. With Geraldine's support, Helena had gone into rehab and overcome her addiction. Aware how precarious the life of an ex-user was, Geraldine lived in fear of her sister reverting to her former habit. Theirs was an uncomfortable relationship, each of them only too aware how easily their situations might have been reversed. Gradually Helena was overcoming her resentment of her sister's success in life, and Geraldine was coming to terms with her own unjustified guilt.

For once, Helena sounded genuinely pleased to hear from Geraldine.

'At last,' she crowed. 'I can't wait to see you again. It's been ages.'

Geraldine muttered about her work keeping her busy. 'This is the first opportunity I've had to get away in weeks.'

'I've got something to tell you,' Helena interrupted Geraldine's mumbled apology. 'What time's your train?'

Geraldine stifled a sigh. She hadn't even committed to going to London yet, and Helena's impatience to see her most likely meant she wanted more money. Conscious that guilt made Geraldine generous, Helena was never shy to make exorbitant demands on her. Afraid that her sister might return to her habit if she was feeling wretched, Geraldine always helped her. Fortunately her salary, together with money she had inherited from her adoptive mother, meant she was able to pay her own mortgage and Helena's rent as well, but until Ian had moved in with her she had sometimes struggled to pay her bills.

'I'm looking forward to seeing you too,' she told Helena, although that wasn't strictly true.

Perhaps because of her former drug habit, Helena was volatile, and likely to fly into a temper without warning. After the miserable youth Helena had endured, Geraldine forgave her twin for attempting to manipulate her, but every time they met, Geraldine felt as though she was entering a garden that might turn into a minefield without any warning. She rang off, already regretting having agreed to meet her twin. But at the back of her mind she knew she was going to London to avoid the risk of seeing Ariadne, and she despised herself for running away.

25

ARIADNE HAD GONE TO meet Geraldine on Saturday, secretly hoping that her friend would be able to share good news about the investigation. All Ariadne wanted to hear was that the real culprit had been identified, and Nico was coming home, instead of which Geraldine had hedged and revealed nothing about the case. Her refusal to talk about work left Ariadne feeling even more dejected than before. Clearly there was no positive news, and Nico was going to continue to languish in custody for an indefinite period. Ariadne couldn't keep the situation to herself for much longer. Her mother in particular would start asking questions, curious to know where Nico had gone. If Ariadne lied, and Nico did end up being convicted, the lies would be exposed. Somehow, she had to discover the truth. She lay awake all night, fretting.

The next morning, she picked up the phone and called Geraldine. They had seen one another only the previous evening, but Geraldine had been cagey, and Ariadne had to find out what was happening. Nearly a week had gone by since Nico's name had first been mentioned in connection with the investigation, and he had been a prime suspect for days. Ariadne's uncertainty about marrying him, her stress over the grandiose wedding orchestrated by her mother and grandmother, the wonderful honeymoon, had all come to this: she was the wife of a man accused of murdering an old woman. It was only a matter of time before everyone she knew heard about the accusation that had been levelled at her husband. And beyond the shock waves it would send around her family and friends, and her own shame and humiliation, was the horrific prospect of a future alone. Of course she would have to divorce Nico if he was guilty. That went without saying. And then she would spend the rest of her life alone, because how could she ever trust another man, if someone as reliable and steady as Nico had actually killed a woman? Even if he had been tormented beyond endurance, it was unforgivable. There could be no excuse for Doreen's murder, no provocation that could justify the murder of a woman in a wheelchair.

The more she thought about what had happened, the less sense it made. Unless he had a secret life, as far as she knew Nico had only met Doreen a few times, and in any case, there was no way he would have strangled a woman in a wheelchair. Flipping back and forth between grief at realising she had never known her husband's vicious nature, and fury that anyone could possibly doubt his innocence, she had to speak to someone before she went crazy. Geraldine had counselled her to be patient, but that didn't help. She needed to know the truth. Nico was her husband. It was unbelievable that she could have been so misguided in trusting him. And through all her misery and confusion, she clung to the knowledge that he was incapable of murder. He was a kind man, a God-fearing man, a man who liked to help people. How could such a man have strangled a helpless victim like Doreen? No, she refused to believe it. In her despair, she turned to Geraldine. They were friends, and Geraldine was working on the case. She would be able to clear up Ariadne's confusion. Whatever else happened, she had to know the truth about Nico before bewilderment and lack of sleep dragged her down into madness.

Geraldine answered the phone straight away, and Ariadne was thankful for that, at least. In Geraldine's place, Ariadne wasn't sure she would have had the courage to talk to her friend.

'Geraldine, it's me, Ariadne.'

'Ariadne, I saw it was you. How are you?'

Geraldine sounded genuinely concerned and for a moment Ariadne struggled to speak.

'I want to know what's going on,' she stammered at last. 'You have to tell me the truth, Geraldine.'

'Thanks for calling,' Geraldine went on, as though she hadn't heard Ariadne's reply. 'I know it sounds like a brush-off, but I really can't chat now. I'm on my way to London to see my sister, you know, my twin, Helena.'

Ariadne nodded, although Geraldine couldn't see her. Geraldine had talked about her identical twin who was as different from Geraldine as it was possible for two women to be, despite their physical similarity.

'Let's talk when I'm back,' Geraldine said. 'I'll call you. Okay?'

'I just want to know what's happening.'

'It's complicated, but there's nothing more to say for now. Nothing's changed, but we're working on it. I promise I'll tell you if there's any news. And you know we're all working flat out to resolve this.'

While buggering off to London for a day out, Ariadne thought bitterly, but she said nothing.

'I'll speak to you soon,' Geraldine promised. 'I'm about to go into a tunnel.'

At that, the line was cut off, leaving Ariadne feeling abandoned all over again. She was angry with Geraldine, even though there was nothing Geraldine could do. In her place, Ariadne would have said the same. She sank down on the floor. There was no one else she could turn to for support or advice. She had many colleagues at the police station, but none of them were close friends of hers, as Geraldine was. If even Geraldine was unwilling to talk to her, how could she expect anyone else to discuss the case with her? The one person on whom she ought to be able to rely on was locked in a prison cell, and her best friend had made herself inaccessible. Geraldine couldn't alter the fact that Nico had visited Doreen on the morning of her death, but she could be devoting her time to finding the real culprit, instead of which she was going to London to see her sister.

Ariadne was seized by a sudden rage. She hurled her phone across the room. It hit the skirting board with a sharp crack. The back flew off and the impact dislodged the battery. She stared at it lying uselessly on the floor. The violence of her throw did nothing to alleviate her fury with Nico, with her family, with Geraldine, and most of all with herself for being stupid enough to get married in the first place. She wondered if she had ever really loved Nico. How could she have done, when she didn't even know him? She had only agreed to marry him because she hadn't wanted to spend the rest of her life alone, and she had ended up more alone than she had ever been when she had been single. And underlying all her misery was the fear that she could not acknowledge even to herself. She was his wife. She had told him she would stand by him whatever happened, for better or worse. But surely that didn't include this?

If he was guilty, what then? Having spent her working life hunting down killers and seeing them brought to justice, how could she continue working as a detective and still remain loyal to Nico? Whatever happened from now on, she was being torn apart. If she didn't get a grip on her thoughts soon, she would lose herself in darkness. Someone who hadn't been trained to focus on evidence might ignore all the signs and believe in the man they loved despite the facts, but she couldn't do that. Not normally one to succumb to self-pity, she caved in and wept uncontrollably, for Nico and for her own shattered life, and for her love that wasn't strong enough.

26

GERALDINE HARDLY RECOGNISED HELENA when they met for lunch in a restaurant near Kings Cross station in Central London. It was a sunny day in April. A few picturesque white clouds floated slowly overhead across a bright blue sky, their indolent progress contrasting with the movement of people scurrying across Granary Square far below. For once, Helena had arrived first. Geraldine failed to recognise her from behind, and could scarcely conceal her astonishment when Helena turned round. Her hair was cut into a short bob and dyed black, like Geraldine's, and when she smiled in welcome, Geraldine saw Helena's front teeth had been capped since their last meeting. Even the shape of her face appeared different, and her skin had improved as well. Pleased as she was, at the same time Geraldine was slightly unnerved at how similar they now looked. It was almost like staring into a mirror. Almost, but not quite. Close up, Geraldine could see her sister was wearing thick foundation, which could not completely mask the pock marks on her face, or the heavy grey shadows beneath her eyes. Years of abuse had left their mark.

'Helena, you look wonderful,' she blurted out, genuinely glad at the transformation. 'You look so different, I hardly recognised you. Your hair looks great.'

She refrained from mentioning Helena's teeth and skin.

'Like yours, innit?'

Helena gave a hoarse throaty laugh, and Geraldine was reassured to discover that beyond her appearance, her sister

LEIGH RUSSELL

did not seem to have changed. It would have been weird, and slightly unnerving, if she had tried to alter her voice to simulate Geraldine's.

'What about me teeth then?' Helena bared them in a grin. 'It don't even hurt now. How's that for a bargain?' She winked.

As she listened, Geraldine realised that Helena's voice had changed almost imperceptibly. With the improvement in her teeth, she had lost her slight lisp, so that although their accents differed, her voice sounded more like Geraldine's than before.

Geraldine nodded. 'You look absolutely amazing.'

'You wanna know where I got me hands on the dosh, don't ya?'

Geraldine shook her head, smiling nervously. Expecting Helena to hand her a bill for her dental work, she was more perplexed than relieved when her sister assured her she had no intention of asking for a penny.

'Them days is gone,' Helena assured her with a complacent nod.

'I'm pleased you're doing so well for yourself,' Geraldine said warily. 'You've got a nice job, haven't you?'

She hoped she hadn't sounded patronising. For several years she had been supporting Helena, and she had come to accept the situation. Now Helena seemed to be intimating that their relationship had changed, and Geraldine wasn't quite sure how to respond.

'Oh yeah, there's me job,' Helena grinned. 'But the thing is, what I wanted to tell ya, is I met this lovely fella,' Helena replied.

'You've met someone?'

'No need to sound so surprised,' Helena retorted with a flash of her former acerbity.

The waiter came to take their orders and interrupted their conversation. When they finished choosing, Helena grinned again.

'He only went and got me this,' she said, pointing to a heavy gold ring on her finger and a matching gold chain around her scrawny neck.

'They're lovely,' Geraldine stammered, surprised.

'Geraldine, he only wants to marry me,' Helena blurted out, unable to conceal her glee any longer.

Geraldine stared at her sister in surprise. 'How long have you known him?' she asked at last.

'Long enough,' Helena said. 'Thing is, it's too much of a good thing to turn down. He's nothing much to look at, but he's loaded.'

Geraldine watched the links on Helena's gold chain quiver as she flung her head back and guffawed.

'Helena, do you love him?'

'Listen, don't you go all soppy on me. I'll be dead happy with him. What's not to like? I told you, he's loaded like you wouldn't believe.'

Geraldine felt a pang of anxiety. She had no reason to think Helena would be miserable, and she certainly deserved some happiness after all that she had suffered. It wasn't concern for Helena's future, and it certainly wasn't jealousy, but somehow Geraldine found it unsettling to realise that Helena was no longer reliant on her. All the time they had known one another, Geraldine had been the successful twin. Now, after living for years as a heroin addict, dysfunctional and struggling to survive from day to day, Helena had succeeded in sorting herself out. She had a job she seemed to like well enough, her own apartment – which admittedly Geraldine was paying for – and now on top of all that, she had found herself a wealthy husband.

'Does that mean you're no longer going to need me to pay your rent?' Geraldine asked, immediately hating herself for sounding churlish.

She expected her sister to snap at her, but Helena smiled contentedly.

'You don't need to worry about me no more,' she said firmly. 'You done enough for me. Lord knows I'd be dead in a gutter years ago if you hadn't come along. But I'm telling ya, I got a lovely fella now and, like I said, he's minted.'

A horrible suspicion struck Geraldine. 'How old is he?' she enquired.

'Sixty-eight. So what? It's not like you and me is gonna see the right side of forty again, innit?' she cackled and her laughter ended in a chesty cough. 'But seriously, Geraldine, he's a good fella and I got no intention of messing this up. Not like everything else in me life.'

Accustomed to being her sister's saviour, Geraldine's pleasure was tinged with dismay.

'That's wonderful news,' she said, doing her best to sound excited. 'I'm so happy for you, really I am. When can I meet him?'

Helena shook her head. 'Best not,' she said. 'I mean, he don't know nothing about me past. What I was. Even you don't know the half of it. What I used to do for me hits. I told him my teeth was diseased and it was genetic, you know, and I swore the dentist to secrecy. With what these gnashers cost, he wasn't going to queer my pitch.' She laughed.

'You know I can be discreet,' Geraldine said. 'You have my word for it that I won't say anything to him.'

Helena heaved a sigh and looked sincerely apologetic. 'Trouble is, if my fella sees you, he'll know what I shoulda been like, if I'd lived a proper clean life.'

'But you look great now, and besides, I'm bound to meet him one day.'

Helena shook her head vehemently. 'Best not,' she repeated, avoiding Geraldine's gaze. 'We can get together like this, you an' me, but it's best you and Glen don't meet. I mean, there ain't no point, really.'

Geraldine didn't answer for a moment.

'You understand, don't ya?' Helena was wheedling now, her head slightly tilted, her eyes bright with hope.

Geraldine sighed. 'Of course, if that's really what you want, you know I'll respect your wishes. I would have liked to come to your wedding though.'

'Yeah, well, it's gonna be a quiet affair. His kids ain't too pleased about it.'

'He's been married before then?'

'Oh yeah, a few times,' Helena replied airily. 'He is nearly seventy,' she added, as though that was reason enough for her fiancé's previous marriages.

They both ordered dessert and over coffee Helena quizzed Geraldine about her own life. She began to talk about her work in general terms

'Never mind all that,' Helena interrupted her impatiently. 'How's things going with you and your fella?'

Geraldine was tempted to confide her fears to her twin. In many ways no one else was as close to her, or understood her quite as well. But she kept her suspicions to herself and smiled.

'It's all good,' she replied.

Helena gazed earnestly at her. 'You would tell me if it weren't? Only we are still sisters, even after everything what's happened. I know I brought you nothing but grief, and your life would be better if I never was born, but that's over now. I won't be a problem to you no more.'

'You were never a –' Geraldine began and paused, deciding not to lie. 'I'm glad you've finally found a decent man,' she said, 'and I hope he's good to you. I mean it, Helena, you deserve to be happy.'

Helena smiled sadly. 'I done nothing but fuck everyone up. If I been lucky, it's not from anything I done.'

Geraldine put her hand on her sister's. 'You're the bravest person I know,' she said.

'Don't talk that shit to me,' Helena replied, but she didn't pull her hand away until their food arrived.

Geraldine was pleased to see Helena looking so relaxed and felt a quiet happiness, knowing she herself had played a part in helping her sister sort her life out and find contentment.

27

IT WAS MONDAY, AND Eddy was fed up. Kylie usually went to work on Mondays, but he had waited until late morning and she hadn't gone out. When she went to work, he had worked out that she did shifts, and he knew what times she left home, but he never really knew where she was on her days off. She might go out at any time, usually to the shops, or sometimes she just stayed at home and he didn't see her at all. But that wasn't all that was upsetting him. Alec had turned up a couple of days ago, and he showed no signs of leaving. On the contrary, he appeared to be making himself comfortable, and taking over the house. Wherever Eddy went, Alec was there, if not in person then in his belongings. His shoes lay discarded in the middle of the hall for Eddy to trip over; in the living room the cloying aroma of hops from empty beer bottles vied with the sour smell of cigarette butts stubbed out in soiled cups and saucers. It was unbearable. Yet all Eddy's attempts to push Alec out had failed miserably.

'This is my house,' Eddy had announced several times.

On each occasion, Alec had merely winked and congratulated Eddy on his luck in inheriting the house, apparently oblivious to his cousin's attempt to seize control of the situation.

Eddy had to make a plan to get rid of Alec, because two was company, and three wasn't. He couldn't remember the exact words, but he knew that meant he could never be happy with Kylie as long as Alec was living in the house. It was Eddy's house now, and he should be allowed to choose who was allowed to live there. But Alec wouldn't go away. 'You're a bad smell,' Eddy muttered to himself. That was what Alec used to say to him when they were children: 'You hang around like a bad smell.' And then Alec would laugh and knock him over. Well, now it was Eddy's turn to send Alec away. He knew exactly what he wanted to achieve, he just didn't know how to set about it. It had been the same at school. He had always understood his goals, but somehow the steps between having a goal and actually achieving it were missing. Other pupils seemed to manage, but he was like someone stranded at the top of a burning building without a ladder.

That Monday, he was at home in the afternoon, and he decided it was time to tackle Alec. His teachers used to urge him to 'have a go'. He remembered one teacher in particular. 'You can do it, Eddy,' she would say, with an encouraging smile. 'What's the worst that can happen? It doesn't matter if you come up with the wrong answer. What matters is that you have a go.' He had asked her how he could have a go when he didn't know what to do, but even she hadn't been able to give him an answer, even though she was trying to help him. 'I can't help you if you don't make any effort for yourself,' she had said, and she had turned away with a sigh. So she had been trying to help him, and she hadn't been able to achieve her goal. And she was a teacher.

But he wasn't at school any more, and this wasn't a test in class. What he was facing now was a real problem, and he had to find an answer. Alec appeared in the kitchen wearing a brown and red dressing gown and red slippers. His legs were bare. Eddy's mother would have scolded him if he had ever come downstairs in what she called 'a state of undress'. Eddy gave a disapproving sniff, but didn't comment on Alec's attire. He had more important matters to discuss.

'You've been here for ages,' he began.

'Since Friday,' Alec replied, nodding and smiling.

He turned his back on Eddy and proceeded to make himself

breakfast, humming cheerfully to himself. He didn't offer Eddy anything. Eddy watched him fill the kettle and make himself a mug of tea. Reaching into his pocket, he drew out a small flat bottle, took a gulp, smacked his lips, and poured a dollop into his tea. He blew on his steaming drink before sipping it, while waiting for his toast to pop up.

'You'll need to nip out and get some bread,' Alec said, without looking round. 'I'd have offered to make toast for you as well, but these are the last two slices.' He began to wolf down his breakfast as though he didn't trust Eddy not to grab his toast.

It occurred to Eddy that they could have had one slice of toast each, but he dismissed the thought. He needed to remain focused on his goal. He still wasn't quite sure how he was going to proceed, but he knew that he couldn't afford to be distracted. That was something his teacher had taught him.

'Focus, Eddy,' she used to say. 'If you don't stay focused, you'll never work out the answer.' At school he had never mastered the secret of how to stop his thoughts flitting around, unpredictably. Now, faced with a real problem, he cleared his throat.

'You could give me one of yours,' he blurted out and stopped, disconcerted by his own words.

'Yes, but then I'd still be hungry,' Alec explained, licking butter from his lips. 'You're going to be hungry anyway, because one slice of toast is never enough. At least this way, only one of us is hungry.' He took a large bite out of his second slice of toast.

Eddy frowned. What his cousin had just said reminded him of the problems he used to be given at school. But this time the answer was easy. Two people, two slices of toast, how many slices each? He shook his head, trying to clear his mind of such thoughts. The toast was a distraction. Staring at his cousin, he tried again.

'You have to go,' he said.

'Oh, I would, but I'm not dressed yet. You could pop to the shops and be back by the time I'm ready to go out. And besides,

I'm broke,' he added. 'Not enough bread to get bread.' He giggled.

Eddy's head began to hurt. It was like being back at school. Everything confused him.

'You have to go today,' he announced, with a sudden burst of confidence, because it was really that easy. All he had to do was say the words. 'You have to leave the house today. I want you to go.'

Alec looked at him quizzically, his head on one side. 'Go where?'

'I don't care. I just want you to get out of my house.'

Alec looked taken aback, but then he smiled, slowly. 'Make me,' he said.

'What?'

'You heard me.' Alec was no longer smiling. 'You want me gone?' He took a step towards Eddy. 'What are you going to do if I refuse to leave? Run to mummy and complain? Oh no, you can't, can you, because she's not here anymore. But I am. So be a good boy, run to the shops and get some bread, because I want another slice of toast.' As Eddy hesitated, Alec glared at him. 'Don't make me ask you twice. And don't worry,' he added, smiling again, 'I'm not going to abandon you. I've come here to take care of you and that's exactly what I'm going to do.'

Somehow, on Alec's lips, the words sounded like a threat.

28

REMEMBERING THE PUB IN Micklegate where Shona had taken her, Louisa felt a frisson of excitement. According to her new friend, the pub was frequented by the best-looking guys in York. Obviously Shona was biased because that was where she had met Benjy, but it seemed like a decent pub, welcoming and comfortable. Anyway, it wasn't as though Louisa had anywhere else to go that evening, or anything else to do. Tired of sitting alone in her lodgings, she decided to go back to the same pub, just for a drink. At least there would be other people there, even if she didn't know any of them, plus there was a chance she might see Stan again. Given a second chance, she wouldn't hesitate to accept his invitation to go out with him. If Stan wasn't there, she might meet another man who showed an interest in her. This time she was determined to dismiss her reservations and be bold. Shona might be there but that didn't matter. Louisa was entitled to go there by herself. She had come to the city looking for adventure. Now she was settled at work, she was ready to go out looking for fun. If she was too scared to try anything new, she might as well have stayed with her parents in Whitby, living in a familiar place with people she had known all her life.

As she entered the bar she removed her mac and was immediately aware of a few men staring at her flimsy top, sizing her up. Suddenly she felt very vulnerable. On her previous visit to the pub she hadn't attracted much attention, but she hadn't been alone on that occasion. Now, she was afraid it must be obvious why she had come there. Wishing she'd worn something less revealing, she looked around as if she was meeting someone, before she approached the bar to order a glass of wine. Even though it was Monday, there were quite a few people there. Two young men were lounging at the bar, one blond, the other dark-haired with soulful brooding eyes. As she was gazing at the dark-haired man, the blond one shuffled over to her and paid for her glass of wine, and his companion drifted away. The blond man smiled a lot, which made him look nervous. That amused her, because he had no idea she had been almost too anxious to go out at all that evening. He introduced himself, telling her his name was Micky. Short and stocky, he wasn't as attractive as Stan, nor did he offer to take her clubbing. But he was there, and he bought her another drink. In the course of a stilted conversation, Louisa learned that Micky had lived in York all his life. She told him she came from Whitby

'That's nice,' he said, nodding.

'Have you ever been to Whitby?'

'No. But I'd like to,' he replied.

'Why don't you then?' she retorted, slightly irked by his lack of initiative. 'I mean, it's not like it's far away.'

By the time Micky offered her a third glass of wine, Louisa had drunk enough and the conversation had faltered. All he seemed to be good for was offering to buy her drinks.

'It's getting late,' she said, refusing his offer. 'I'd best be getting home.'

'Shall I walk with you?'

'No, thanks. I don't live far from here.'

He leaned forward as though to kiss her, but she stood up abruptly, avoiding the contact. He clambered awkwardly to his feet.

'Well, goodbye then. Will I see you again?'

Although she had no wish to spend any more time in his dull company, Louisa was flattered that he was interested in her, and she felt slightly guilty. He had bought her a couple of drinks. It would be churlish of her to simply walk off, even though she didn't particularly want to see him again.

'Maybe see you in here next week,' she muttered as she turned away.

The rain had held off and it was a mild evening, and the streets were busy. That was one thing she liked about York. There were usually other people around, which she found reassuring, unlike Whitby which could be very quiet in the winter. Leaving the main road, she turned into her side street, and was struck as always by her isolation. For once, it didn't bother her. Perhaps it was because she was tipsy but, for the first time, the atmosphere in the empty street didn't seem sinister after the lively bustle of the town centre. Laughing at her customary anxiety, she reminded herself that she was a grown woman, living independently, with a steady job, and an apartment in an exciting city where she had just been out and met an eligible man. This was what she had left home to find. This was living. This was adventure. She was determined to ignore the negative aspects of her life: the dingy apartment, the dead-end job, and the dull man who had offered to buy her drinks although he had nothing to say to her. There would be other men, and if she worked hard she would find a better paid job once she was more experienced. Intent on examining her life and congratulating herself on her success so far, she didn't try to walk quickly, nor did she worry about being followed. She felt completely free, and it was glorious.

She was nearly home when a blow struck her on the side of her head with such force that she staggered and almost lost her footing. Grabbing the top of a low wall with her flailing hand, she succeeded in keeping her balance, but before she could turn or run, someone shoved her really hard in the back, causing her to stumble and fall to her knees. Frantically she fumbled with the zip on her bag so she could fish out the rape alarm her mother had thrust at her before she left Whitby. With a sickening lurch she remembered she had switched bags before going out.

The alarm was in the bag she had left carelessly on her bed. Whimpering with fear she scrambled to her feet and fled. She wasn't sure if she was being pursued, or if what she could hear was an echo of her own footsteps, but she didn't pause to find out. She had nearly reached her own building when she tripped and fell. Burning pain shot along her arm and her face seemed to be crushed by a tremendous weight before she blacked out.

29

GERALDINE HAD PREPARED CAREFULLY for Ian's return, planning her cooking for Monday evening and making a list before shopping to make sure she had everything she needed. She had intended to make a Thai curry, but arrived home far too late to create such a complicated dish. When Ian called to say that he would be back later than he had originally intended, and wasn't going to be home in time for supper, she was both disappointed and relieved. She still needed to finish her laundry and do some housework to make sure the flat looked as tidy and clean as possible. It was half past ten by the time he walked into the kitchen, brandishing a large bouquet of flowers.

'I'm afraid they got rather battered on the way home,' he said.

'It's the thought that counts,' she replied with a smile.

'Well, my thoughts should count for a lot, because I've been thinking about you constantly while I've been away.'

He leaned down and kissed her gently on the lips.

'I was just putting the kettle on,' she told him. 'Or there's some beer in the fridge if you prefer?'

She tried to remain calm but was sure her excitement on seeing him was apparent in her eyes.

'Let's share a bottle of wine,' he replied, smiling. 'I'm feeling pretty wiped out to be honest. It's been a tiring few days. All I want to do is put my feet up, have a drink and a chat with my girl.'

After Ian had talked at length about his visit to London and his reunion with his brother, the conversation moved on to Geraldine's case. Ian was shocked to hear that Ariadne's husband was still a suspect in the murder investigation.

'I thought you knew,' Geraldine said.

It was strange to realise how much had happened in the short time since Ian had gone away. He was keen to hear how Ariadne was coping with the situation.

'I thought he'd have been released by now. I can't imagine what she must be going through,' he said. 'How is she taking it?'

Geraldine shrugged. 'It's difficult to say, really. I mean, she hasn't talked about it much, not to me at any rate. The last time I spoke to her she kept insisting Nico was innocent, which is understandable, I suppose. She called me yesterday morning, but I was on my way out to see Helena, and didn't have time to talk. I said I'd call her back, and haven't yet, but it's a bit late now.'

'Poor Ariadne.' Ian commiserated with their colleague in her absence. 'What a horrible situation to find herself in. It must be hard for you too, seeing your friend going through such a difficult time.'

'Well, yes, that has been hard, especially with you away as well, but that's nothing compared to what Ariadne must be suffering. I just wish there was something we could do to help her.'

'Finding out the truth is the only thing any of us can do for her,' Ian said. 'Uncertainty must be the most difficult thing to deal with. If Nico *is* guilty – and I'm sure we're all hoping he's not – the sooner Ariadne finds out the better, so she can begin to think about how she's going to deal with the situation.'

'Yes,' Geraldine agreed. 'At the moment, she won't know what to think or how to prepare herself. You said we're all hoping Nico's innocent,' she went on and broke off, uncertain how to continue.

Ian nodded expectantly.

'The thing is,' Geraldine resumed, 'that's not quite true.'

Ian looked puzzled. 'Go on,' he prompted her at last, 'what do you mean?'

Hesitantly, Geraldine described how Eileen had insisted that Nico was guilty.

'What I mean is,' she went on, fumbling for words, 'there's something not quite right about her.'

Ian looked even more baffled. 'What do you mean?'

'It's just that to begin with she was absolutely sure Eddy was guilty and, just like that, she's now convinced Nico is the killer. Her views seem, well, capricious, as though she's selecting a suspect based on a whim, without waiting for irrefutable evidence to persuade her.'

Ian laughed at her. 'You've never really got on with Eileen, have you?'

'Ian, this isn't funny and it has nothing to do with whether or not I get on with Eileen. I may not particularly like her, but I've always respected her. This is different. She seems to have changed, and I'm worried about her. She's – well, there's something wrong with her. Just watch her and make up your own mind, but I think she may be ill.'

Ian didn't answer for a moment. 'Ill how?' he asked at last.

Geraldine hesitated. 'This is between us,' she said at last, 'but I think she might be suffering from some kind of breakdown. It could be early onset dementia, or stress related, I don't know, I'm not a doctor and I can't diagnose her problem, but I think there's something going on with her. She just seems, I don't know, erratic.'

Ian was silent, waiting, but Geraldine didn't say anything else.

'Can you give me a concrete example?' he asked at last.

'No one can confirm this,' Geraldine replied, 'but I'm pretty sure she forgot my name when I was alone with her.'

'Easy to get muddled, I suppose, when she has so many names to remember.'

'No, it wasn't just my name. I don't think she knew who I

was. There was a moment when she actually didn't recognise me. She asked me if I remembered when I had long hair. I've never had long hair. And she called me Susan. It was only for a moment, but nothing like that has ever happened before. And then she flipped out of it and didn't seem to remember what had happened. And she just seems generally a bit confused and all over the place.'

'All over the place?'

'I can't be more specific, and it could just be me looking for things that aren't there. I mean, no one else has mentioned anything to me. I'm hoping you'll keep your eyes open.'

Ian laughed, but he looked worried. 'I hope I can do that. I wouldn't be much use as a detective if I walked around with my eyes shut.'

'I'm serious, Ian. Watch her and then let me know if you think my fears are groundless.'

But they both knew she would never have mentioned the subject if she wasn't convinced something was wrong.

'Anyway,' she said, 'enough about work. I didn't want to worry you and it could just be me, mistaking Eileen's single-mindedness for something else. And it's possible she's just stressed about the investigation.'

They both knew if the detective chief inspector was struggling to cope with the demands of an investigation, they had a serious problem, whatever the cause of her temporary confusion.

30

VOICES TRICKLED INTO HER ears, interrupted by an intermittent buzzing in her head.

'Are you all right?'

Louisa struggled to open her eyes and saw a blurry face peering at her from above.

'We were just driving past and we saw you lying on the pavement so we thought we should stop and see if you needed help,' the voice continued. 'So, are you all right?'

The face came more clearly into focus; a young woman with a furrowed brow was staring at her with a troubled expression. She was wearing glossy pink lipstick and her bright yellow jumpsuit seemed to flicker in the light from the streetlamp.

'Did you see who it was?' Louisa asked. Her words sounded slurred and she wasn't sure if she was making any sense. 'Did you see anyone?'

'We haven't seen anyone else along here, only you,' the woman replied. 'We were afraid you'd tripped over or passed out or something.'

'I'm not drunk,' Louisa protested, although she could smell alcohol on her breath. No doubt the stranger could smell it as well. 'Who are you?'

'My name's Yvette Johnson, and this is my friend, Tim. Like I said, we were just driving past and we stopped to see if you needed any help. Is there anything we can do for you? Is there someone we can call? Are you hurt?'

Louisa sat up cautiously, trying not to move her arm. 'No, I'm fine.'

'Your nose is bleeding,' Yvette said.

That must have been from when she hit the ground. Gingerly Louisa felt her nose with the tip of one finger. As far as she could tell it didn't seem to be broken, but it felt swollen and sore, and blood was dripping down her upper lip.

'Can you breathe through both nostrils?' Yvette asked.

'What?'

'That's how to tell if you've broken your nose. As long as both nostrils are clear, your nose isn't broken.'

Louisa tried and found she could breathe through both sides of her nose.

'Good, that's okay then,' Yvette said. 'You don't have a deviated septum.'

'Are you a doctor?' Louisa asked.

Yvette shook her head. 'No, but my brother plays rugby. He's broken his nose more times than I can remember.' She gave an awkward little laugh.

Louisa tried to stand up and cried out in pain. 'I think my arm's broken,' she gasped.

'Can you wiggle fingers and move your elbow?' Yvette asked.

Louisa found that she could and Yvette announced that her arm wasn't broken, only badly bruised. All at once, Louisa just wanted to get home away from this brisk stranger who kept assuring her she hadn't broken any bones, although she wasn't a doctor and probably didn't know what she was talking about.

'I live just over there.' Louisa pointed. 'I can get myself home. I'm fine, thank you.' She looked around. 'Have you seen my bag?'

'No. It looks like you've been mugged and your bag was taken.'

Louisa scowled and let out a groan.

'Was there much in it?'

'What?'

'In your bag. Was there much in it?' Yvette wanted to know.

Luckily Louisa had her keys in her pocket. Just her purse and make-up were in her bag. With a sinking feeling, she remembered her phone was in there as well.

'I'm fine, really,' she insisted. 'It's only a bag. There was nothing in it.'

That was a stupid lie, but she just wanted to be left alone. All the same, she could hardly be rude after Yvette had been kind enough to stop and check she was all right. She supposed she was fine, really, but her head was pounding and her arm hurt. With an effort she clambered to her feet and froze, afraid she was going to be sick.

'Do you want to report the robbery?' Yvette enquired. 'You really should tell the police what happened.'

Louisa shook her head and flinched at a spasm of pain in her neck. 'My phone's gone.'

She wished this stranger would stop fussing.

Yvette pulled out her own phone. 'We can report it if you like.'

'What's the point, Yvette?' her companion interrupted impatiently. 'The police are hardly going to be interested in a stolen phone. The mugger could be anywhere by now. Come on, let's go. You can see she's all right.'

'If you're sure you can manage?' Yvette asked her. 'We could drive you to the hospital if you like.'

'Yvette,' her companion hissed, 'she's dripping blood.'

'It's all right, I'm fine now, really,' Louisa insisted. 'I'll just get on home, thank you. I don't need any help.'

Yvette and Tim returned to their car and watched Louisa for a few seconds as she hobbled along the pavement, nursing her bruised arm, before they drove away. She was alone again, but this time she was in pain and her phone had been stolen. Limping home as quickly as she could, she cleaned herself up in the shower. Her arm was aching horribly but she thought it felt a little less painful than when she had first regained consciousness. There were dark contusions along the outer edge of her upper arm, right up to her shoulder. Her knee was bruised as well, and her nose looked puffy and red. The impact of her fall had been spread between her arm, her knee and her face. Studying her battered face in her bathroom mirror, she wondered whether she should call police after all. But that would involve borrowing a phone, and she didn't want to give her landlady the impression that she was in any trouble. Then again, the landlady might offer her sympathy.

Tears slid from her eyes as she thought how supportive her mother would have been if this had happened at home in Whitby. On balance she decided there was no point in making any kind of fuss, or reporting the incident to the police. As Tim had pointed out, no one would be interested in a mugging. No one but her mother, that was, and she was the last person Louisa wanted to learn about what had happened. It wasn't even as though she had been attacked. As far as she could remember, she had tripped and fallen over. In a way it was a mugging, because her phone had been stolen, but she didn't know it would be classed as one.

'I've been mugged,' she whispered aloud, testing out the words.

She made herself a cup of cocoa and went to bed. She was afraid she wouldn't be able to sleep but the next thing she knew was when she was woken by a loud knocking at her front door. For a moment she lay perfectly still, rigid with panic. It might not be sensible to pretend no one was in. Burglars liked to break into empty premises. On the other hand, her mugger knew she had no phone. So did Yvette and Tim. There were at least three strangers who might realise she could be alone in her apartment without any means of contacting the outside world. All at once she felt giddy and confused. The room seemed to be spinning around her. The knocking came again. She slid out of bed and crept to her front door on trembling legs.

'Who is it?' she called out in a voice barely louder than a whisper. 'If you don't go away I'm calling the police.'

The knocking came again.

'Are you there? Louisa? Louisa, are you there? It's me, Shona, I've been trying to call you all morning.'

With a sob, Louisa opened the door, forgetting in her relief how dreadful she must look.

'Oh my God, what happened to you?' Shona cried out.

'Nothing, it's fine. I'm all right. I was mugged. What time is it?'

'It's past midday.'

'Oh no, I should have been at work hours ago.'

'Never mind that. We need to get you to a doctor.'

'No, no, it's fine.'

Shona insisted on Louisa seeing a doctor and called a cab to take them to the hospital. Too weak to resist, Louisa gave in to the shock she had been fighting to control ever since the attack, and wept all the way there. Tears mingled with blood from her nose and soaked through nearly a whole roll of toilet paper that Shona had thoughtfully brought with them in the taxi. Together they made their way up to the desk.

'My friend's been mugged and I think she's hurt,' Shona announced.

'Where is your friend –' The receptionist broke off, catching sight of Louisa. 'Yes, I see. Take a seat and a doctor will be out to see you soon.' She pointed to a row of chairs. 'You can wait over there. It shouldn't be long.' She handed Louisa a form. 'While you're waiting, can you fill this out?'

31

ON TUESDAY MORNING, GERALDINE was pleased to see Ariadne back at her desk. Her head was lowered, and she appeared to be concentrating on a file in front of her. When Geraldine went over and greeted her she merely grunted in response, as though unwilling to be distracted from her task. Stifling a sigh, Geraldine left Ariadne to her work, although she was fairly certain her friend's show of industry was a ruse to avoid contact with her colleagues. Geraldine could understand why Ariadne might not want to talk. With her husband in custody as the main suspect in a murder enquiry, it was only natural that she would be feeling confused and upset, and perhaps a little embarrassed.

Geraldine prevaricated for a moment over whether to approach her friend again, but decided it was best to leave her alone. Conscious of Ariadne's eyes on her, she walked past without looking directly at her. If Ariadne wanted to know how the investigation into Nico was progressing, she could ask. In the meantime, Geraldine might have to accept that she was unlikely to engage in a normal friendly conversation with Ariadne until the case was resolved, one way or another. She hoped Nico would be exonerated. The trouble was, if Nico was innocent, that only left Eddy as a suspect and Geraldine was not convinced he had killed his mother.

With Ariadne off the case, Eileen moved Ian on to the team.

'She said it wouldn't be for long,' he told Geraldine when he went to tell her about his reallocation. 'She seems pretty convinced we have the right suspect safely behind bars.'

'On circumstantial evidence,' Geraldine replied.

Ian gave her a quizzical look. 'Are you sure you're not allowing yourself to be influenced by the fact that the suspect is married to one of our colleagues, who happens to be a friend of yours?'

Geraldine bristled. 'I think you could give me credit for being a bit more professional than that. Do you really think I'm incapable of looking at things objectively?'

Before Ian could respond, they were summoned to a briefing and hurried away without exchanging another word. Eileen strode in shortly after they arrived, a ferocious scowl on her face as she crossed the room.

'She looks happy,' someone muttered audibly.

The room fell silent as the detective chief inspector turned to face the team. There was nothing unusual in Eileen looking irritable when she addressed the team at a briefing. As long as an investigation was open, she never appeared to relax. Geraldine had not been alone in finding this disconcerting.

Ian clearly thought the same. 'It can't be good for the DCI to be so stressed all the time,' he murmured to Geraldine as they waited to hear what Eileen had to tell them. 'Apart from ruining her health if she runs herself into the ground, she'd probably be better at her job if she took a break now and then to recharge her batteries. She's only human.'

Geraldine was on the point of retorting that humans didn't have batteries. She suspected Ian was really aiming a veiled criticism at her for being obsessed with work whenever she was on a case. But before she had a chance to reply, the detective chief inspector glared around the room, as though she suspected her colleagues of hiding information or being incompetent. Either way, something appeared to be upsetting her more than usual.

'We have a serious problem,' Eileen announced in an unnecessarily loud voice.

She paused as though she was steeling herself to continue, and there was silence for several seconds. A few of the assembled officers shuffled and fidgeted. Others stood absolutely motionless. All of them were waiting to hear what their irascible senior investigating officer was going to say next.

'What sort of problem?' Ian prompted her at last.

He had been working with Eileen for several years, and never appeared to be intimidated by her frosty manner, although even he had noticed how stressed she was.

'There's a problem with our suspect,' Eileen replied. 'It seems a neighbour has come forward who thinks she saw Nico leave Doreen's house at shortly after midday on the Saturday she was killed.'

'That doesn't necessarily change anything,' Geraldine said. 'We know it's possible Doreen was killed around midday. Jonah said it was impossible to narrow down the time of death precisely. He could only conclude she was probably still alive at two. She might even have been killed before midday.'

Eileen shook her head impatiently. 'No, no, no. You need to listen.'

The desk sergeant who had taken the neighbour's statement explained. 'The woman who lives across the road from the victim says she saw Doreen in her wheelchair at the front door, waving Nico off. The witness even claims she heard Doreen call out to him as he was walking away.'

'What did the neighbour report hearing her say?' someone asked.

'She thanked him for his help, something like that.'

'Which makes sense because Nico went there to help her sort out her financial affairs,' Geraldine murmured.

Eileen glared at Geraldine. 'The point is,' she resumed, 'we have a witness who gave a statement asserting that Doreen was alive and talking quite happily when Nico left Doreen's house at just after twelve, and she closed the front door after he reached the gate.'

'Is the neighbour sure it was Nico she saw?' Geraldine asked. 'Julie didn't see him leave and she seems to see everything that goes on next door.'

'The neighbour who gave her statement was walking past and saw a man who she described as looking like Nico coming out of the house,' the sergeant said.

'If she can positively identify him in a line-up as the man she saw leaving the house at midday, then we have a problem,' Eileen said. She sounded cross. 'She lives a few doors away and knew Doreen, and unless there was another woman in a wheelchair who looked just like Doreen, she was still alive when Nico left her at around midday.'

'That's it then,' Geraldine said. 'Nico was telling the truth when he said he left Doreen at around midday and she was alive when he left her. It ties in with the pathologist's estimated time of death as well. And we know he was in town having lunch at one, so he can't have returned and killed Doreen.'

'But it means we have to release him, and now we're back to square one,' Eileen snapped, as though it was a bad outcome that an innocent man was no longer a suspect.

Geraldine glanced at Ian who was looking worried.

'You see?' she hissed at him.

Ian shook his head. It wasn't clear if he meant that this was not the place to discuss their concerns, or if he was disagreeing with Geraldine's suspicions that Eileen was unwell.

By the time Geraldine returned to her desk, Ariadne had already heard the news and was chatting excitedly to a couple of other colleagues. She looked up at Geraldine, her eyes shining.

'So that's it then,' she blurted out. 'I knew he couldn't have done it. I just knew it.'

'Have you spoken to Nico yet?' Geraldine asked.

'Yes, I've spoken to Nico – I've seen him – and he'll soon be on his way home. It's all over.'

For a moment, Geraldine was afraid her colleague was going

to burst into tears, but Ariadne recovered her composure and suggested they go to the canteen together for a coffee. Geraldine was more relieved than she could say. She and Ariadne had been close friends and it had been awkward seeing her when they had both known Geraldine was working on the case that had threatened to put Ariadne's husband behind bars for a long time.

'You have no idea what it's been like,' Ariadne confessed, when they were seated together with coffee and celebratory doughnuts. 'I really had no idea – I mean, I always thought he couldn't possibly have done it, but then when the results of the DNA analysis came through –' She shook her head, with a faint shudder. 'I mean, how do you really know what's true and what isn't? If all the evidence points to something being true, it's so hard to keep hoping it's all just a horrible mistake. I mean, you keep hoping against all the odds, but it's so hard.'

'How's Nico now?'

Ariadne shrugged. 'He seems pretty cut up about the whole thing, to be honest, but I'm sure he'll get over it. He's a level-headed kind of guy.'

'I suppose something like this is enough to disturb anyone's equilibrium. But you're okay, aren't you? I mean, you and him?'

'Why wouldn't we be?'

Geraldine hesitated. 'It's just that he left you, didn't he?'

'Oh, that was only temporary. It didn't mean anything. It was because of all this.' Ariadne spread her hands, scattering sugar and crumbs on the table. 'We'll be fine now that everything's back to normal. And I'm going to be back with you, working on the case again.'

She smiled. Geraldine felt really pleased, and said so. With Ian back home and Ariadne working with her again, her friend was right when she said that everything was back to normal.

'I can't tell you how relieved I am about everything,' she said, returning Ariadne's smile.

Ariadne grinned. 'I don't suppose Eileen was too happy about losing a suspect,' she muttered.

Geraldine bit into her doughnut and shook her head, glad to have an excuse for not answering. Ariadne nodded, drawing her own conclusions from Geraldine's silence.

32

TOO TIRED TO EXPLAIN that she didn't think there was any point in reporting the attack, Louisa agreed to speak to the police. The constable who visited her in hospital that afternoon was nothing like the dismissive policeman Louisa had been expecting. Blonde, pretty and kind, and not much older than Louisa, she seemed genuinely concerned about the mugging. Louisa thought wistfully that, under other circumstances, they might have been friends, and felt an unexpected stab of nostalgia for the schoolmates she had left behind in Whitby. Not that many of them were still living there. Most, like her, had left, at least temporarily. And it wasn't as though she had many friends anyway.

Introducing herself as Constable Naomi Arnold, the police officer explained that she was there to talk to Louisa about the incident.

'You don't have to answer any questions you don't feel comfortable with, but there have been a few similar attacks recently,' she said, her curly hair bobbing about as she shook her head. 'Anything you can tell us about your attacker would be really helpful. We need to make sure he can't cause any more damage. You were fortunate to get off with just a few bruises, but his attacks seem to be growing more aggressive, and the next victim might not be so lucky. '

Louisa didn't feel very lucky but she nodded uncertainly. 'There's nothing more I can tell you. I didn't see anything. It was dark and I didn't even know anyone was there.'

'What happened? Please tell me everything you can remember. The smallest detail could turn out to be significant. It's really important we find this mugger and stop him before he causes any serious injury.'

'Well, he didn't actually hurt me, not really. I mean, I fell over after he'd gone,' Louisa explained. 'That is,' she added awkwardly, 'he did hit me but I don't think he knocked me over.' She frowned. 'To be honest, I can't actually remember exactly what happened. It's all a bit hazy and,' she paused before muttering, 'and I'd been drinking. Not that much, only a couple of glasses of wine, but I wasn't completely sober when it happened. I think that's why I wasn't being careful.'

'In what way were you not being careful?'

'Just that usually I try to keep an eye out for anyone following me, you know. And I've got a rape alarm my mother gave me, but I'd left it at home.'

She broke off, hoping the police officer wouldn't think she was a complete idiot, rambling incoherently about her experience. But the constable seemed nice and Louisa felt like a responsible citizen, doing her duty by helping to keep the streets of York safe for other women to walk around in. Even so, after a few minutes the questions grew tiresome.

'No, I didn't notice his voice.' She frowned, trying to remember if the mugger had said anything before attacking her. 'I'm not sure he said anything to me, actually. I'm sorry, I just can't remember.'

'Well, if you think of anything else, please let me know.'

The constable sounded disappointed and Louisa wished she could have recalled more about the mugger. The trouble was, the whole incident had happened so fast, it was just a blur. Only after the constable had left did Louisa wonder whether she ought to have mentioned her suspicion that she was being followed. She had repeatedly noticed a figure out of the corner of her eye when she was going to work, and again when she was on her way home. She wondered whether to contact the constable, but she had been so vague about the mugging, it would be embarrassing to mention the possibility she was being stalked. The police would only want to know details, and she couldn't give any. Until the attack, she had almost convinced herself she had been imagining someone was stalking her. Now she wasn't so sure. She didn't have long to ponder the situation because soon after the police officer left, Louisa heard a disturbance in the ward and her mother appeared, rushing past the other beds towards her, crying hysterically. Louisa drew in a deep breath, cursing to herself. She should have anticipated this.

'Louisa, are you all right?' her mother demanded, shouting to her while she was still a few beds away.

'Yes, mum, thank you, I'm fine. Just a bit bruised. They're not even keeping me in overnight. I'm fine, really,' she insisted, barely managing to control her fury. She had just finished answering questions from the police and now she had her mother to deal with, when all she wanted to do was sleep. 'Actually,' she muttered, 'I'm tired. I hardly slept at all last night. So can you just give me a bit of space, please? I really need to rest.'

'Well, that settles it,' her mother said firmly, without listening to a word Louisa was saying. 'Enough is enough. You're coming home with me right now. I've spoken to the nurse and everything's settled.'

'Hang on, mum, where I go when I leave here is my decision. And I'm staying right here in York. Apart from anything else, I have a job to go to.'

Her mother looked shocked. 'Are you out of your mind? No way are you going back to work in your condition,' she snapped. 'It's out of the question. Louisa, you're not thinking clearly. Now, let's stop this nonsense, shall we? I've got the car here and I'm taking you home.'

Louisa hesitated. She was tempted to capitulate and return to Whitby where she would be looked after and could feel safe and protected, letting her mother do the laundry and prepare dinner, and take care of everything.

'You can put your feet up and recuperate, for as long as it takes,' her mother continued, perhaps sensing that Louisa's resolve was wavering.

'No!' Louisa shouted suddenly, even surprising herself. 'You need to understand,' she continued in a lower voice, 'I live in York now, and I'm not going back to Whitby, with or without you. I'm staying here.'

As she spoke, a nurse appeared beside her bed.

'Is everything all right here?' she enquired. 'We heard raised voices and have to ask you please to respect the other patients. If you can't talk quietly, we'll have to ask you to leave.'

'It's fine,' Louisa's mother replied quickly, shifting her plastic chair closer to the bed. 'My daughter's just a bit upset by her experience.'

Louisa glared at her mother. 'Yes,' she said, 'everything's fine. My mother was just leaving.'

'Louisa, don't be awkward,' her mother said. 'It's all been a bit of a shock, all this,' she added, looking up and smiling at the nurse. 'But she'll be all right. We'll take care of her.'

The nurse nodded and moved away. Louisa restrained a crazy impulse to call after her with a plea to be rescued from her mother's suffocating attention.

'Thank you for visiting me,' she said frostily, 'but you're overreacting. There's nothing wrong with me, just a few bumps and bruises, and I'll be back at work tomorrow. So you can stop telling yourself that I'm coming back to Whitby with you.'

Her mother gazed earnestly at her. 'Louisa, listen to your mother. I know what's best for you. Didn't I tell you all along it was a mistake coming to the city all by yourself? It's a miracle you weren't raped and murdered. Surely you've seen the news? A girl was murdered in the city only a week ago. It's not safe for you here. You've already been attacked once. You were lucky to escape with your life. Next time you might not be so lucky.'

'Don't be daft. I wasn't attacked. I tripped over.'

'You were mugged.'

'No, after I fell over someone stole my phone. That's all.'

'That's all? Louisa, you could have been killed. I'm going straight to the police.'

'You can save yourself the bother. They've already been here and taken my statement. Please accept I live in York now, because I really don't want to fall out with you, but I'm not going back to Whitby and that's final. So, thank you again for coming, but you can stop worrying about me, because I'm fine.'

She closed her eyes and listened to the noises of the hospital ward: footsteps, muffled voices, and the occasional high-pitched beep that had been disturbing her sleep. Eventually she drifted into an uneasy doze and when she opened her eyes again, her mother had gone.

33

A FEW OF HER colleagues arranged to go for a quick drink after work, but Ariadne was keen to get home. Nico would be waiting for her, and she was keen to see him as soon as she could. Having assured Geraldine that everything was fine in her marriage, she hoped that was true, but Nico had seemed strained and awkward ever since he had left her, and she drove home with increasing trepidation. For once, the traffic seemed light and the journey didn't take very long. She almost wished there had been a delay so that she could have spent longer preparing herself to see him. Arriving home, she entered the hall with an uneasy feeling, almost like a premonition. If she believed in such things, she would have been seriously worried. As it was, she was gripped by a strong sensation that something was wrong. Nico did not come out into the hall to greet her. She assumed he was asleep upstairs, but then she heard a faint clattering in the kitchen and relaxed slightly. He was in the kitchen preparing supper and hadn't heard her come in.

'Hello,' she called out as she unzipped her jacket, kicked off her shoes, and wriggled her feet into her slippers. 'Nico, I'm home.'

Nico didn't answer. She hurried to the kitchen and saw him seated at the breakfast bar, a bottle of beer on the table in front of him. He glanced up and immediately looked away, picked up his bottle and took a swig, all without acknowledging her arrival.

'Nico,' she said, taking a hesitant step towards him. 'I'm so happy you're home. I can't tell you how happy I am to see you here. It must have been really awful for you. How are you feeling?'

He didn't answer but just grunted without looking at her.

She pulled out a stool and sat down opposite him. 'Nico, look at me. What's wrong?'

'What's wrong?' he echoed, finally looking up and staring directly into her eyes.

His expression was difficult to read but he seemed distant. It was almost like looking at a stranger.

'Nico, something's not right. Talk to me. Tell me what's going on.'

He stood up and turned his back on her. 'What's going on is that I was arrested on a murder charge.'

His voice was taut with suppressed emotion.

'Yes, I know. Do you really imagine for one moment that I could think about anything else while you were locked up? But that's not what I meant. I want to know what's going on right now between us. First you walked out on our marriage for no reason, and now you've come home, you're refusing to talk to me. So tell me what's going on here, with us. I'm your wife, Nico. Don't shut me out like this, I can't bear it. There's obviously a problem, and we need to talk about it.'

He turned back and sat down again, staring at the table between them.

'No reason?' he said, and his voice came out in a kind of hiss. 'Your people arrested me and interrogated me and locked me in a cell. I thought I was never going to be released.' His voice rose until he was almost incoherent in his anger. 'Doreen Lewis was murdered and everyone thought I did it. Can you imagine what that was like, knowing that everyone thought I'd killed a helpless old woman? She was in a wheelchair.'

'I never thought that for one moment,' she blurted out, reaching out to him with both hands in a gesture he ignored. 'I always knew you were innocent.'

'But you did nothing about it.'

She was shocked at his bitterness. 'What do you mean? What could I have done? You'd been arrested. The evidence pointed to you. I couldn't remove your DNA from the scene, could I?'

'Why not, if you were so sure I was innocent? Why didn't you do something? Anything? I'm your husband. How could you just leave me there, locked up in a cell?'

Ariadne contained her emotion with difficulty. 'Did you expect me to tamper with the evidence? What are you talking about? Listen, you need to calm down. You're not thinking clearly. This hasn't been exactly pleasant for me, you know.'

He snorted. 'You should try being locked in a cell, not knowing if you'll ever be let out. Then you'll know what it means to experience something that's not exactly pleasant.'

He stood up and stalked out of the kitchen, leaving Ariadne sitting alone, shaking. After a while, she heard the front door slam. Nico had gone, leaving her alone again. Finally, her composure crumbled and she began to cry, tears sliding down the inside of her wrists as she covered her face with her hands. Nico had been exonerated, but he had left her, and her marriage was over. Giving up any attempt to control herself, she rested her arms on the breakfast bar and let her head sink forward as she wept without restraint. All she could think of was how keen Nico had been to build a breakfast bar in the kitchen, and how pleased he had been when she had agreed.

'It'll be great, you'll see,' he had promised her. 'In the mornings, when you're in a rush to get off to work, I'll have your breakfast waiting for you right here.'

'I won't have time,' she had protested, laughing.

'You'll make the time,' he had replied solemnly. 'We'll always have time for each other once we're married. Promise me, Ariadne.'

She had kept her promise, as far as she had been able to. He had walked out, not her, but she was the one who had caused the rift. Somehow he must have sensed that she hadn't trusted him.

Her emotions had been in turmoil and she had been incapable of thinking clearly, but the fact remained that she hadn't trusted him at a time when he needed her most. The hand on her shoulder was so unexpected, she spun round and almost seized Nico's arm in a well-trained response to an aggressive approach.

'You're crying,' he said, gently wiping her cheek.

'I thought you'd left me,' she stammered. 'I thought you were angry with me.'

'I was,' he replied simply. 'I was furious with you, with your fucking police force, with that stupid old woman who went and got herself killed with my DNA in her hair, with life, with everything.' He took a bottle from the bag he was carrying. 'And then I calmed down and bought this to celebrate. It's over, Ariadne, and we can get back to our lives.'

He placed a bottle of Champagne on the breakfast bar that he had so carefully constructed for them to share.

'Any marriage has its good times and its bad times,' he said, smiling sadly at her. 'You have to admit this was a particularly bad time, but we can get past this, can't we? I was just angry. I'm over it now.'

She smiled back at him. 'And I was just sad. I'm over it now you're back.'

And, just like that, her feeling of impending disaster vanished.

'I do love you, you know,' she said.

'Well, I should hope so,' Nico replied. 'You married me.'

She was glad he had no idea how uncertain she had been about her feelings for him until she had been afraid she had lost him.

34

IAN WAS PLAYING IN a five-a-side football league that evening, so Geraldine decided to pop into a pub near the police station. Her colleagues often gathered there for a sociable drink after work. Ariadne had declined to join her, but Geraldine decided to have a look in the bar anyway. If none of her colleagues was there, she wouldn't stay. Entering, she saw two of her colleagues engrossed in conversation. Naomi's blonde head bobbed up and down as she talked, while dark-haired Matthew listened. Tall, slim and good-looking, Detective Inspector Matthew Morrison had recently joined the police station in York. He was intelligent, with an air of confidence and a cheeky sense of humour. And he was separated from his wife. Geraldine had not been surprised to notice a few of her colleagues flirting with him. If she had been single, she might have been attracted to him herself. Naomi was one of the officers who was friendly with him. In her late twenties, bright and ambitious, she was conventionally pretty and seemed to be looking for a partner. She had been interested in Ian at one time, before he moved in with Geraldine.

Matthew smiled and beckoned to Geraldine to join them.

'What's going on?' she asked, pulling a chair over to their table.

'Naomi's just ranting about muggers,' Matthew replied with a tolerant smile.

'The trouble is, it's not dramatic enough to attract much attention,' Naomi said. 'No one takes it seriously, but it's getting way out of control. There are muggings happening every day and we really should be stepping up and doing something about it.'

'It's hardly a daily incident,' Matthew replied. 'Unless you count school kids nicking each other's phones.'

'Yes, if you ask me, we certainly should count that,' Naomi said. 'Of course we should. We should take it very seriously. But no one takes much notice, and that's just where we're going wrong, because that's where all the trouble starts. And it's not school children we're talking about, it's school bullies and thieves, many of them well into their teens. But that's beside the point. I don't care how young or old they are, what they're doing is stealing, and they ought to be caught and punished. The real issue is that we're too busy dealing with other more grown-up crimes, so they get away with it time and time again. We've gone completely soft on youngsters, but these kids grow up to be adults who believe they're above the law and no one can touch them. It's that kind of low-level misdemeanour in the young that leads to worse crimes later on. We should be targeting the youngest offenders, not waiting until they're too old to change their ways, at which point we run around trying to find them and lock them up. Instead of that, we should be working to sort them out while they're kids, so they don't become criminals when they're adults. We go about it in completely the wrong way.'

She seemed set to continue with her diatribe, but Matthew had finished his pint and interrupted her.

'I'll get the next one, shall I?' he enquired.

Geraldine smiled. She wasn't surprised to learn that Naomi had bought the first round. She had probably instigated her visit to the pub with Matthew.

'What brought this on?' Geraldine asked while Matthew was at the bar. 'Don't tell me someone was stupid enough to try and mug you on your way to the pub?'

Naomi shook her head. 'No, no, not me, it was a woman I was

sent to question in hospital today. She'd been injured, allegedly in a fall, and said she'd been mugged, but she couldn't remember anything about her attacker so it was all a complete waste of time. It's a pity because she's only been living in York for a few months.'

'Do you think that makes the crime worse than if she'd lived here all her life?' Geraldine enquired with a faint smile.

'No, of course not,' Naomi replied quickly. 'That's not what I meant. It's just that we don't want the city to get a bad reputation as a place where it's not safe for a woman to walk around alone.'

'What's this?' Matthew asked, sitting down again. 'Who's getting a bad reputation, and what for? I hope you weren't gossiping about me, ladies,' he added with mock solemnity. 'I'd be horrified to hear that my wicked deeds have been discovered, after I was so careful to cover my tracks.'

Naomi laughed a little too loudly, and Matthew sipped his beer, seemingly oblivious to her admiring glances. Geraldine felt a flicker of sympathy for her young colleague, and hoped she wouldn't get hurt. Ever since Geraldine had saved Naomi's life, she had felt irrationally protective towards her. But Naomi was nearly thirty, and an intelligent woman. Her personal life was really no concern of Geraldine's.

'I was just telling Geraldine about the latest victim of a mugging on the street,' Naomi told Matthew. 'The poor woman ended up in hospital.'

'Was she badly injured?' Geraldine asked.

'She was bruised where she apparently tripped while she was running away. She fell on her face and suffered quite extensive contusions. She was lucky her nose wasn't broken.'

'So she sustained whatever injuries she had by falling over? The mugger didn't physically attack her? But she must have had a reason to be running away from him?'

'He hit her head, pushed her so hard she fell over, and stole her bag with money and her phone in it,' Naomi replied. 'If that's not a physical attack, I don't know what is.'

As they drank, they discussed what difference it made if the victim had been thrown to the ground or fallen as a result of being hit. Matthew wasn't as upset by the incident as Naomi, while Geraldine declined to comment on a specific case she knew nothing about, but they all agreed in principle that mugging should be dealt with severely.

'If the woman I saw today had brittle bones, or a heart condition, or had hit her skull when she fell, she could have been killed,' Naomi pointed out.

Geraldine nodded. Such an attack could happen to anyone, and the fact that a woman had recently been murdered in York was making everyone a little jumpy.

The conversation drifted on and Naomi offered to buy another round. Geraldine declined the offer, saying Ian would be home soon. Actually, she wasn't expecting him home for another hour at least, but she wanted to prepare dinner.

'It's all right for you, being single,' she added, smiling at Naomi whose eyes flicked to Matthew to see whether he reacted to the hint. 'Ian'll be waiting for me at home.'

She was thinking about the reported mugging as she drove home.

35

ALTHOUGH ARIADNE WAS CLEARLY tired, she looked cheerful, and Geraldine even heard her humming to herself as she worked.

'I told you,' Ariadne murmured, looking up and catching Geraldine watching her.

Geraldine smiled. 'Yes, you did,' she agreed. 'You know,' she went on, feeling slightly awkward, 'You know I was –'

'Only doing your job, yes, I know, I know,' Ariadne interrupted her, but she was smiling.

Taking a break from her own work, Geraldine glanced through the other recent incidents that had been logged, curious to see whether Naomi had been exaggerating the extent of the recent spate of local muggings. On her way into work that morning, she had half listened to a call-in programme on the radio. The presenter had talked in sweeping terms about how the streets of London had become a jungle in many areas. Some callers had agreed with the presenter, others had dismissed his opinions as sensationalist scaremongering. Of course many assaults were never reported to the police, so it was impossible to know the real extent of mugging on the streets, but the topic had come up twice recently, and she wanted to find out whether it was as much of a problem as some people appeared to suggest. Checking through Naomi's report, she was surprised to recognise the victim's name. This was the second time Louisa Thomas had been brought to her attention in a week. Clearly that was a coincidence, but she decided to speak to Louisa again when she had a free moment.

The next morning, she called on her at home. Louisa looked faintly annoyed when she opened the door after establishing who was on the other side.

'Is this going to take long, only I'm due at work.'

'What time do you need to be there?' Geraldine enquired, glancing at Louisa's dressing gown and pyjamas.

Louisa hesitated then admitted she had been given the rest of the week off. It was only half past eight and Geraldine realised she had roused Louisa from bed.

'Can I come in? I'd like to speak to you.'

'Is it about the mugging?' Louisa asked.

Geraldine nodded. 'Yes, I'd like to ask you a few questions, if that's all right.'

'No,' Louisa snapped. 'What I mean is, there's really no point. I already spoke to the police and told them everything I could.'

When Geraldine pressed her, Louisa caved in and led her to a small sparsely furnished living room. Geraldine sat on an upright chair and Louisa sank down on the solitary armchair with a sigh of annoyance. There was no other furniture in the room, apart from a television that was too large for the space, and a small coffee table in the centre of the room.

'Now, I know you've already spoken to my colleague and made a statement, but I'd like to find out more about what happened. What can you tell me about your mugger?'

'Nothing at all, because I didn't see him. That is, I did catch sight of him, but only out of the corner of my eye, and I didn't see his face at all. He was very careful to keep that hidden from me so that he was just a shape. He came up behind me and the first time I knew he was there was when he hit me on the head. It really hurt. Before I knew what was happening, he shoved me really hard. I think he was trying to make me fall over. I managed to keep my balance and ran, only then I fell over – I think he may have pushed me a second time. But he was wearing a hood and his face was completely hidden all the time, so I couldn't see him.'

'But you knew it was a man who attacked you?'

Louisa nodded. 'Of course. I said so, didn't I?'

If it was true that she hadn't seen his face, then she could only be that sure her attacker was male if she had heard his voice.

'What did he say to you?'

'Nothing,' Louisa replied promptly. 'He didn't say anything. I didn't hear his voice.'

'Then can you be sure your mugger was a man?'

Louisa hesitated and looked vexed, as though she had been caught out inventing a story. 'I can't be sure, not really. You just assume, don't you? That is, I assumed it was a man. He shoved me pretty hard, so I think whoever it was he must have been strong. That's what I thought at the time, anyway. Yes, I'm as sure as I can be that it was him.'

Geraldine didn't pounce on Louisa's use of the pronoun, even though it sounded as though she knew more about her mugger than she wanted to admit.

'Did he take you by surprise?'

'Of course he did. I mean, you don't expect to be mugged on the street, do you?'

There was something about Louisa's indignation that bothered Geraldine. She looked away from Geraldine, and seemed inordinately flustered. Without knowing what it might be, Geraldine was almost certain Louisa was hiding something.

'Did you suspect this might happen?' she asked gently. 'Louisa, tell me who you're afraid of.'

All at once, Louisa broke down in tears. When she had recovered sufficiently to speak coherently, she stammered that she thought she was being stalked. Little by little Geraldine managed to prise out of her that Louisa had seen a hooded figure following her on several occasions.

'I thought at first I must be mistaken,' she said, and paused to blow her nose. 'I mean, there are lots of people walking around, aren't there? I thought I was just being paranoid. I guess moving to the city has that effect on lots of people, doesn't it? I mean, my mother was worried about my moving here and she really put the wind up me. But I shouldn't have listened to her, should I? I mean, it is silly to be so paranoid, isn't it? Lots of people live in York and they aren't scared of walking around, are they? I didn't want to say anything. I mean, I didn't even mention it to the other policewoman because – well, there's nothing to say really. Nothing happened. Until I was mugged. But I don't think that had anything to do with – the other thing. I'm pretty sure I was just imagining that someone was following me.'

She was asking for reassurance, but Geraldine made no response and only sat listening. When people were nervous, they often talked just to fill the silence. In such circumstances, careless chatter could lead to indiscretion, but Louisa fell silent.

'Do you think your mugger was the same person who was stalking you?' Geraldine asked when it became clear that Louisa wasn't going to say any more.

'I don't know, I don't know,' Louisa admitted, sobbing again. 'But I'm not going back to Whitby,' she added inconsequentially.

Geraldine left. She was no better informed about the recent muggings than she had been when she arrived, but if Louisa was genuinely being stalked, then it was possible the attack on her was a different kind of crime altogether. And Geraldine had a feeling she might know who was responsible for the assault. She just had to find proof that her theory was correct, and she needed to establish the truth soon, before there was another attack on Louisa.

36

EDDY DIDN'T APPEAR SURPRISED when Geraldine called on him. He readily agreed to accompany her to the police station, and shuffled over to the waiting car without remonstrating. Far from protesting, he actually seemed pleased at the interruption to his day.

'It's not as if I've got anything else to do today,' he said cheerfully as a uniformed constable led him away. 'And it gets me away from Alec telling me what to do all the time.'

His next-door neighbour was standing on her doorstep watching, with a sour expression on her face. Eddy scowled at her but she continued staring without moving a muscle. Slightly surprised by Eddy's willingness to return to the police station, Geraldine assumed he was bored and lonely without his mother. They had always lived together and he must be missing her.

'That doesn't mean he didn't kill her,' Ian pointed out, when Geraldine arrived at the police station and told him that Eddy had been remarkably amenable about returning to the police station for further questioning. 'Just because he misses his mother doesn't change anything. It's not unheard of for people to bump off someone they're living with. Don't tell me the thought has never crossed your mind since I moved in with you?'

Refusing to be goaded, Geraldine laughed. When the solicitor and the social worker arrived, Geraldine went to question Eddy.

'Why am I here?' he asked, gazing around the room. 'And when are you going to tell me who killed my mother? I know that's what happened. She explained it all to me.' He pointed to the social worker and then turned back to Geraldine with a worried expression. 'I know what's going on and I know it's your job to put the killer in prison where he belongs.'

The constable who had collected Eddy reported that he had seemed quite cheerful about travelling in a police car, but his lawyer's presence seemed to wake him up to his situation and he grew fretful, whining that he wanted to go home. The lawyer looked as though he had neither changed his clothes nor washed since the last interview. He sat frowning, seemingly resentful at having been summoned back for the same client. His eyes were restless in his wily face, but Geraldine had the impression he was not very interested in the proceedings and was eager for the interview to draw to a close. She wondered how much he knew about Eddy, and whether it was more than he was prepared to share with the police. She tested a faint smile at him, which he ignored, before turning her attention to Eddy, who was fidgeting and gazing anxiously at her.

'I want to go home,' he blurted out. 'I want to go home now!'

'Of course,' Geraldine responded quickly, before the lawyer could reply. 'Of course you do. And we don't want to keep you here any longer than we have to. We just want to ask you a few questions and then you can be on your way.'

Eddy turned to the lawyer. 'Do I have to answer any of her questions? I don't want to. I don't have to say anything, do I?'

Geraldine interrupted before he had finished speaking, giving the lawyer no time to reply.

'It will be better for you if you co-operate with us,' she said firmly. 'Otherwise we're going to suspect that you're hiding something, and then we'd probably want to keep you in a cell for hours and hours while we search your house.'

Eddy looked startled. 'You can't do that.'

The lawyer grunted, but he made no comment.

'Let's talk about the woman you call Kylie,' Geraldine said.

The lawyer stirred in his seat and glared at Geraldine, his

head on one side in an interrogative pose. He mouthed the word, 'Kylie', and looked at Eddy for an explanation.

'This is Kylie, isn't it?'

Geraldine placed a copy of a photo of Louisa on the table in front of Eddy. He leaned forward in his chair and stared at the image, his face suddenly flushed. There could be little doubt that he recognised the face displayed in front of him.

'Well?' Geraldine demanded, impatient to hear the truth.

Eddy nodded wordlessly.

'Is this Kylie?' Geraldine pressed him. 'Eddy, I need an answer from you. Do you recognise this woman?'

Eddy nodded. 'That's Kylie,' he muttered. 'That's her.'

'Are you sure?'

He nodded again, without lifting his eyes from the photo.

'That's Kylie,' he confirmed aloud at last. 'That's her all right.' He paused and smiled. 'I'd recognise her anywhere. She's got a special mark, see? Just there. It's a birthmark. Not many people have that,' he added as though proud of Louisa's birthmark. 'She was given it as a baby so that her parents could identify her. That was clever, wasn't it? Babies can get lost, can't they? Or mixed up. It was in a film.'

What Eddy said made no sense but Geraldine looked where he was pointing, indicating a dot on the woman's temple that was clearly a mole.

'This woman in the picture isn't called Kylie, is she?' Geraldine asked suddenly. 'She never was called Kylie. You gave her that name because you don't know her. Let me introduce you now. This is Louisa Thomas and she has no idea who you are. So, let's start again, shall we?'

Eddy stared at Geraldine as though she was speaking a language he didn't understand, his face devoid of emotion.

'You told us you were with Kylie when your mother was killed, but that's not true, is it? You made that up. You never met her. Your relationship was all one big lie, so you could pretend you had an alibi for the time of the murder. You must think we're stupid.'

Eddy shook his head. 'No, no, I don't think you're stupid. I don't. I don't.'

'Didn't you realise we would trace Louisa and question her about you?'

Eddy was shaking his head furiously. 'No!' he shouted. 'No! That's not true. You're the one who's lying. You, it's you. You're the liar.' He was nearly crying now and trembling so that he could hardly speak.

There was something unnerving about Eddy's outburst. Whatever the truth, Geraldine wasn't sure he was ever going to disclose where he had been on the morning of his mother's death. They were going to have to rely on whatever evidence they could find, and so far that pointed to Eddy being guilty. She decided to try one last time.

'Tell me what you did on the Saturday when your mother was killed,' she urged him gently. 'If you keep lying to me, I won't be able to do anything to help you, and I do want to help you. But you have to tell me the truth.'

At Eddy's side, the dishevelled lawyer stirred but didn't speak.

'I followed her – I went with her to her work,' Eddy said. 'And then I waited for her to finish and went back home with her.'

He spoke so earnestly, that it was hard to doubt that he at least believed what he was telling her. Remembering Louisa's claim that she was being stalked, Geraldine hesitated. Eddy knew where Kylie lived, and where she worked. Geraldine was almost certain now that he had been following Louisa to and from work. Thoughtfully, she went to see the visual identifications and detections team with her theory.

'You want us to see if we can find any sign of him loitering in Dale Street, and hanging around outside the hotel?' a constable asked.

'Exactly,' Geraldine replied. 'We need to trace his movements that day and find out if he's telling the truth about where he went.'

Eddy was still the obvious suspect, since he had motive and opportunity to kill Doreen. His alibi had been demolished, depending as it did on the word of someone who denied knowing him. Nevertheless, there was a slight possibility that Louisa was the one who was lying, so Eddy was allowed to return home, with a warning to remain in York.

'Where would I go?' he answered. 'I live here.'

37

LOUISA HAD THE WEEK off work. Her manager had been surprisingly sympathetic and had given her paid leave. Admittedly it was the middle of the week and housekeeping was generally uneventful once the rooms had been cleaned. There was the occasional request for extra towels or shampoo, but generally nothing much happened and there was little changeover of guests.

She went into town and spent the afternoon looking round the shops. Even though she didn't know anyone, the other customers were company of a sort. She ended up buying new trainers, which were far too expensive, and new jeans. She had intended to do her food shopping on the way home, but instead went to a cheap Chinese buffet where she ate alone in the noise and bustle of other customers. By the time she was on her way home, carrying her purchases, the sun had set. The pavement was lit by the soft glow of street lamps, along with intermittent bright flashes from car headlamps speeding past, while the cold glare of a thin crescent moon gave little light. When she left the main road she started to feel nervous, because this time there seemed little doubt she was being followed.

She began to hurry. After passing a few houses she dared to glance over her shoulder in the hope that she was mistaken. But a hooded figure was there, scurrying along behind her. She broke into a run, and sprinted to her front door, reaching it before her pursuer could reach her. Shaking, she fumbled to turn the key and almost fell through the door as she pushed it open. She was home, unharmed but frightened, trying to convince herself that she must have been mistaken. Someone else had chanced to be walking along Dale Street at the same time as her, that was all. There was no reason to suppose anyone had been following her. It was time to give herself a severe talking to. She had been unlucky to be mugged a few days earlier, but that happened to lots of people. She had been weak to allow the incident to unnerve her, but now she had to get over it and carry on with her life.

She took a cup of cocoa to bed and lay awake until past midnight. At last, she turned the light out and lay down. She wasn't sure if the sound of footsteps woke her, or if she had not yet fallen asleep, but she was instantly awake, convinced there was someone in her flat. She could hear them moving around just outside her bedroom door. She held her breath and listened, trying to persuade herself she must be mistaken and the noise was coming from one of the neighbouring flats. It was dark in her room, but gradually her eyes became accustomed to the dim light from a street lamp outside her window. Slowly she raised herself on her pillow, straining to hear. Waiting until her next payday, she had as yet done nothing about replacing her phone. Now, not only was she alone, but she couldn't summon assistance. Cautiously she slid back down under the cover and waited for a few moments. Nothing happened.

Then she heard footsteps again.

Lying in bed, wearing only an old T-shirt, she felt horribly vulnerable. She might as well have been naked. As quietly as she could, she reached down to rummage in a pile of clothes that were lying on the floor beside the bed, finding what she wanted more by feeling than sight. The clothes were waiting to be washed, but nothing was really dirty. Fumbling in the dark, she pulled on a pair of jeans. She didn't bother with underwear. Irrationally, covering herself up gave her courage and she told herself crossly that she was being ridiculous, believing someone else was in her flat. In any case, if there really was an intruder, the last thing she wanted was for him to find her in the bedroom where she would effectively be trapped. Cautiously she opened her bedroom door, intending to try and creep out of her flat and escape, even though she was still telling herself she was overreacting to a few creaks in the woodwork, or a noise from the flat upstairs.

Seeing there actually was a figure standing nearby, half concealed in shadow, she heard herself scream. Nothing like the screams of women in films, this was a low thin sound, almost a whistle. The intruder's face was concealed by a large baggy hood. As though watching in slow motion, she saw him walk towards her. She had left the bedroom without arming herself with anything that could serve as a weapon. Clenching her fists, she struck out in panic, but the intruder seized her arm as she attempted to hit him, and twisted it so roughly she was forced to her knees. As she was clambering to her feet, he grabbed a bottle from the table and swung it at her. Missing her head, the bottle glanced off her shoulder. She ducked away and made a dash for the hall.

Managing to reach her front door, she wrenched it open. With a flash of relief that she had thought to pull on her jeans, she fled. She ran as far as the stairs and flung herself forwards. Hurtling downwards, she lost her footing and slipped. There was a resounding crack as her head crashed into the wall, and a bright red light flashed inside her head. After that, she was aware only that she was sliding, sliding, into darkness, while pain sliced through her brain.

When she came to, her head was throbbing painfully and she couldn't see. With an effort she moved her arm and felt around, with no idea of what she was searching for. She tried to scream for help but she couldn't cry out. Patting the floor, she felt a wet sticky mess beside her and realised she was bleeding from a head injury. With a sudden shock, she understood that she might die if she didn't receive medical attention soon. Her lips moved helplessly but no sound came out. She blinked and heard a faint moaning followed by an odd kind of rasping sound. Through the silence of the night, she remembered her mother's warning.

'It's dangerous here, Louisa. It's time to come home.'

'I want to come home,' she tried to answer the voice in her head, but she couldn't speak.

The worst had happened, and it was more painful than she could possibly have imagined.

38

While Geraldine was keen for Doreen's killer to be discovered, she remained unconvinced of Eddy's guilt, although her colleagues all seemed convinced that his lies were sufficient to condemn him. Geraldine tried to explain her reservations to Ariadne who, like the rest of the team, remained positive that Eddy had killed his mother.

'He told us he had a girlfriend called Kylie, but in the end she turned out to be a woman called Louisa who doesn't even know him,' Ariadne pointed out. 'How much more proof do you need that he's hiding the truth? We can't trust anything he says, and he's the only one with a motive.'

'Yes, I know all that, but I still don't think he's lying,' Geraldine replied. 'It's just a feeling I have.'

'Well, we know he's not telling the truth, so it's hard to see how you can say he's not lying.'

'What I mean is, he may be deluded and fantasising, but that's not the same as deliberately lying to conceal the fact that he's guilty. And it doesn't mean he killed his mother.'

Ariadne shook her head. 'It comes to the same thing. He's not telling the truth about where he was when Doreen was murdered. You can think of it as delusion or fantasising or deliberate lying, but ultimately it makes no difference what you choose to call it. Whatever your "feelings" about him are, he's not telling the truth.'

'If he's lying to cover up the truth then he's clearly done something wrong, but if he's a fantasist, we can't automatically assume he's guilty.'

'There's nothing to suggest he's innocent.'

'Innocent until proved guilty?'

'Oh, for goodness sake,' Ariadne burst out, 'I don't know why you have to be so obstinate. It's like you're determined to be different for no reason.'

'Of course I have a reason,' Geraldine protested. 'I don't think we can be sure beyond any reasonable doubt that he's guilty.'

'Well obviously he's guilty. I just don't understand why you can't see it. Everyone else can. And in any case, it's not up to us to make that call. It's for a jury to decide.'

Doreen had one sister, Mary, who lived in Saddleworth, and a local constable had been sent to speak to her. According to Mary, no one in her family had seen Doreen or her son for many years after a falling out. She wasn't able to pass on any information about Eddy, whom she hadn't seen since he was a child. She called her local police station after she had been questioned, to state that Eddy had been prone to fits of temper as a child, during which he could become quite violent. His school record confirmed that he was easily frustrated, although he had never assaulted another pupil. Eddy had no other relatives and no friends that the police were able to trace. While they were discussing Eddy, and whether he was responsible for his mother's death, they were summoned to the incident room. Hoping that more evidence had been discovered that would confirm the situation concerning Eddy one way or the other, they made their way along the corridor. If Eddy had been captured on CCTV following Louisa to work on Saturday, Geraldine thought it was possible his alibi might stack up after all, even though Louisa insisted she didn't know him. With mixed feelings, she waited to hear what Eileen had to tell them.

'SOCOs must have found evidence that proves it was Eddy, not to mention his fake alibi,' Naomi said. 'The sooner we get him locked up the better, if you ask me.'

There was a murmur of agreement from several of their colleagues, but before Naomi could continue, Eileen entered the room and they all fell silent. There was something in her expression that sent a chill through the assembled officers. Before she spoke, everyone knew that something was wrong. For a few seconds, Geraldine was afraid the detective chief inspector had lost control of herself.

'We have another victim,' Eileen barked. There was a fleeting hiatus while she appeared to struggle to control herself. Geraldine had never seen her looking so agitated. 'The body was discovered lying in the road,' she resumed after a moment. 'It would be quite a coincidence if this murder was not connected in some way with the murder of Doreen Lewis.' She paused to allow that information to sink in.

'Is there anything specific that links this body to Doreen's case?' Geraldine asked, wondering why Eileen was assuming the two deaths were related.

'It's possible this second body was left in the road with the deliberate intention of misleading us into believing the victim was run over,' Eileen continued, ignoring Geraldine's question. 'We have to consider every possibility.'

The detective chief inspector now sounded so reasonable, Geraldine wondered if she had imagined that her senior officer was ill. Perhaps Eileen had just had a bad day. It happened to everyone.

'All we know so far is that this second victim is a woman, and her injuries are not consistent with damage caused by a traffic incident,' Eileen continued. 'Her body was found lying in the street, although we don't yet know for certain whether she was killed there. There is some evidence she was killed elsewhere and the body was moved post mortem. As I said, we need to keep an open mind at this stage.'

'If she wasn't run over, how did she die?' a constable asked.

'We don't yet know,' Eileen replied. 'The body's gone off for examination and no doubt we'll hear more in due course.'

Geraldine and Ariadne drove to the site in Dale Street where the body had been discovered, coincidentally not far from where Louisa Thomas lived. The road was dominated by a forensic tent and although it was early, a small cluster of curious neighbours had already gathered on the pavement nearby. As she drew close, Geraldine saw there were only three women and a couple of men there. No doubt the fine drizzle that was falling had kept away all but the most inquisitive of onlookers.

'Hey, what's going on?' a stout woman demanded as Geraldine and Ariadne approached, and a uniformed constable moved aside to let them pass.

'Some poor soul's been run over,' a woman in a grey coat replied. She spoke authoritatively. 'They only put up those tents if there's a body in there. That's how you know someone's died. If you ask me, some bastard knocked her down in the night and drove off. He was probably drunk.'

'She might have been drunk,' one of the men pointed out. 'You don't know it was the driver's fault. She might have walked right out in front of him.'

'We saw the mortuary van leaving,' another man chimed in. 'So they've taken the body away.'

'If you ask me, it was a hit and run,' the woman in the grey coat insisted. 'Otherwise there wouldn't be so many police here, would there? And they wouldn't put up that tent if it wasn't a crime scene.'

'Did you see who it was?'

'Didn't see anything.'

'I mean the body.'

'No. They kept us well back. All we saw was a covered stretcher.'

'Was the head covered up as well?'

'Has someone been bumped off then?' a tall man asked, joining the group of onlookers.

'Hey, show some respect, will you?' the woman in the grey coat snapped suddenly. 'Someone died here.'

'Who was it?' the tall man asked.

'Doesn't matter now, does it?' the stout woman replied. 'Whoever it was, she's dead now.'

'But how do you know it was a woman?' another man asked.

'Could've been a man,' the woman in the grey coat replied. 'But if you want my opinion, it was a woman.'

The three women nodded solemnly, as though the victim of a hit and run was somehow more likely to have been a woman than a man. Geraldine and Ariadne pulled on their protective clothing and entered the tent, but the body had already been removed so there was not a great deal to be seen other than scene of crime officers beetling around in and out of the tent, taking photographs and gathering samples, scrutinising every inch of the surrounding tarmac.

Geraldine addressed the nearest officer. 'What do we know?'

He shook his head and above his mask she saw his eyes narrow as though he was screwing his face into a grimace before answering.

'Not a lot, to be honest. She wasn't killed here so there's nothing much for us to find. We're taking measurements of any footprints and tyre marks we can spot, but it's going to be a long job. It's always a problem when a body is found in the street. So it looks as though it's going to be down to any eye witnesses or CCTV you can find. Honestly, there was next to nothing of any use to us here at all, just a load of messy footprints. She was carried here wrapped in a bed cover that we are almost certain was brought with her from elsewhere. I mean, no one leaves a large throw on the pavement for someone else to deposit a body on, do they?' He shook his head, and Geraldine wasn't sure if he was smiling. 'We can't say yet whether she was carried here or driven here in a vehicle, but we're working on it. The bed cover has gone off to the forensic team and hopefully they'll be able to tell us more.'

Geraldine questioned him further about the death, but he just told her she would have to ask the pathologist when he carried out the post mortem, and insisted there was nothing more he could tell her. There was no point wasting any more time at the scene where the body had been discovered, so she and Ariadne left the scene of crime officers to their painstaking work. They didn't even know where the unidentified victim had been killed, only that her body had been left lying in the road. Without expecting to learn much, Geraldine went to question the person who had reported finding the body.

39

THE BODY HAD BEEN found by a young boy out on his paper round. He was now sitting in the front room of his home in Moss Street along with his parents, who seemed far more shocked than their son by what had happened. Two untouched mugs of tea stood on the table in front of them. His father's expression was tense and his mother sat quietly watchful, while the boy's greenish eyes shone with excitement. He seemed to be finding it hard to sit still. He brushed his ginger curls off his forehead in a pointless gesture and looked as though he was trying not to grin.

'I saw her. I was cycling past,' he blurted out as Geraldine sat down. 'She was just lying in the road, a real dead body, and it was me that found it. Do the police think I had something to do with it? Have you come to arrest me? Only you don't have any evidence, do you? I know I haven't really got an alibi, I was just there on my bike, but I didn't run her down. I didn't do anything.'

His mother was holding what looked like a damp handkerchief, twisting it in her fingers, and dabbing at her nose with it from time to time. 'He's a good boy,' she kept repeating. 'He's a good boy.'

It took Geraldine a few minutes to persuade the boy to calm down and stop talking so she could reassure his distraught mother that no one suspected her son of being in any way responsible for the body that he had discovered, and Geraldine had not arrived to drag him off to a prison cell.

'So you're not going to arrest me?' he asked, wide-eyed.

'Not unless you've broken the law,' Geraldine replied solemnly. 'Discovering a body and reporting it to the police isn't a crime. On the contrary, it's a very responsible thing to do. You must have been worried when you saw the victim out in the street. You could have just left her for someone else to find, and it could have been someone walking by with a very small child who came across her, or someone who was very old who might have found it very upsetting. So you did absolutely the right thing, Tommy. Now, I need you to take a moment to stop and think and then you can tell me exactly what happened.'

With a sob, his mother nodded and wiped her nose with her handkerchief.

'Yes,' she whispered. 'He'll tell you everything he can, won't you, Tommy?' She turned to Geraldine. 'He's a good boy.'

Tommy's father spoke for the first time. 'He's missing school,' he said gruffly.

Tommy grinned. 'I can't help that, can I? I'm helping the police with their enquiries. It's the responsible thing to do when you find a dead body. She said so.'

'That's right,' Geraldine agreed. 'Now, I need you to tell me what you can about how you came across the body. It's just for our information and if you can't remember what happened, that's fine. But anything you can tell us might help us to discover who left the woman in the road where you found her. And we do need to find out what happened, so we can make sure it can't happen again. You understand that, don't you? I know it's been a shock for you, but I'm asking you to help us. No one else can tell us what you can tell us, because you were the one who found the body. So it's very important you don't leave anything out.'

The boy nodded. As Geraldine had hoped, emphasising the importance of his witness account was enough to persuade him to make the effort needed to calm down and deliver a coherent account of what had happened.

'I was out on my paper round,' he began. 'I've been doing it for weeks. Dad makes me do it before school,' he added with a touch of sullenness. 'But it was my idea and I get paid every week.' He paused, his face almost relaxing in a smile and then growing solemn again as he recalled his situation. 'I never got it done this morning because when I was on my way to collect the papers I saw... should I say her or it?' He didn't pause for an answer but continued, with a resurgence of his former excitement. 'Anyway, I saw the body on the road but I didn't know that's what it was, I mean I didn't know she was dead.' His eyes shone at the memory. 'Just wait till I tell everyone at school! Will I be in the papers?' He laughed. 'I'm the one who delivers the papers, and now I might be in them!' His eyes opened wider. 'I might be on the telly! Do you think I'll be on the telly?'

'I don't know,' Geraldine replied.

'Just answer the policewoman's questions, Tommy,' his mother said.

'When did you realise you ought to call for help?' Geraldine asked.

'He came straight home,' Tommy's mother answered for him. 'As soon as he thought she was – injured, he came straight home and told us. So we went to look. That is, his father went with him. I wasn't even dressed yet.'

Tommy's father took up the story. 'We saw her lying there, just as the lad said. So that's when we called you and, well,' he shrugged. 'It was clear she was in some sort of trouble, unconscious or dead, so I called for an ambulance as well. Anyway, the ambulance came pretty sharpish I must say, and they called the police who started asking all sorts of questions.'

His wife broke down in tears, whimpering into her handkerchief and mumbling about the shock. Muttering her thanks for their co-operation, Geraldine stood up.

'Will anyone else be coming to speak to us?' Tommy asked

eagerly. 'I don't mind staying off school to help you with your enquiries.'

Geraldine smiled at him. 'I don't think that will be necessary,' she said. 'But you've been extremely helpful and the police are very grateful to you.'

His face fell. 'So you don't need me anymore?'

Thanking Tommy and his parents again, Geraldine took her leave.

40

JONAH WAVED A REDDENED glove at Geraldine without looking up, and she waited for him to complete the procedure he was engaged in. Usually when she arrived, his pug-like features were creased into a welcoming grin, after which he seemed to operate in a state of relentless good humour, entertaining her with his wisecracks. She had never before observed him absorbed in his work to the exclusion of everything else. Now that he wasn't charming her with his banter, his face wore an expression of intense concentration, and she realised how ugly he truly was, with his squashed nose, overhanging brow and small deep-set dark eyes. Not for the first time, she wondered if he had chosen to work with the dead because they could not be repulsed by his appearance, but then she remembered that he was happily married, and had a teenage son of whom he was excessively proud. It was so foolish, and yet so easy, to judge people by their looks. Lowering her gaze, she studied the subject of Jonah's scrutiny.

The dead woman was lying on her back, her eyes open and staring up at the ceiling, half of her face concealed by her light brown hair which had fallen forward across her brow. A neat line had been scored across her chest, doubtless by Jonah in the course of his examination, and there was a bald patch on her temple, where he had shaved her hair to examine the side of her skull.

'There's a head injury, as you can see, and her left shoulder was fractured and badly bruised while she was still alive, although possibly unconscious,' Jonah commented, looking up at last. 'It looks as though she fell.' He paused, frowning. 'If she was holding a bag in her right hand, or over her right shoulder, she might conceivably have put out her left arm in an attempt to break her fall, but it rather looks as though she fell from some height, possibly down a flight of stairs. There's flakes of paint under her fingernails and she has extensive bruising down her left side, as you can see.'

'What was the cause of death?' Geraldine prompted him after a few seconds.

'I'd say she tripped and hit her head. But the officers who examined the scene seem to think she was moved after she fell.' He frowned. 'And if I'm right in my hypothesis that she fell down some stairs, as her bruising and the flecks of paint would seem to indicate, then that would confirm she didn't die on the road where she was found.'

'Was she still alive when she was moved?' Geraldine asked.

She wondered if someone had tried to help the dead woman, unaware that it was already too late to save her. Perhaps the attempt to help her had itself proved fatal.

Jonah nodded. 'Well, yes, it's possible she was still alive when she was moved. It's difficult to be sure, but some of the bruising on her arms suggests someone may have manhandled her after she fell, and before she died.'

'So what exactly was the cause of death?' Geraldine repeated her question.

'The head injury caused a deep bleed in the brain.' Jonah indicated a saturated mess of bloody tissue in a dish, which meant nothing to Geraldine. 'Death would have been quick, but not instantaneous in this case. Not that it ever is,' he added and paused thoughtfully. 'Even severing the neck completely won't cause instantaneous death. I've never examined a body immediately after decapitation, of course. You probably think that would cause death instantly, but you'd be wrong. Removing a head from a body isn't what kills the brain. No, it can continue

223

to function, apparently for as long as ten seconds, until blood loss and lack of oxygen lead to unconsciousness and death. The exact time will vary from person to person, depending on the nature of the fatal blow. But death after decapitation's not something I've ever corroborated for myself.'

'Fascinating,' Geraldine interrupted his monologue. 'But hardly relevant.'

She could have added that what he was saying was quite disturbing, as was his ability to chat about murder victims without showing any emotional reaction. Added to that, he was highly intelligent. In another life, he might have made a very successful killer. With a faint shudder it occurred to her that exactly the same accusation might be levelled against her.

'True. This woman definitely wasn't decapitated,' Jonah agreed, with a return of his familiar cheerful grin. 'At least that's one thing I can confirm without any doubt.'

'Can you tell me anything about her I don't already know?'

Jonah's grin widened. He seemed to have snapped out of his pensive mood.

'She seems to have been healthy and well nourished – perhaps a touch too well nourished.' He paused and tapped the dead woman's rounded belly. 'In her early thirties, I'd say. There or thereabouts. Her last meal, ingested a few hours ante mortem, contained noodles, a few prawns and vegetables. She'd been drinking, not excessively but moderately. A couple of small glasses of wine, perhaps.'

'Have you discerned any signs of a struggle?'

Jonah shook his head. 'There are no defence wounds, and nothing to indicate she resisted an attack, so I'd think she probably fell or was deliberately tripped up or pushed. Don't quote me on any of this, of course. My conclusions are no more than informed guesswork.'

Geraldine nodded. Jonah knew he could rely on her discretion and, in return, he was always ready to share his theories with her. Intelligent and knowledgeable, his speculation was often very helpful in suggesting possible avenues to investigate.

'I wonder if she knew her attacker,' Geraldine mused aloud.

Jonah smiled. 'That's for you to determine. You're the detective. I'm just a humble pathologist.'

Geraldine gazed down at the body. With a gesture that almost looked like a caress, Jonah brushed the dead woman's hair gently off her face. Watching, Geraldine let out a cry of surprise.

'I know who she is,' she blurted out, staring. 'I didn't recognise her until I saw that mole on her temple. I can't believe I didn't identify her as soon as I walked in.'

'Death changes people. They can look completely different,' Jonah said. 'Who is she?'

'Her name is Louisa Thomas and she was helping us with the investigation into Doreen Lewis's murder.'

'So is she another victim of the same killer?'

'Possibly. But the methods of killing are quite different, aren't they?'

'Yes, Doreen was strangled with a length of rope, and this victim died from a head injury caused by a fall. I can't see anything to connect the two deaths just by examining the bodies, but of course that proves nothing.'

'No,' Geraldine agreed with a sigh. 'That proves nothing. What can you tell me that might be helpful?'

Jonah looked serious for a moment as he said, 'I'm sorry, Geraldine. You know I'd love to help you if I could. If I could examine this poor girl and tell you who did this to her, I would. If this was a film, I would be able to tell you the killer was six inches taller than his victim, and left handed, and he walked with a limp. But the fact is, this body hasn't told us anything about her attacker at all which, in itself, is unusual. She could have been ruthlessly attacked by a violent thug who pushed her downstairs, or this could have been an accidental death. I can't even tell you for certain this woman was murdered. Doreen

Lewis was clearly deliberately strangled. That can't happen by chance. But a head injury?' He shook his own head and raised his arms in a gesture of helplessness.

'SOCOs were sure the body was moved post mortem,' Geraldine said. 'So someone knew she was dead, even if they hadn't killed her. But why else would they have moved the body, concealed in a duvet, if they weren't trying to put some distance between the site of the murder and the body?'

'Yes, moving the body certainly indicates foul play,' Jonah agreed.

'But even that isn't positive proof. Is it possible she fell and injured herself, then dragged herself out on to the street wrapped in a duvet against the cold, and died there?'

'It's highly unlikely, if not impossible. It's certainly implausible but on the basis that anything's possible I suppose you can't absolutely rule that out. Her injuries don't give us a very clear account of how she died.'

Geraldine nodded. She understood Jonah was only telling her the truth, but she wished he could have been more helpful.

'If I find a clue to the killer anywhere on this body, you'll be the first to know,' he called out after her as she reached the door.

'I know you're doing what you can,' she replied.

'We all do our best. That's all any of us can do, Geraldine. Don't expect miracles from anyone, not even yourself,' he added softly.

Geraldine took a last look at the body lying on the cold slab. It had taken her traumatic death for Louisa to receive close attention from another human being, and that was no more than a clinical and impersonal examination. Between her infancy and now, she probably hadn't experienced much physical contact with another human being. With a surge of pity for the dead girl, Geraldine felt more determined than ever to find out who had committed this atrocity.

41

EILEEN'S TAUT FEATURES BROKE into a grin when she heard the identity of the second murder victim.

'It can't be a coincidence, Louisa being so closely associated with the main suspect in Doreen's murder. So there it is, then,' she announced with evident glee. 'We've got him now. There's all the proof we need.'

'Proof of what?' Geraldine blurted out in surprise.

'The proof that Eddy's guilty,' Eileen replied quickly. 'He's our murderer. I knew all along we should never have let him go. Send a car to pick him up, Geraldine, and let's put him behind bars where he belongs. And then we can start preparing the paperwork to get this case wrapped up.' Seeing Geraldine hesitate, Eileen snapped at her. 'What are you waiting for?'

'I'm on my way, Ma'am,' Geraldine replied, and Eileen grunted in satisfaction.

'Is it just me, or does this all seem a bit rushed to you?' Geraldine muttered to Ariadne when she returned to her desk. 'I mean, granted Eddy is a link between the two victims, but that doesn't necessarily mean he killed either of them, does it?'

Ariadne shrugged. 'Maybe not, but it's a pretty good start. And it's not as if we've got any other suspects,' she added, with undisguised satisfaction.

'Just because we have no other suspects doesn't mean Eddy's guilty,' Geraldine protested.

'Well, someone must have strangled Doreen,' Ariadne said, turning back to her screen.

'So what? It might as well have been Eddy? Is that what you're saying? Don't you care whether he's guilty or not?' Geraldine asked.

'That's not for us to say, is it?'

A SOCO team was sent to Louisa's apartment block to examine the stairs leading up to her flat and it didn't take them long to discover a few minor scratches on the skirting board, the paint of which was an exact match to the flakes of paint discovered underneath Louisa's fingernails. With conclusive proof that Louisa had died indoors and her body had been moved, Geraldine went to question Eddy who was waiting for her in an interview room. He was sitting with his head lowered, displaying a round bald patch on the top of his head, like a miniature tonsure. When he looked up, she scarcely recognised him. His eyes were half closed as though he hadn't slept for days, and his face looked ashen beneath his uneven stubble. Geraldine wondered if his mother used to prompt him to shave, or if he had stopped caring about himself because he was grieving for her.

The lawyer stifled a yawn before launching into a routine diatribe. 'Yesterday you questioned my client at great and, if I may say, quite unnecessary length, in an unconscionable attempt to browbeat him into confessing to a crime of which he is innocent. You found nothing that could possibly incriminate him, and had no choice but to let him go. You still have no reason to accuse him of the slightest wrongdoing, let alone the horrendous crime of murdering his mother, yet you seem intent on harassing him. It's a monstrous allegation to make in the absence of any proof.'

Geraldine had the impression the lawyer was going through the motions of defending his client. She suspected he could be a persuasive advocate when he chose, but Eddy had evidently failed to engage his sympathy. She wondered whether he had reason to believe his client was guilty, or if he had simply accepted the fact that Eddy was unlikely to convince a jury that he was innocent. The social worker sat silent, apparently brooding on having been summoned to accompany Eddy at yet another interview.

'You seem to be forgetting he gave us a false alibi,' Geraldine pointed out calmly. 'That's hardly likely to win a jury over.'

'I don't like it at home without my mother,' Eddy interrupted in a whining voice. 'She used to have helpers who came in, you know. They helped me too. I'm not sure what I'm going to do now. And I don't know how to get rid of Alec,' he added plaintively.

'Who's Alec?'

Eddy explained that his cousin had come to stay with him. 'I don't even like him,' he added sullenly. 'I know he's my cousin and that means we're family, but I don't like him. He thinks he's better than me and he expects me to do all the shopping as well as looking after the garden. He doesn't even give me any money. Why should I buy his food? All he does is cook and eat and cook and eat, and I don't like him.' He looked up and stared at Geraldine. 'I want you to make him go away.'

'I'm afraid we can't do that,' Geraldine said.

Eddy seemed more upset about his cousin's arrival than about his own threatened arrest. He kept insisting that Geraldine send his cousin packing.

'That's not something we can do,' she repeated.

'Why not? You're the police, aren't you?'

Geraldine put a photo of Louisa on the table.

'What can you tell me about this girl?' she asked.

'That's Kylie,' he muttered. 'And I told you that before.'

'When did you last see her?'

Eddy frowned. 'I looked for her yesterday but I couldn't find her. I guess she had a day off work and I missed her. When she isn't working I don't know what time she goes out,' he added earnestly.

He seemed to be saying that he hadn't seen Louisa on the

day she was attacked, but of course that was what he would say if he had killed her. They knew that Louisa had suffered a fatal injury at home and her body had been moved post mortem. Geraldine had set up a VIIDO team to trace and observe any security camera footage from properties in Dale Street. The body must have been deposited there during the night, and a couple of nearby street lights had not been working, making it difficult to make out what was happening. In any case, the video footage of the actual street was limited, and they found nothing helpful. At one point, the team thought they picked up some suspicious sounds on one of the films, shuffling that could have been the noise of a body being dragged along the ground. Without any visuals it was impossible to be sure what was going on, and they had no information about who was in the street at that point.

That evening Geraldine listened to Ian clattering about in the kitchen. Thinking how lucky she was to be living with a man who enjoyed cooking, she remembered Eddy's complaint about his cousin. 'All he does is cook and eat and cook and eat.'

'I wonder if we should go and speak to this cousin of Eddy's?' she said when Ian sat down at the table with her. 'I suppose he's come to take care of Eddy now his mother's gone.'

'What?' Ian's face creased in perplexity.

Geraldine explained what she meant and Ian shook his head with a sigh.

'Can't you forget about work for a few hours? There's nothing you can do until the morning, so you might as well relax and enjoy the evening.'

'I'm sorry, I can't stop thinking about Eddy.'

'How about thinking about me instead?'

Ian leaned over and put his arm around her and she laughed. 'Stop it, will you?'

'Give me one good reason why I should. And don't say it's because you want to think about work.'

'What if I say I don't want to ruin this wonderful dinner you just made by letting it get cold?'

Ian smiled. 'Well, I can't argue with your logic there, Inspector.'

Still laughing, Geraldine turned her attention to her curry.

'If there's one thing you know how to do, it's make a good curry,' she said at last, as she put down her spoon and fork with a sigh of contentment. 'That was good. And now I've eaten way too much.'

'Is that the only thing I know how to do?' he replied, laughing and pulling her towards him.

For the rest of the evening, Geraldine really tried to put work out of her mind, but her thoughts kept straying to Eddy and his uninterested lawyer. She knew it wasn't fair to ignore Ian when he clearly wanted to spend time with her, and she felt guilty that she wasn't giving him her full attention. With a faint pang of nostalgia, she remembered the solitude she had enjoyed when she had lived alone. It wasn't that she regretted allowing Ian to move in with her, but her home life had undoubtedly been simpler when she had only had herself to please. She could hardly complain that Ian was needy, but he was living with her, and it would be unrealistic to expect him to demand no attention from her at all. However accommodating he was, she was finding it difficult living with someone else while she was preoccupied with a murder investigation.

42

GERALDINE DROVE SLOWLY TO the hospital the next day, her leisurely pace not solely dictated by Friday morning traffic. She was in no hurry to reach the mortuary. Viewing dead bodies did not bother her unduly, but she always found it upsetting having to deal with the bereaved. She firmly believed it was her duty, as a principled human being, to do her best to make the world a better place. That was what had motivated her to pursue a career as a detective in the first place, and she remained dedicated to her work, seeking justice. Refusing to allow evil to define her world, she fought against it, but all too often she seemed to be struggling on the losing side. Despite her efforts, there was nothing she could say to comfort those who had lost loved ones due to the evil that existed all around them.

Steeling herself to face Louisa's parents, she pulled up in the hospital car park. A steady drizzle had set in under a lowering sky, which made her feel even more dejected.

However reluctant she was to face her morning's task, she could not shirk it, and in any case doing so would not help the bereaved parents who were waiting for her when she arrived. It was clear at a glance that Louisa took after her father in appearance. A quiet man who looked considerably older than his wife, Mr Thomas was fairly short and stout. He had a pasty face and rimless glasses which kept slipping down his nose. He pushed them back in position with resigned regularity, and refused to meet Geraldine's gaze. In contrast to her husband and daughter, Mrs Thomas was tall and lanky. She looked like a sportswoman or a PE teacher. Her face appeared flushed and her eyes were red-rimmed and swollen, which was hardly surprising given her recent loss. She sprang from her seat and almost leapt at Geraldine as soon as she stepped into the hushed waiting room, where relatives of the dead came to the hospital to identify the bodies of their loved ones.

Gently, Geraldine explained the procedure to them, advising them that there was no need for both of them to see their daughter. Mr Thomas sat motionless, listening, while his wife fidgeted with the strap of her bag and shifted from foot to foot, unable to keep still. On being assured they both wanted to be shown the body, Geraldine led them into the viewing room. For a moment the two parents stood staring at the dead woman in silence. All at once, Mrs Thomas began to shake so violently that, for an instant, Geraldine was afraid she was about to suffer a fit of some kind.

Mr Thomas nodded. 'That's her. That's our girl.' Tears glistened on his eyelashes.

Back in the waiting room, Louisa's father sat down heavily on the sofa, his hands on his knees, his head bent forward, his eyes fixed on the floor.

'Something inside of me died today,' he said quietly.

His wife remained on her feet, curiously animated.

'How did it happen? How?' she demanded. Her voice shook with emotion. 'Who was it? Who did this to her?'

'Stop it, Beattie,' her husband said, raising his eyes from the floor. 'It's not going to bring her back.'

'Something happened to her and I want to know what. Young girls don't just fall down dead. It shouldn't have happened, not like that. My baby. She was my baby. Please,' she hissed. 'Who did this to her? We have a right to know. We need to know what happened to her. Please. You have to tell me everything you know.'

'What difference does it make now?' her husband said in a flat voice.

Mrs Thomas turned on him. 'Shut up, Adam, just shut up. You don't know what it's like. She was my baby. My baby. I can't bear it. I can't bear it. How did she die? Please, we need to know what happened. Who did this to her?'

There was a manic quality to the woman's grief that Geraldine had witnessed many times before. Being called on to identify the corpse of a murdered child was possibly the worst experience anyone could have to suffer. Speaking very gently, Geraldine invited Mrs Thomas to take a seat. She didn't sit beside her husband on the sofa, choosing instead an upright chair where she sat, staring intently at Geraldine, while Mr Thomas continued gazing at his feet.

'We are investigating the circumstances of your daughter's death,' Geraldine began carefully.

'Circumstances? What do you mean? What circumstances? What are you investigating? Are you saying she was murdered?' Mrs Thomas interrupted, sounding almost hysterical. 'Well? Is that what you're saying?'

'We're investigating her death,' Geraldine repeated calmly. 'We're not convinced your daughter died of natural causes,' she added. 'But we don't yet know exactly what happened.'

'Well? Have you got him?' Mrs Thomas demanded, rising to her feet in her agitation.

'Have we got who?' Geraldine prevaricated.

'The man who did it? Have you caught him? The scum who took our daughter from us?'

Geraldine hesitated. The police had a man in custody who was suspected of killing Louisa, but he had not yet been convicted and even though the rest of the team seemed confident they had caught the killer, Geraldine wasn't convinced they were right. Eddy had undergone a psychological assessment and Eileen had been jubilant when the report stated that he was able to comprehend the nature of the charges that had been brought against him, and could be held responsible for his actions. But it also confirmed that Eddy lived with a neurologically divergent condition, and in addition was possibly detached from reality. Geraldine found it rather ambiguous, but she appreciated that psychological conditions were tricky to assess. The professional who carried it out was understandably circumspect in reporting his findings.

'The important thing is to establish whether he's guilty or not. We need to know if he's a danger to others and if he is, he has to be kept in a secure institution, whatever form that takes,' Eileen had said. 'Whether or not he's responsible for his actions isn't the issue.'

Geraldine cleared her throat. Louisa's parents were waiting for her response.

Mrs Thomas's face turned a darker shade of red and her eyes glared with a wild despair.

'Well?' she demanded. 'Has he been caught? What are you doing?'

'What difference does it make?' her husband repeated dully without raising his head. 'She's gone and we can't bring her back.' His voice broke and he dropped his head in his hands.

Muttering useless platitudes, Geraldine left them to their grief. They seemed an oddly matched couple, and something about them had struck her as out of kilter. Mrs Thomas had become really quite aggressive in her demands. Geraldine knew that grief affected people in different ways, and anger was not an uncommon reaction in the bereaved. She pictured the two of them returning to Whitby to wait to bury their only child, and she felt a wave of compassion for them, with all their hopes for the future wiped away in one cruel blow.

43

Determined to leave no loose ends in her pursuit of the truth, Geraldine decided to question Eddy's cousin to see if he could add anything to what they already knew about the suspect. According to what Eddy had told them, Alec had turned up shortly after Doreen's death. If Alec was unable to reveal what had happened on the day his aunt was killed, he might at least be able to shed some light on Eddy's relationship with his mother. He had allegedly been living with Eddy for about a week, and it was possible he might have heard something about what had happened. It was certainly worth questioning Alec, if he even existed. They only had Eddy's word for that, and Geraldine already suspected that Eddy's imagination peopled his solitary world. On leaving the hospital, she drove straight to Portland Street. The rain had given over, and the sun now shone intermittently between patches of grey cloud moving swiftly across the sky.

The door was opened by a man who looked around thirty. He was wearing dark jeans and a white T-shirt, yet he contrived to look well dressed, and his smile radiated warmth and intimacy, as though he was genuinely pleased to see her.

'Hello, hello, how can I help you?' he asked. 'If you're looking for Doreen, I'm terribly sorry to tell you she passed away three weeks ago. It was a great shock to us all.' His smile now appeared to be tinged with sadness.

Wondering if his grief was genuine, Geraldine introduced herself as a member of the police team looking into the circumstances of Doreen's death.

'Are you Alec?'

He nodded.

'And you're Doreen's nephew?'

'That's right.'

Eddy had been telling the truth about his cousin, at least.

'So you're here with the police,' Alec said smoothly. 'The police,' he repeated, smiling sadly. Geraldine wondered if he was covering up a momentary confusion as he repeated his earlier question. 'How can I help you?'

He appeared relaxed, but there was something ingratiating in his smile that put Geraldine on edge. Members of the public were often obsequious when they learned they were talking to a police officer. She preferred people to be embarrassingly servile as opposed to openly hostile, which was another common reaction she had from strangers, but Alec seemed almost too keen to please her. He stood leaning against the door frame in an ostensibly casual pose. She might have been reading too much into his posture, but it suggested a reluctance to move inside to allow her to enter. She stared back at his sharp black eyes, noting his neat black moustache that gave him a slightly dashing air, which she found pretentious. She had the impression that he was carefully masking his irritation at her arrival and decided to be forthright.

'I want to talk to you about your cousin, Eddy.'

'Oh yes, poor Eddy. What is it you want to know about him?'

'Can I come in?'

For the first time, Alec appeared uncertain as he muttered that it wasn't his house.

'It's not really for me to ask you in,' he added apologetically. 'I don't live here. I'm just staying here temporarily as Eddy's guest, looking after things for him for a while. Just while he needs me here.'

Geraldine suggested he might prefer to accompany her to the police station, confident he would decline her invitation.

'No, no, that is, I'm sure it'll be fine. Please, do come in,' he replied. 'I'm sure Eddy won't mind. And of course I'm desperate to do anything I can do to help him.

Once again smiling, he ushered her into the front room. But his mask of insouciance had briefly slipped, and Geraldine determined to watch him closely.

The last time she had entered that room, Doreen had been lying on the carpet, dead. The place looked very different now. Magazines that had previously been lying in a tidy pile on the table had slipped on to the floor, and lay spread out in a jumble. Some of the pages were torn as though they had been carelessly stepped on. The chairs in the room were no longer tidily arranged, but stood around haphazardly. Balls of wool that had once been organised in a basket lay in a tangled mess on the floor, and the ornamental cats that Geraldine remembered seeing arrayed in a neat line on the mantelpiece had disappeared. She couldn't see any scissors in the wool basket, but that didn't really mean anything.

'Can you tell me why you're here?' she enquired as she sat on one of the armchairs.

Alec nodded as though he had expected the question. 'I wanted to check on my cousin. Eddy's not – that is, Eddy finds things hard. I'm sure you've noticed,' he added, with a conspiratorial smile, as though he and Geraldine shared a secret together.

'What do you mean?' she asked curtly, refusing to submit to his crass attempt to charm her.

'Just that he doesn't really know how to look after himself,' Alec continued, his smile now expressing regret and compassion. 'Aunty Doreen used to look after him.' He heaved a dramatic sigh. 'Now she's gone I thought I'd better move in here for a while. Keep an eye on things for him. Keep him company. That's all there is to it, Inspector. I'm just trying to do a good deed.' He put his head on one side with another winning smile. 'And it's lucky I turned up when I did. Eddy must be relieved to know that I'm here to keep an eye on things.'

Geraldine politely returned his smile. 'What things are you keeping an eye on?'

She glanced at the empty mantelpiece, wondering who had removed the ornamental cats and what had happened to them. They were unlikely to be worth much, but Alec might have sold them, all the same.

'I've been in touch with a lawyer friend of mine to sort out Eddy's affairs, the house and that,' Alec explained airily, as though coming into possession of a house was an insignificant matter. 'Probate is a complicated business and I'm not sure Eddy's up to dealing with it. You know Doreen owned this house?'

'Which Eddy owns now,' Geraldine replied sharply. 'He'll need an independent advisor to help him manage Doreen's estate.'

She wasn't sure Alec's friend was on the level. He might not even be a lawyer. She wondered whether Nico might be able to help with that, but it wasn't her place to intervene. Besides, after his terrible experience, Nico probably wanted nothing more to do with Doreen's family. Eddy's inheritance was not Geraldine's responsibility. She didn't trust Alec, but if he saw a way to benefit from the situation that was nothing to do with her, as long as he wasn't breaking the law.

'I came here to ask you about Eddy,' she said, feeling her way carefully.

'Poor Eddy. He doesn't really know what he's doing most of the time.'

Geraldine let that pass for a moment, although it possibly suggested Eddy might not always be in full control of his actions.

'Did he get on well with his mother?' she enquired.

For the first time, Alec looked uncomfortable. 'Not really,' he admitted, squirming in his chair. 'They used to argue a lot. But that's nothing unusual in families, is it? I don't mean to suggest there was anything out of the ordinary. But if I'm honest, I have to admit they had a difficult relationship. Eddy wanted his independence, but he wouldn't have been able to handle it. Aunty Doreen had to take care of him, and he resented what he saw as her interference. He believed she was trying to control his life, but the truth is he needs someone to supervise him. That's why I decided to come and stay with him for a while, just until he sorts himself out. And now, of course, he resents me. I can just imagine what he's been saying about me.' He shrugged. 'I'm sure he'll be all right before long, with a little help. He just needs to manage the adjustment from total dependence on his mother to coping on his own. I think he's bound to struggle to begin with. I want to help him as much as I can.'

'What about your own life?'

'My life?' Alec looked surprised.

'Don't you have a job?'

'Oh, I've taken time off. I work short-term contracts, so it's not a problem. I was due a break anyway, and it's nice to have some time to myself for a change.'

Geraldine didn't point out that no if he was busy taking care of his cousin, he might not have much time to himself.

'What did you mean when you said Eddy doesn't know what he's doing? Have you ever seen him lose control of himself?'

Alec's smile faded. 'I'd rather not answer that,' he said.

Geraldine nodded. 'I think you just have.'

'I want you to know that Eddy's innocent,' Alec said earnestly. 'Anyone who thinks he could have killed his own mother couldn't be more wrong. I don't believe for one moment that he could do anything so dreadful. Not my cousin Eddy. He's a gentle soul, usually.'

'So you'd describe him as placid?'

Alec looked thoughtful. 'No,' he replied. 'Not exactly. I mean to say, he's got a temper, of course, like many people, and he can lose control of himself when he's provoked, but that doesn't mean he's capable of killing his own mother. That's a preposterous accusation to level against anyone.'

By the time Geraldine had finished questioning Alec, it was time to go home. Ian would be waiting for her. She had learned nothing that helped to confirm whether Eddy was guilty or not, and it had basically been a waste of time talking to Alec. Yet she couldn't shake off the feeling that she was missing something obvious. No one else seemed to share her unease. Eileen had been almost childish in her glee, and Geraldine had caught sight of her punching the air when she thought no one was looking. Such elation seemed curiously out of character for her, and reinforced Geraldine's impression that something was not right with the detective chief inspector. That evening, she reiterated her concerns to Ian, who dismissed her misgivings with a wave of his hand.

'I'm sure we'd know if something was wrong,' was all he said, but this time he sounded unconvinced.

'You've known her for a long time,' Geraldine said and hesitated, seeing Ian's worried frown.

44

THE NET SEEMED TO be closing around Eddy. Geraldine had been the only member of the team to doubt he was responsible for Doreen's murder. Now even she was having to accept he had probably killed his mother. Everyone else at the police station seemed happy to accept the investigation was concluded. Eddy had been the obvious suspect all along, and there was no good reason to doubt that he was guilty. Having established he could be violent, it was a short leap for him to become the sole focus of their investigation into Louisa's death. Eddy had fantasised she was his girlfriend when, according to her, they had never met. He hadn't even known her real name. And now she was dead.

Shelving her reservations about his guilt, Geraldine joined in the general relief on Saturday morning. She had always trusted her instincts in the past, but occasionally her hunches had let her down, and she concluded that she must have been distracted by Ian's absence. All the same, she was dismayed that her gut feeling about Eddy could have been so wrong. It was all over, bar the collating of evidence for submission to the Crown Prosecution Service. But when Eileen called a briefing that morning, it was no longer possible to ignore her bizarre behaviour. She let out a curious sob as she faced her colleagues who shuffled and fidgeted awkwardly, staring at their feet or fiddling with pens, embarrassed by their senior officer's display of sentimentality.

Gathering herself up to her full height, Eileen barked with something like her usual ferocity. 'Do I have your attention?

I want you all to share in the triumph of another successful investigation.'

A sigh rippled around the room as the assembled officers waited to hear what had happened. Geraldine was puzzled because, as far as she was aware, Eddy had not confessed, yet there was no other obvious explanation for Eileen's exultant claim. What followed raised an ineludible question over the detective chief inspector's state of mind.

'The VIIDO team have come across something that nails our case against Eddy Lewis. Believe me, I know it may not seem fair after all the hard work you've put into this case that the conclusive evidence comes from CCTV, but it seems that with this evidence we'll be able to make a murder charge stick after all.'

There was a hiatus as everyone waited to hear the new information.

'So what is the evidence?' Geraldine asked.

'One of the neighbours along the street has been away,' Eileen resumed. 'When he came home yesterday he responded to the appeal for recorded security footage filmed on the day of the murder.' She broke off, apparently too overcome to continue. Flapping one hand at her perplexed colleagues, she cried out, 'It's all over, it's all over!' before she covered her mouth with her other hand and rushed from the room.

'Now tell me there's nothing odd about her behaviour,' Geraldine muttered to Ian.

'What the hell is wrong with her?' a constable asked.

'And what are we supposed to do now?' another voice chimed in.

In the absence of a senior investigating officer, Geraldine stepped forward before the assembly fragmented into pockets of discussion about Eileen's bizarre behaviour. As the most experienced detective inspector in the room, she informed her colleagues that she would check with the VIIDO team and report back. If there was indeed evidence that would convict

Eddy, she would inform them and log the details for the whole team to see. In the meantime, she suggested they all return to their desks and continue to pursue their allotted tasks. Until confirmed otherwise, although Eddy remained their prime suspect, the case was not yet formally closed.

Geraldine went to speak to the visual images identification and detection team straight away. They had been studying CCTV of the area around Doreen's house for two weeks. Searching for any sign of someone approaching and leaving before and after the estimated time of Doreen's death, they had been particularly interested in anyone who appeared to be in a hurry. And they had been looking specifically for Eddy. A slim dark-haired constable told Geraldine that Eddy had been recorded on a home security system, walking away from Doreen's house at half past seven. He had returned briefly at one fifteen before going out again after ten minutes.

'That would have been long enough to kill his mother?' Geraldine asked.

'Just about, it would seem.'

Geraldine watched the tape with her colleague. The quality was poor, but it was clearly Eddy going out and coming back, and he had a strangely furtive air as he returned home and departed again, scurrying along the street. Geraldine watched it several times. The first time he left the house, he was hurrying, looking straight ahead. On his return home, at one fifteen, he kept glancing around as though checking that no one was observing him. Far from exonerating him, the evidence proved that he had gone home for around ten minutes at one fifteen, which confirmed that he could certainly have been there at the time of his mother's death.

'But would he have had time to kill her?' Ian asked when Geraldine reported what the video evidence had revealed.

'Only if he went in, killed her and left, all within the space of ten minutes.'

'So either this was the result of a very sudden flash of anger or –' Naomi said.

'Or this murder was premeditated and he returned home with the express intention of killing his mother,' Ian completed her sentence.

'Would Eddy really be capable of such planning?' Geraldine asked. 'Would such an idea even occur to him?'

'The question is, did he do it?' Ian replied. 'Our job is not to act as psychologists, deciding on a suspect's intellectual capabilities, but to establish facts.'

Geraldine nodded. Ian was right. The evidence was irrefutable.

'So it was Eddy after all,' she said. 'I have to say I'm surprised. I never thought he would have had it in him.'

'Who knows what anyone might do if pushed?' Naomi replied. 'We don't know that Doreen was very kind to him. She could have been bullying him for years.'

Geraldine nodded again. There was nothing else to say. And there remained the unresolved problem of Eileen and her strange behaviour. She and Ian discussed what they ought to do over supper that evening.

'Why do I feel like Fletcher Christian in Mutiny on The Bounty?' Geraldine asked, frowning. 'But we can't ignore her emotional outburst. Something has to be done.'

'Don't frown,' Ian replied, dodging the issue. 'If the wind changes, you'll get stuck looking like that.'

'No, I won't, and you're avoiding answering the question.'

Ian shrugged.

'We can't leave the investigation in the hands of someone who's clearly ill,' Geraldine insisted. 'Apart from anything else, her judgement could be impaired.'

'At least she's fixated on the right suspect,' Ian said.

'That's not the point, and you know it. What if she'd got it into her head that it was someone else?'

'All right, of course, I agree something has to be done, but there's nothing we can do about it right now, so let's just forget about work and enjoy the evening. How about a Chinese take away? My treat.'

Geraldine laughed. 'Because it's your turn to cook? All right, but you're paying.'

45

THERE WAS NO LONGER any serious question over Eddy's guilt, and everyone on the team was elated at the successful conclusion of the investigation. Not only did they have the proof needed for a conviction, but the killer was already in custody. Yet even though the killer was safely behind bars, Geraldine resolved to carry out a further investigation of her own.

'It's impossible to be too thorough,' she had said to Ian. 'And we still can't be sure he was responsible for both murders.'

'That's for a jury to decide,' he agreed. 'Unless he confesses.'

'Or new evidence comes to light.'

'Meaning what, exactly?' he asked.

'Meaning I'm going to do a little digging, just to tie up one or two loose ends.'

'It's the weekend,' he protested, half laughing. 'You are incorrigible. Eddy's clearly guilty. There's no need to continue investigating on your own.'

'We don't have absolute proof he killed Doreen,' she replied. 'I know it looks that way, but he doesn't seem clever enough to have plotted it so carefully. And we have no evidence he bought the rope himself.'

'Even if he didn't buy the rope himself, he could have used it.'

'As for Louisa, we don't know if he ever even met her,' Geraldine went on. 'Admittedly it looks as though he killed Doreen, but what about Louisa? Who killed her?'

'Eddy was stalking her, and her body was found after he had killed his mother. It all seems pretty conclusive to me, in fact to everyone but you. Would you be so scrupulous if you hadn't kept insisting we had arrested the wrong man?'

'Of course,' she replied, a little too indignantly.

Ian was right to suspect the reason for her reservations over whether Eddy could have planned and carried out a murder, but that said, there was no downside to double checking the evidence. First of all, she returned to Eddy's house to have another word with his cousin, Alec. A scowl replaced his smile when he opened the door and saw who was calling on him.

'Don't tell me he's getting off on a technicality?' he asked, before she had even spoken. 'Poor Eddy. I hope he does get off. He doesn't deserve to be locked up. I mean, he's hardly a risk to anyone else. I know him and he wouldn't willingly hurt a fly. But Aunty Doreen did drive him crazy,' he added softly.

'Crazy?'

Alec just shrugged.

'No, we're not letting him go,' she went on. 'He's still under arrest. I just wanted to have a word with you.'

Alec nodded. 'Very well,' he replied. 'But it's not terribly convenient right now. I have a visitor.'

Geraldine could hardly insist. Alec wasn't a suspect, and she had been given no official instruction to talk to him again. Nevertheless, she persisted.

'I just want to ask you a few questions.'

Alec heaved a resigned sigh. 'I don't know what you hope to gain by pestering me like this,' he grumbled. 'Eddy's the one you should be talking to.'

'I'm just looking for answers to a few more questions, and I think you can help me. It won't take long.'

'Very well, but I don't understand what you could possibly want with me.'

He didn't invite her in.

'You came to stay with Eddy after his mother was killed, and you were probably the last person to speak to him before his arrest. It might really help us if you would agree to co-operate and answer a few questions.'

'Do I have any choice in the matter? Come on then, ask your questions. You're sure he did it, then?'

Geraldine sighed. 'I'm afraid it's looking that way, yes.'

Alec's smile faltered. 'Poor Eddy,' he said, shaking his head. 'He never had much of a chance in life, did he? But I must say I never thought he would do something like this. I wouldn't have thought him capable of killing her. Are you sure it was murder? I mean, she couldn't have slipped and caught herself in something, could she? You do know she couldn't walk unaided? She was always falling over.'

'Your aunt was strangled,' Geraldine replied gently.

'There's a lot of wool lying around the house,' Alec pointed out hopefully.

Geraldine recalled how neatly Doreen had kept her wools.

'I still can't believe she was murdered,' Alec said.

'Think carefully, Alec. Did Eddy ever say anything that might suggest he was planning something like this?'

'Something like this?'

'You said earlier that his mother drove him crazy. Did he used to get angry with her?'

'Oh, yes, all the time.' He broke off, frowning. 'What I mean to say is, he was living with her, and so naturally he found her irritating. But I don't believe for one moment that he killed her.'

'Why not?'

'I mean, it's not something you think will happen to someone you know, is it?'

His words reminded Geraldine of something else she had heard recently, but she couldn't remember what it was. She pressed on with her questions, but there was nothing more to be learned from Alec. As she was leaving, she turned to him.

'If you were involved in your aunt's murder, if you had anything to do with it, you know we'll find out. You can't hide the truth forever. So are you sure there's nothing else you'd like to tell me?'

She watched his reaction closely, but he didn't flinch as he batted away her accusation with assurances that he only wanted to help his cousin. There was nothing for her to do but thank him for his help and leave. Driving home, she fretted, and tried to work out what was troubling her. All she was sure of was that it had something to do with Louisa's parents. She didn't go home, where Ian was bound to distract her, but drove to the police station. Settled at her desk, she reread her notes carefully. On a second reading of her report on her meeting with Louisa's parents, she spotted what had been bothering her. It was perhaps a trivial point, but Mrs Thomas had not waited to be informed that Louisa's death had not been an accident. Alec had said murder was not something you expect to happen to someone you know, yet Mrs Thomas had immediately assumed her daughter had been murdered, and had wanted to know who was responsible.

'Who was it? Who did this to her?' she had demanded.

The question puzzling Geraldine was why Mrs Thomas had been so convinced Louisa had been murdered when nothing had yet been broadcast to that effect in the media. Thoughtfully, she returned home and discussed her suspicion to Ian.

He shrugged. 'Perhaps she thought the city wasn't a safe place for her daughter. People from small towns often seem to get the idea that life in the city is fraught with danger.'

'Why do some people always assume the worst?'

Ian shrugged again, a characteristic gesture. His shoulders looked increasingly hunched as he approached middle age. Looking at his careworn face, Geraldine felt a desperate urge to protect him, and her affection for him seemed to her almost maternal.

'I don't know,' he admitted.

'Well, we're going to find out what it's all about,' Geraldine said fiercely.

Ian looked at her in surprise. 'You mean why people think the worst?'

'No,' Geraldine laughed. 'No, no, I'm talking about Louisa's mother.'

'I'm sure you know what you are talking about,' Ian replied, smiling.

46

THE NEXT MORNING, GERALDINE decided to drive to Whitby to speak to Louisa's parents. She had spoken to them before, at the mortuary, but this time she was investigating a disturbing suspicion of her own. Understanding that she considered Louisa's parents as potential killers, Ian offered to accompany her and she accepted his offer gladly.

'You know, I've never been to Whitby,' she said.

Ian told her it was a quaint town on the coast, which she already knew, and before long they were driving along its picturesque winding narrow streets past a view of the harbour, looking for somewhere to park. The weather had hit a warm spell, and the sun broke free of a bank of clouds as they stepped out of the car. Watching people sauntering past along crowded pavements, Geraldine wished she and Ian were there as holidaymakers, instead of as detectives pursuing a darker purpose. It was Sunday, and for a moment she allowed herself to imagine they were simply out for a day's enjoyment, innocent and uncomplicated.

'We should come here one day, just for a day out,' she said.

'We could be doing that today if you weren't so set on suspecting everyone of murder,' Ian replied.

'Hardly everyone,' she retorted, peeved by his accusation.

It didn't take them long to find the Thomas's house, which was situated on a corner not far from the harbour. The ground floor was occupied by a small gaudily painted café which boasted 'The Best Tea Cakes in Whitby'. Perhaps in a nod to the famous

Whitby jet stone, the tables and chairs were black, but the floor and walls were green and white. Geraldine recognised Beattie Thomas straight away, and the other woman's eyes narrowed on seeing them enter her premises.

'What can I do for you?' she asked with a sour scowl.

'We'd like a few words with you in private, please,' Geraldine replied quietly.

Beattie grunted and summoned her waitress, a short, plump girl in a white apron. Having told the girl she was taking a break and would be back soon, she led Geraldine and Ian through the kitchen to a back door leading up a narrow staircase to her living quarters above the café. Where the café downstairs was bright and cheerful, the flat above it was dingy and bordering on squalid, with rubbish bags piled up on the landing next to a full basket of laundry. The walls were painted a dull khaki above a scuffed grey carpet, and the place smelled musty.

'We're in a bit of a state.' Beattie cast an apologetic glance at the bags of rubbish. 'After what happened.'

Geraldine gave a sympathetic grunt, although the clutter looked as though it had been accumulating for a while.

'I can't stay long, mind,' Beattie fussed. 'I have to get back soon and see how Daisy's getting on downstairs. She's very young. I haven't left her on her own before, and we're busy at the weekends.'

The room into which she took Geraldine was small and cramped and smelt faintly of mould. Adam Thomas was slouching awkwardly on an upright wooden chair facing an oversized television. Geraldine sat down on another wooden chair. Ian elected to stand, probably because there was very little leg room for those who were seated. Geraldine wished she had remained on her feet as well. Flat cushions had been placed on the chairs, but the seats felt hard and she could feel ridged wooden slats through the thin hassock. Apart from the chairs, the only other furniture in the room was a low wooden chest on which the television stood. This appeared to be the living room where the Thomas's spent their evenings after work. It was an unpleasant place for a family to spend their leisure time. Geraldine was not generally claustrophobic, but she couldn't wait to escape the stultifying atmosphere of the room where it felt as though the window was never opened to let in fresh air.

'We would like to ask you a few questions,' she began.

Adam stared at the television, even though it was not turned on. His wife sat on a chair beside him, fidgeting with her apron, her bright eyes fixed on Geraldine with a faintly hostile expression.

'It's not easy,' Adam mumbled. 'Beattie works hard in the café but it's hard. We wanted the girl – we thought she would take over one day –'

'We do our best,' his wife interrupted him sharply. 'There's nothing else to be done. I have to get back downstairs,' she added suddenly, rising to her feet. 'But I'm sure Adam will answer all your questions, won't you?'

Her husband didn't respond. She turned to leave, but Geraldine detained her with a shake of her head.

'I'd like you to stay.'

With Ian standing in the doorway, there was nothing Beattie could do without becoming involved in an awkward scuffle. Grumbling about leaving Daisy on her own, she perched on her chair again.

Geraldine started with a direct question. 'What led you to suppose that Louisa was murdered?'

Beattie didn't falter for a second. 'You told us,' she replied quietly. 'You said she was killed – that someone took our girl from us –'

Geraldine shook her head. 'No one mentioned murder until you wanted to know who had done this to Louisa. In fact, you were very insistent, asking who killed her. But you already knew the answer to your question. You knew all along who had killed her, didn't you?'

Adam stirred in his chair. His apathy gone, he sat upright, glaring at Geraldine.

'What are you saying?' he asked in a hoarse voice. 'Beattie, what is she talking about?'

Beattie shook her head. 'I've no idea. I don't know what any of this is about.'

'I think you'd best be leaving,' Adam said gruffly.

Geraldine spoke gently, holding Beattie's gaze as though there was no one else in the room, just the two women talking. 'Tell me what happened,' Geraldine said softly.

All at once, Beattie began to tremble. 'I never meant to harm her,' she whispered.

'It may have been an accident, but you were there when it happened, weren't you? Did you push her?'

Beattie shook her head, her eyes wide with alarm. 'I didn't mean it. It wasn't supposed to happen like that. I never meant to harm her, I just wanted to frighten her so she'd come home where she'd be safe.'

All the time she was speaking, her husband was staring at her in disbelief.

'Don't look at me like that,' she snapped.

'You killed her,' he whispered. 'It was you?'

'No, no, it was an accident. I never meant to harm her. I just wanted to keep her safe. There are dangerous people out there. I wanted to keep her safe.' She was sobbing now. 'I wanted to protect her. But she slipped and fell down the stairs. It happened so fast, there was nothing anyone could have done. I didn't do anything. I didn't do anything.'

Adam was on his feet, his face pale and twitching, his fists clenched. 'You – you – monster!'

'No, no, it wasn't like that. It wasn't like that,' Beattie insisted.

'What *was* it like?' Geraldine asked but Beattie buried her head in her hands and didn't reply. Her shoulders shuddered as she sobbed.

47

GERALDINE SUSPECTED ADAM THOMAS would never really recover from the death of his daughter. How could anyone find their way back to any kind of normality after their only child had been murdered? And now his wife had been taken as well. After years devoted to supporting his family, he had lost the two women he had loved. One was dead and the other would doubtless be convicted of assault and concealing a terrible crime. Reluctant to leave him alone, Geraldine contacted his sister who agreed to visit her brother the following weekend.

'We were all so shocked to hear about my niece,' Adam's sister said. 'But I don't understand what's going on there now. Why is Adam on his own? What's happened to Beattie?'

'Nothing's happened to Beattie,' Geraldine replied, 'but we've asked her to come and help us with our enquiry for a few days. I'm afraid I can't tell you any more than that for now.'

'I don't understand how you can be so callous. Surely Adam and Beattie should be together at a time like this.'

Geraldine ended the conversation. They left Adam sitting on his uncomfortable wooden chair, staring vacantly at a blank television screen. There was nothing more she could do for a man who had lost everything that had given his life meaning. If loving someone meant giving 'hostages to fortune', then fortune had been particularly cruel to Adam Thomas.

Daisy had been left to run the café by herself. Her blonde hair was tousled, and she looked harassed and slightly sweaty. The fallout from a murder touched on so many lives.

'I suggest you close the café for the rest of the week,' Geraldine told her.

The young girl stared back at her. 'I take my instructions from Mrs Thomas,' she stammered.

'We're taking Mrs Thomas away, and I'm afraid she won't be back for a while.'

As Geraldine faced Beattie across the table later that day, it struck her that the interview room at the police station was more comfortable than the living room where they had left Adam, still in shock and not yet able to give voice to his grief and anger. She wondered how his sister would fare when she went to visit him, assuming she kept her promise to check on him the following weekend.

'Tell us what happened,' Geraldine urged, staring at Beattie.

The duty brief was a nervous-looking young woman with ginger hair. She glanced anxiously at her client, who sat pouting in silence like a sulky teenager.

'It will help your case if you co-operate with us,' Geraldine said.

'Yes,' the lawyer echoed. She had a slight lisp that made her sound very young. 'It will help your case if you co-operate fully.' She smiled anxiously at Beattie.

'Nothing can help me,' Beattie replied dully. 'She's gone and it's over. You can't bring her back. No one can.'

Her expression didn't alter, but tears slid down her cheeks.

'Tell me what happened,' Geraldine said, as though she and Beattie were the only people in the room, and they were just two friends having an intimate chat. 'What were you doing in York?

'I came to see her, of course. I wanted to persuade her to come home. I told her and told her.'

'What did you tell her?'

'That it's dangerous in the city. That's why she needed to come home with me. I told her she'd be safe with us.'

Geraldine thought she began to glimpse the truth. 'And when

she refused to listen to your advice, that's when you decided to frighten her into leaving York?'

'Please don't put words in my client's mouth,' the lawyer began, but Beattie interrupted her.

'Yes, yes,' she cried out, 'I had to make her see reason. I thought if she could understand how dangerous it was, living in the city, she'd come home.'

'But as it turned out, the only threat to her was you,' Geraldine pointed out.

Louisa might have been stalked by Eddy, but although he had fantasised about her, he had intended her no harm. Geraldine had been right to suspect Beattie.

'So it wasn't Eddy after all,' Eileen said, beaming, once the interview was over and Beattie had been charged. 'It's time to summon the team and tell everyone the good news.'

Eileen gazed around at the assembled officers. 'It was Beattie all along, wanting to terrify her daughter. Well, she went too far, stupid woman. But I don't understand why she killed Doreen. Was that all part of the same attempt to frighten her daughter, by showing her how dangerous a place the city is?' She looked genuinely perplexed.

While the detective chief inspector was speaking, Geraldine experienced a strange sensation, as though cold fingers were tracing a line down her spine. She caught Ian's eye and saw that he was also troubled by Eileen's assumption. Because Beattie had confessed to killing Louisa, Eileen was somehow jumping to the conclusion that she had also murdered Doreen.

'There's nothing to implicate Beattie in Doreen's murder,' Ian pointed out.

'Only that she killed Louisa,' Eileen replied, with an exaggerated show of frustration. 'What are the chances someone else killed Doreen? Louisa was linked to her by Eddy, wasn't she? It can hardly be coincidence they were both killed. We can't have two killers in York, both at the same time.'

'Just because we know she killed Louisa, that doesn't make her a suspect in Doreen's murder,' Geraldine said quietly.

Eileen's face reddened.

'Have you questioned Beattie about Doreen?' Eileen demanded. 'We had no idea she killed Louisa until she confessed. All we need now is a second confession from her.'

Geraldine shook her head.

'We need to interview Beattie again, and this time let's make sure she tells us everything. And now, it's time to congratulate the team on a successful double investigation. Drinks after work this evening, everyone. The first round is on me. So get started on your paperwork and I'll see you later.' She beamed. 'Another triumph. The streets of York are safe once more, thanks to your efforts. Well done, all of you. This is a feather in all of our caps.'

As Geraldine had suspected, Beattie denied knowing anything about Doreen's death. Puffy eyed from crying, she shook her head and repeated that she didn't know anyone called Doreen, and had never met a woman in a wheelchair who lived in York. She had confessed to killing her own daughter, but was adamant she had not harmed anyone else. There was nothing to link her to Doreen, except Eileen's glib accusation. And in the meantime, if Beattie hadn't killed Doreen, then whoever had strangled her was still at large. Until resources were released to continue the investigation into Doreen's murder, nothing could be done. Geraldine fretted under their inactivity and Ian agreed with her that the situation was unsatisfactory. Together they went to confront Eileen, who smiled in welcome as they entered her office.

'Another triumph,' she greeted them. 'Detective Chief Superintendent Wells is delighted with us. A double murder solved in record time. That showed them I never lost control of the investigation!' she added, her elation fading as she grew earnest. 'There was talk, you know,' she said.

'What kind of talk?' Geraldine asked.

'They were saying that I was incompetent, that I've lost my grip. Me! I have enemies everywhere, people who want to see me put out to pasture, like a knackered horse. Can you believe it? I told the DCS I'm still as good at my job as ever. They can't manage without me.' She gazed intensely at Geraldine. 'Was it you who complained about me?'

Ian stepped forward. 'Eileen, don't you think it's time you took a break?' Even if he hadn't spoken with conviction, his addressing the detective chief inspector by her first name said far more than his words. 'We're afraid you've been overworking and exhaustion is making you confused.'

Eileen drew in a breath and seemed to expand in stature. 'Who thinks that?' she hissed. 'You don't know what you're talking about.' But then she seemed to droop.

'We think you may be confusing the two cases,' Geraldine explained gently. 'We're not convinced Beattie killed Doreen. She might have done, but there's no evidence to support that theory, and without evidence –' She shrugged.

There was no need to complete the sentence.

48

On Monday morning, the whole station was summoned to a meeting. Wondering what was happening, Geraldine joined the line of officers entering the incident room where Eileen was staring rigidly at the clock, avoiding meeting anyone's eye. She was standing absolutely straight, her arms pressed against her sides. At her side, Detective Chief Superintendent Wells stood equally upright but, unlike Eileen, he didn't seem tense. A powerfully built man in his fifties, with greying hair and a large square face, an upright bearing appeared to be his natural posture.

'So that's it, I'm taking leave,' Eileen announced to her colleagues in an unnecessarily loud voice.

There was a faint murmur of voices expressing regret, some perhaps tinged with relief. Still Eileen stood staring at the clock on the wall.

'It seems I have lost the confidence of my team,' she continued. Her eyes flicked coldly round the room before resuming their scrutiny of the clock. 'Officers I have supported for years have turned against me.'

'Come along now,' the Detective Chief Superintendent urged her gently. He gazed impassively at the assembled officers. 'Eileen has discussed her position with me, and we have agreed the time is right for her to step back from her duties, while she recovers from the stress she has been struggling with recently. I know you will share my deep regret at losing so outstanding a DCI. Eileen has served with dignity and integrity for many years, but now she's going to take a break, until she has made a full recovery.'

'Take a break?' Eileen muttered sourly, her words clearly audible to everyone in the room. 'I've been pushed out is what you mean.'

Scowling, she accompanied the detective chief superintendent from the room, dismissing the polite applause of her colleagues with a quick shake of her head. Watching her leave, Geraldine wondered how she herself was going to behave on the occasion of her own retirement. Hopefully she wouldn't succumb to the stress of the job like her senior officer. All the same it would be tough having to acknowledge her career was over, and she felt desperately sorry for Eileen. But the detective chief superintendent had been right. It was no longer possible for Eileen to continue in her post. The need to get the job done was more important than the desires of any one individual, and Eileen was no longer competent.

At least Ian would be at Geraldine's side when she faced the end of her own career. Eileen had dedicated herself to her work, but now the police had no place for her, and there was no one waiting for her at home. Geraldine had seen other committed officers retire, often reluctantly, and perhaps for the first time she truly appreciated how fortunate she was to be in a long-term relationship with a man she loved. Her life would continue after her career was over. Together, she and Ian would find a new way of living. They might even appreciate being able to spend more time together. It was difficult to see what kind of life Eileen could look forward to now.

But Geraldine couldn't dwell on her compassion for Eileen; she had work to do. It was possible that whoever had strangled Doreen was still free to wander the streets of York. Not only must the killer face justice, but, if they were still at large, they had to be apprehended before they could strike again. Shrugging off her pity for her colleague, Geraldine returned to her desk and settled down to work. Nico had been cleared of any involvement in Doreen's murder, which meant their only viable lead so far was Eddy, so she focused her attention on him. Just because Eddy hadn't attacked Louisa didn't guarantee he hadn't killed his mother. Yet they had already questioned him, and Geraldine struggled to believe he could have planned such an efficient operation. It was frustrating. She seemed to be going round in circles, with Eddy at the centre of her speculation.

That afternoon, the new detective chief inspector arrived and introduced herself to the team. Binita Hewitt was slim, with black hair and searching eyes, and a clear complexion. There was something birdlike in her rapid movements, and her delicate physique made her appear as vulnerable as a child. She was not much older than Geraldine, who had been on track for promotion to DCI herself before she had blotted her record with a flagrant misdemeanour, when she had broken protocol to protect her twin sister. The experience had been devastating, but at the time Geraldine had felt there was nothing else she could have done. She still stood by the decision which had almost destroyed her career. She had been lucky to be reinstated to the rank of inspector following a mortifying period of demotion, and she had come to terms with the knowledge that she would never rise any further in her chosen career. She was just thankful to have been made an inspector again. All the same, it gave her a faint twinge of regret on meeting her new senior investigating officer, knowing that she could have attained that rank herself had she not been demoted.

Binita smiled at her colleagues and assured them she was on top of the investigation so far.

'Which is more than we can say,' Geraldine murmured.

'So our focus now is on Doreen,' Binita said, frowning at Geraldine. 'What are you all doing?'

Geraldine hesitated, slightly thrown by Binita's collaborative approach. In the middle of a faltering investigation, everyone wanted to hear clear and decisive directives but, to be fair, it wasn't easy to pick up the reins of an ongoing investigation. Binita really had little choice other than to consult the officers who were already working on the case. Briefly Geraldine outlined what they knew about Eddy.

'So he had motive because he expected to inherit his mother's house,' Binita said. 'He clearly had plenty of opportunity, we know he was with his mother on the morning of her murder, and he had the means. Doreen was strangled, possibly by gloved hands, which could have been accomplished by anyone who managed to overpower her.' She frowned. 'But he's been arrested and interviewed, and now you want to send him home?'

Geraldine nodded. 'That's correct.'

'Why?'

Geraldine shook her head.

'Come on,' Binita urged them. 'You must have had a reason for wanting to release him.'

'Eileen – DCI Duncan – thought one person had killed Doreen and Louisa, because the two women were possibly linked by Eddy's interest in Louisa.'

Binita frowned. 'Do you agree with DCI Duncan?'

For a moment no one spoke; it was not their place to criticise a senior officer's decisions. In the end, Geraldine broke the awkward silence.

'I don't know what you've heard, but DCI Duncan had been overworking for some time,' she said carefully. 'The detective chief superintendent was afraid her judgement might have been affected by exhaustion. That's the reason she was removed from the case.'

'DCI Duncan has taken early retirement,' Binita snapped. 'There was no question about her fitness to continue working. She left voluntarily.'

'She left in the middle of a case,' Naomi murmured.

Binita bristled, and Geraldine hurried to smooth over the incipient difference of opinion.

'Eileen would be the first to admit she was worn out,' she said. 'Of course there was no question that she was fit to continue, but she made a rational decision to step down. She wouldn't have wanted her personal fatigue to impact on the investigation. Eileen was a dedicated officer.'

She stopped, aware that her words sounded like a valedictory speech. It was not her place to comment on Eileen's performance.

'I see,' Binita said, in a disapproving tone of voice. 'Indeed.'

49

THE NEW DETECTIVE CHIEF inspector seemed to be under the impression that the team was in disarray and it was her job to lick the officers into shape. She spent very little time seated behind her own desk, choosing instead to prowl around the offices, talking to different members of the team. Some of Geraldine's colleagues felt Binita was checking up on them; others seemed to welcome the new face of authority stamping its mark on the investigation.

'As if we weren't working hard enough already,' Naomi complained in the pub that evening. 'Anyone would think we've been sitting on our arses doing nothing.'

'Rampant bureaucracy,' someone else grumbled.

'Bureaucracy gone mad,' Naomi added, putting her pint down with such force it nearly slopped over the rim of the glass.

A few other officers who had gathered in the bar after work grumbled into their pints. Geraldine listened sympathetically and gave a noncommittal grunt. The new detective chief inspector had tasked them all with checking through the reports they had submitted, to make sure no detail had been omitted or left obscure, and not everyone was pleased with this new directive.

'There's nothing ambiguous about my reports,' one constable protested. 'I've been doing this job for more years than any of you –'

'Yes, grandad,' someone said.

Several of his colleagues laughed, and the old-timer gave

a tolerant smile as the conversation descended into cheerful banter.

Geraldine agreed with the new senior investigating officer that it was always a good idea to review what they had done, and she frequently did just that herself. Nevertheless, running an effective team took more than sensible ideas, and Geraldine was concerned that Binita had not yet gained the unquestioning support of the team. Taking over partway through an investigation was bound to be challenging, but unless Binita earned the respect of her colleagues, the task might become unnecessarily difficult. That wouldn't help anyone, least of all the rest of the team.

Geraldine intended to discuss the issue with Ian that evening, but by the time he returned home from playing five-a-side football, he was too tired to talk about work. They had dinner and went to bed early.

The next day, Geraldine discovered some of her fellow officers approved of Binita's methods.

'At least something's getting done,' a grey-haired constable said.

'Yes, Eileen was all over the place,' a female colleague agreed.

'We never knew from one day to the next what was going on. First one suspect was definitely guilty, then it was another suspect, and now we've gone backwards and we don't know who to suspect. I mean, what was that all about, bouncing us backwards and forwards between suspects?'

Geraldine was cautiously relieved that not everyone resented Binita's approach to the investigation, but she was concerned that the team was splitting into two factions. One group seemed to think that Binita had arrived like a battering ram, muscling in on an established investigation without first finding out the facts, while the other group welcomed the arrival of the new detective chief inspector.

'It's always good to have a new broom,' someone said, and several colleagues nodded.

It didn't take Geraldine long to complete her review of her own decisions and actions since she was in the habit of rereading her reports regularly anyway. Her paperwork up to date, she went to speak to Alec again. It would be interesting to find out more about Eddy from his cousin.

Alec came to the door. 'Well?' he drawled, leaning against the door frame and smiling at her with a familiarity that still contrived to be respectful. 'How can I help you, Inspector?'

'You told me Eddy found his mother irritating,' Geraldine said. 'What did you mean by that?'

Alec looked uncomfortable. 'Just mother and son, you know. Normal tension. He said she was ruining his life, you know, that kind of thing, but he never meant her any harm. She was his *mother*, for Christ's sake. They loved each other. He was her son.'

Geraldine thanked him and returned to the police station to question Eddy again.

'Eddy,' she said. He didn't stir. 'Eddy, I need to ask you a few questions. Eddy? Can you listen to me, please?'

'What's the point?' he replied, his voice devoid of any feeling.

His hair was lank and speckled with dandruff, and as Geraldine leaned forward she became aware of a miasma of urine mingled with stale sweat. He was wearing the same clothes as the last time she had seen him, and she suspected he had slept in them.

'Ask as much as you like,' he mumbled. 'Nothing matters now. She's dead and you can't bring her back.' He let out a sob. 'She'll never know how much I loved her.'

'I'm sorry, I know you're grieving, but I do need to ask you some questions.'

'There's no point. I loved her.' He sobbed again. 'I was going to ask her. I needed more courage but I would have done it, and she would have said yes.' He raised his head and gazed at

Geraldine with an earnest expression, his eyes rheumy.

'What were you planning to ask her?'

'To come and live with me, of course. We were going to get married. We belong together. I don't want to live with Alec. He bosses me about all the time and I have to do what he tells me. I don't like Alec. He's a bully. I just want her.'

It took Geraldine a few seconds to realise that Eddy was not talking about his mother. He was referring to his plans to invite Louisa to live with him. Now that Beattie had confessed to accidentally killing her daughter, Geraldine needed to move the conversation on to Doreen.

'Eddy, I'm here to talk to you about your mother's death,' she said gently. 'You need to come with me.'

He shook his head. 'She's dead too,' he whispered. 'They're all dead. First my dad, then my mum, and now Kylie, all dead. I saw it, you know,' he added, gazing up at Geraldine tearfully. 'Her picture was on the telly and they said she was dead.'

He accompanied Geraldine and the constable with her to the interview room without demur. Facing Geraldine and Ariadne once more across an interview table, Eddy sat beside his lawyer with his head lowered.

'Tell me how your mother died,' Geraldine urged him gently.

For the first time, she thought Eddy looked scared as he shook his head.

'Eddy, how did she die? It's time you told me everything.'

Beads of perspiration formed on Eddy's upper lip. He shook his head, scattering flakes of dandruff on to the table in front of him. 'No, I can't answer any questions. It's not safe, and I don't have to speak to you.'

The lawyer intervened quickly. 'You don't have to answer any questions. My client is feeling uncomfortable with your harassment.'

Geraldine spoke very gently. 'It's all right, Eddy, you can tell me everything.'

At his side, the dishevelled lawyer stirred, watching her intently.

'He told you what to do, didn't he?' Geraldine asked. 'I don't believe you wanted to kill your mother. It wasn't your idea at all.'

She wasn't sure she was right, but Eddy's next words confirmed her suspicions.

'He made me do it,' he blurted out. 'It was his idea, not mine. I didn't even want to do it. He's a big bully. He made me do it. He said it was the only way to get Kylie to come and live with me, but now it's all gone wrong. Everything's gone wrong and now she's dead too and I don't know what I'm supposed to do. He said if I kept quiet it would all go away. He said no one could prove anything as long as I didn't talk to you.'

The lawyer intervened. 'Don't say another word,' he warned his client, but Eddy ignored him.

'I didn't want to do it,' he said, 'but Kylie was never going to come and live with me while my mother was alive. That was why I had to do it. And I might as well not have bothered, because now they're both dead so there was no point.' He began to sob.

'Tell me what you did, Eddy?'

'I had to get rid of my mother, didn't I?' he said, sniffling. 'How else was I going to get Kylie to live with me? Alec told me it would be all right. He promised me I wouldn't get in trouble. He said if I kept quiet, no one would ever know it was me who killed her.'

Before Eddy could continue, his lawyer interrupted, insisting on a break.

'My client is overwrought,' he said. 'He's fragile. He can't cope with this intensive questioning.'

'Take as long as you need,' Geraldine replied quietly. 'But we will resume the interview today.' She looked at Eddy, who was staring at her in horror. 'Whoever promised you all this would go away if you refused to talk to us was lying. We're not going anywhere.'

'And nor are you, Eddy,' Ariadne added with grim satisfaction.

50

'IT WASN'T MEANT TO be like this.' Eddy dropped his head, hiding his face in his hands. 'It wasn't meant to be like this.'

'Like what? Tell me what you mean. Eddy, look at me. What wasn't supposed to happen?'

When he eventually lowered his hands to look at her, he was in tears, and it took Geraldine a while to coax him into talking to her, while the lawyer muttered irately, reminding Eddy to keep quiet.

'He said if I had my own house,' Eddy mumbled. He wiped his nose on his sleeve, leaving a line of mucus glistening like a snail trail. 'He said I'd be free to do anything I wanted. He said everything would work out the way I wanted it.'

'And what did you want?'

He looked directly at her then, blinking tears from his eyes. 'To be with Kylie, of course. Once the house was mine, she was going to come and live with me. He said that was the key to our future, me and Kylie. It was the key. We were going to live together. Once my mother had gone, there would be nothing to keep us apart.'

Naomi had suggested Doreen might have bullied her son, and that had driven him to kill her. Geraldine had agreed it was possible. It was now apparent that it wasn't Doreen, but someone else, who had been bullying him.

'Who told you all that?' Geraldine asked, although she already knew the answer.

'Alec, of course.' He seemed surprised by the question. 'He said with my mother out of the way the house would be mine and then Kylie would come and live with me. Nothing would come between us after that, he said.'

'Eddy, I want you to think very carefully now. What did you use to strangle your mother?'

He just shrugged and closed his eyes.

'Eddy, we know you used a length of rope. Where did you buy it?'

The lawyer warned Geraldine to desist, and barked at Eddy to say nothing more.

'But I didn't buy any rope,' Eddy replied, with a cunning smirk. 'So you can just stop telling lies. If you tell lies, no one will believe you.'

Geraldine tried again, speaking very gently. 'Where did you get the rope you used to strangle your mother?'

'Nowhere,' he replied. 'It was just there.'

However Geraldine worded the question, Eddy came up with the same answer. He had found the rope at home. Eddy's story made a terrible sense. Alec had successfully bullied Eddy all his life, until he had finally exerted his influence to such an extent, he had persuaded Eddy to commit murder. It was not difficult to work out a motive for Alec's behaviour. With Doreen dead, and Eddy in prison for her murder, Alec was planning to keep his aunt's house for himself. It was a fiendish scheme. So Eddy was guilty of matricide after all although, in a way, Geraldine had been right about him, because Eddy had not planned the murder himself. His cousin had come up with the idea, ostensibly to help Eddy win the affections of Louisa, a woman who had not even known he existed. It was a sordid and pathetic story, with a devastating outcome.

Geraldine went to discuss Eddy's accusation with the detective chief inspector.

'So it was Eddy,' Binita said, with a grim smile. 'Well, well.

So now we know who killed Doreen, and we have him in custody.' She paused and shook her head. 'He murdered his own mother.'

'Under orders from Alec, who we know had bullied Eddy throughout his childhood.'

'All the same, it was Eddy who killed her, and now he's confessed, which makes our lives a whole lot easier. Well done on a successful result, Geraldine.'

'What about Alec?' Geraldine asked. 'We can't just let him walk away and keep Doreen's house.'

'I'm not sure what else we can do. We can't touch him. He's bound to deny any responsibility, and it was Eddy who committed the murder. He's confessed to it, hasn't he?'

'So Alec will keep Doreen's house, after he set the whole thing up?'

'We don't know he did that,' Binita pointed out. 'It's Eddy's word against Alec's and, in any case, Eddy has confessed. By all means go and talk to Alec again, but unless you can persuade him to confess to being responsible for talking Eddy into committing murder, I don't think there's much we can do. We can't prove he forced Eddy to kill his mother. He might have manipulated him into doing it, with false promises about Louisa, but it was Eddy who strangled her.'

Geraldine was fairly certain Alec would bat away any uncomfortable questions, but there was a chance she could rattle him into making a mistake. Returning to Portland Street, she posted a uniformed constable at the back door. With another couple of officers at her side, she rapped at the door and rang the bell. There was no answer. She knocked again, more loudly this time, and shouted through the letterbox. Still no one answered. Julie was standing motionless on her doorstep, and a neighbour over the road was also watching.

'Let's get in there,' Geraldine said. 'We need to speak to Alec and get him to confirm that Eddy's telling us the truth.'

'How are we going to manage that?'

Geraldine shook her head. 'I don't know,' she admitted. 'Now, let's crack on and find out if he's in there.'

Her colleague nodded. Leaving one officer on guard at the front door, she led the other one round the house and instructed him to break open the back door. He rushed at the door which flew open with a sound of splintering wood. Geraldine ran in accompanied by one of her team, and together they searched the house. There was no sign of Alec.

Leaving the house under surveillance, Geraldine dispatched two officers to question the neighbours while she returned to the police station. She was determined to find Alec and force him to confess to planning Doreen's murder.

'I understand you're feeling frustrated, but you can't pin anything on Alec,' Ian told her when she arrived home that evening, vexed with Binita for telling her to forget about Alec. 'It's his word against Eddy's, and Eddy's hardly persuasive, whereas from everything I've heard about him, Alec is articulate and credible. Unless you can prove Alec was there at the time of the murder, it's all just talk.'

Aware that Ian was right, Geraldine studied any CCTV footage she could find of Eddy returning home to murder his mother. In one frame of one film, there was a faint tremor in the curtain in Doreen's front window.

'Could someone be there?' Geraldine demanded excitedly.

'It looks like it,' the visual images and detection officer agreed cheerfully. 'But wasn't the woman in a wheelchair? She was likely to be home, wasn't she?'

The faint movement of the curtain in Doreen's front room was inconclusive. There was only a chance it was an indication that someone was in the house with Doreen, waiting for Eddy to walk through the front door. It could just as easily have been Doreen herself, or a slight breeze, or a trick of the light. Geraldine was determined to investigate and make sure she had not missed anything that might implicate Alec in his aunt's murder, but it was difficult to see what she could do.

51

THERE WAS NO SIGN of Alec in Eddy's house, but there was one other person Geraldine thought might be able to help her, and she went to speak to him that evening. Ariadne answered the door. Her smile of welcome faded as soon as Geraldine asked to speak to Nico.

'What do you want with him? Hasn't he been through enough already? Go away, will you, before he sees you here. You have no idea how upset he's been about this whole incident, and we just want to forget about it. I'll see you tomorrow. Now, please leave.'

As Ariadne was speaking, they heard Nico call out, wanting to know who was at the door.

'It's no one,' Ariadne called back. She turned back to Geraldine and started to close the door. 'He doesn't want to speak to you again.'

'Ariadne, I'm sorry but I really do need to speak to him about the case. He could be a key witness,' Geraldine hissed. 'It will be easier for him if I see him here.'

Before Ariadne could answer, Nico appeared in the hall behind his wife. His face fell when he saw Geraldine standing on the doorstep.

'You're here to see Ariadne,' he said, backing away. 'I'll leave you to it. Don't be long, will you?'

'Actually, I wanted to have a word with you,' Geraldine said quickly before he could disappear back inside the house. 'Can I come in?'

With a sullen expression, Ariadne finally drew back to allow her to enter.

'What do you want with me?' Nico asked. He refused to meet Geraldine's eye as she followed him indoors and they sat down. 'I've already told you everything I know. I've told you the truth. I don't have anything more to say to you.'

He looked so dejected, Geraldine wondered if she had made a mistake in going to see him. He was an innocent bystander who had been caught up in a murder investigation in which he had been unjustly suspected. The episode had threatened to take away his freedom, and had almost cost him his marriage. And now, just when he thought it was all over, Geraldine had returned to question him all over again. She could understand why Ariadne was annoyed with her, but Geraldine knew her colleague would appreciate that the murder had to be thoroughly investigated, regardless of Nico's feelings.

'I want you to think very carefully,' Geraldine began.

'He knows the drill,' Ariadne interrupted curtly. 'But I don't know what you think you're doing here. We've got the CCTV evidence backed up by a confession, and there's no question Eddy killed her, so why aren't you satisfied?'

Geraldine sighed. She didn't want to upset her friend.

'Listen, Nico. You don't have to talk to me if you don't want to. I'm not here officially. It's just that I think you might be able to help with a query that's come up. It will only take a minute, but there's a question I'd like to ask you.'

Ariadne began to berate her, but Nico held up his hand to silence her.

'Go on, then,' he said to Geraldine. 'What is it you want to know?'

'Think back to when you last visited Doreen,' Geraldine began.

Ariadne scowled and drew in a breath as Nico tensed at her side.

'Was there anyone else in the house with Doreen and Eddy

that morning?' Geraldine went on, ignoring her friend's angry scowl.

'Apart from me, you mean?'

'Yes, apart from you.'

Geraldine waited and then Nico nodded.

'There was someone,' he said slowly. 'I didn't see who it was, but I heard someone running up the stairs while I was waiting for Doreen to come to the door.'

'Wasn't that Eddy?' Geraldine asked.

'No. Doreen told me Eddy had gone out. Otherwise he would have opened the door for me.'

Ariadne interrupted, looking startled. 'What's going on?' she demanded. 'The investigation is over. It was Eddy. He's confessed.' She turned to look at her husband. 'And what are you talking about, Nico? You never mentioned there was anyone else in the house before now.'

Nico shrugged. 'No one asked me,' he replied simply. 'The fact is, I was so flustered, I wasn't thinking straight. In any case, I didn't see who it was, and he didn't see me.'

'So you definitely heard someone run upstairs before you went in?'

'Yes. I'm pretty sure I did.'

'And did you hear anyone go in or out of the house while you were there?'

Nico shook his head. 'I don't think so, but I was talking to Doreen in the front room.'

'Which is next to the hall, so you would have heard if anyone came in or went out while you were there?'

'Not necessarily. I mean, like I said, I was talking to Doreen.'

'Could someone have left the house before you?' Ariadne asked, catching something of Geraldine's excitement.

Nico frowned with the effort to remember. 'Not long before I left there was a thump from upstairs,' he said slowly.

'A thump?' Geraldine repeated.

'Yes. There was someone up there and he – or she, I suppose – must have dropped something.'

It was frustrating that Nico had been unable to see the other person in the house. Study of the CCTV along the street, and door-to-door questioning of neighbours, indicated that apart from Doreen's carer, no one had arrived at Doreen's house before Nico, which suggested that whoever had run upstairs had been there all along. Geraldine went to speak to the social services carer who had visited Doreen on the day she died.

'Poor woman,' the carer said, shaking her head.

She was a thin woman, who must have been physically stronger than she appeared. Her pale face looked careworn, but she was keen to answer Geraldine's questions.

'If there's anything I can tell you that can help put her killer behind bars, I'll be only too pleased. Poor woman,' she repeated. 'She was a nice lady. How could anyone do such a terrible thing?'

The carer said she visited Doreen for about half an hour, from around eight thirty every morning.

'I go in – that is, I went in – to help her wash and dress in the mornings, and then I go – used to go – back at around nine in the evening to help her get ready for bed. Other than that, she lived quite independently. Or rather, she wasn't living on her own so she didn't need any help during the day. It was just the washing and dressing she couldn't manage by herself.'

Geraldine asked the carer the same question she had asked Nico.

'Someone there?' the carer repeated, looking baffled. 'Her son was there, Eddy. He did the shopping and sometimes helped her with the cooking, but he wasn't much help otherwise.' She lowered her voice. 'He wasn't good for anything much, that one. Not quite all there, if you know what I mean.'

'Did you see Eddy that morning?'

The carer frowned. 'No, I don't think so. But he was there.'

CCTV had shown Eddy leaving the house at half past seven.

'How do you know he was in the house if you didn't see him?'

'I heard him moving around upstairs.'

'Could that have been someone else?'

The carer looked puzzled.

'If you didn't see him, could it have been someone else?' Geraldine repeated.

'Well, yes, I suppose so.' She sighed. 'I couldn't believe it when I heard what happened to her. The poor woman. But I was gone by nine and the first policewoman who questioned me told me poor Doreen wasn't killed until later on. She was certainly very much alive when I left her that morning,' she added, suddenly defensive.

Everything seemed to indicate that someone else had been in the house on the day Doreen was murdered.

52

BY THE NEXT DAY there was still no sign of Alec at Doreen's house. Apart from the boarded-up back door and mess everywhere, the house seemed undisturbed by the recent events. Alec's mother lived in Saddleworth where a local team were sent to search for him, but no one in his village claimed to have seen him for a few weeks. Geraldine read through the reports with increasing frustration. His mother and sister independently said he had gone to see his cousin in York. When asked if he often went to York, their responses were vague, but neither of them expressed any surprise at his recent visit.

The constable who spoke to them wrote in his report that Alec's sister had been noticeably hostile in her responses. 'There's no law against a man visiting his cousin, is there?' she had demanded, allegedly quite aggressively.

'He was very fond of his cousin,' his mother had said.

'Did he often visit Eddy?'

'No, but he was very close to his cousin when they were children.'

Asked directly where Alec was now, his mother replied that she believed he was still in York, giving his cousin moral support in what she called his 'troubles'. His sister said she had no idea where Alec was, adding that he was her brother, not her child.

Scrutiny of CCTV from the train station confirmed that Alec had not left York by public transport in the three days since Geraldine had last spoken to him, nor had he travelled by taxi. He had no car of his own, and had not hired one. The only way he could have left York unseen was if he had hitched a lift, perhaps with a stranger, or stolen a car, either of which was possible.

'So what do we do now?' Naomi asked.

'We find him,' Binita said firmly.

For the first time, Geraldine sensed a ferocious determination in the detective chief inspector who had just joined them, and she faced her senior officer with a new respect.

'Yes,' Geraldine said. 'We'll find him.'

The search focused on York and the surrounding area, but everyone understood there was a risk Alec had slipped away unnoticed, before he was suspected of being an accessory to murder. Local patrol cars kept an eye on Alec's mother's house, his image – with and without his moustache – was circulated to the police forces around the country; stations, bus depots and airports were notified, and a nationwide alert was issued for his immediate detainment. There was little more they could do.

'Someone must know where he is,' Geraldine said, discussing the situation with Ariadne in the canteen one lunchtime. 'I think we ought to question his mother and sister again. There could be another relative or a friend sheltering him somewhere. He can't have just vanished.'

Geraldine decided to drive to Saddleworth and do some investigating of her own. It was raining, and the traffic was heavy, so the journey took her longer than she had expected. She had not even checked that Alec's mother would be at home, and was afraid her journey might be a complete waste of time. By the time she was halfway there, she was already regretting having set out, but something drove her to keep going. It was still raining when she found the narrow terraced house she was looking for halfway up a hill, and rang the bell. After a few minutes a voice called out, asking who was there. Geraldine announced herself and the door opened very slowly to reveal a slight grey-haired woman in a pink candlewick dressing gown.

'What do you want?' Mary Norris asked. 'If you're looking for Alec, I've already told you people he's not here and I haven't got the foggiest idea where he is, so you can just get lost. I'm sick of you lot pestering me.'

With that, she slammed the door. Geraldine knocked again.

'What is it?' Mary snapped, opening the door again and glaring at Geraldine. 'I told you, I've got nothing to say to you.'

'You must want to help us to find out who murdered your sister?' Geraldine asked.

'She was no sister to me.'

'When did you last see her?'

Mary sniffed. 'I told your lot I haven't seen her in years. There's nothing more to say so you might as well save your breath.'

Clearly there was little point in persisting with Alec's mother, so Geraldine asked to see his sister.

'Judy?' Mary said, her aggression undiminished. 'What do you want with her?'

'I just have a few questions for her. It won't take long and then I can be on my way,' Geraldine replied, doing her best to be patient.

The rain was lighter now, but water had already seeped through the seam where her hood was attached to her jacket, and the back of her neck was uncomfortably damp.

'Wait here then.'

With that, Mary slammed the door, leaving Geraldine on the doorstep, feeling damp and wretched. She waited for about five minutes for the door to be opened by a skinny woman of about thirty who looked like a younger version of her mother. A cigarette wedged in the corner of her mouth sent a faint smoke trail wavering upwards, making her squint.

'I already spoke to the police,' she said, snatching at her cigarette, oblivious of the ash that dropped to the floor.

The rain had stopped altogether but there was a stiff breeze blowing, stirring the branches of an old tree. Geraldine shivered but, like her mother, Judy didn't invite her to step inside.

'Judy, we want to speak to your brother. We need you to tell us where he might be.'

Judy grunted, and Geraldine understood that Alec's sister was not going to co-operate with the police.

'He's not here,' Judy said.

'That's right. Alec went to help his cousin,' her mother called out, shouldering Judy out of the way. 'I told Alec to leave him alone, but he insisted Eddy was going to need his help. He said he couldn't abandon his cousin. Well, my sister and her son abandoned me. But if you want Alec, that's where he's gone.'

'I've just come from York, and Alec's not there,' Geraldine replied. 'I understand you don't know where he is right now, but can you tell me where he might be? Does he have any particular friends or other relations he might be visiting? We really want to have a word with him as we think he can help us with our investigation. He's not a suspect,' she added, although that was no longer strictly true. 'But we think he might be able to help us if we could just have a quick word with him. It won't take long.'

Judy shook her head.

'Well, do contact us if you hear from him.' Geraldine handed Judy a couple of cards. 'If either of you hear from Alec, please tell him to get in touch with me. The sooner we can clear this up, the sooner we can stop calling on you. It really would be best for everyone if he could speak to us as soon as possible.'

Judy nodded and reached to close the door. There was nothing Geraldine could do but leave. Miserably she drove back to York, aware that she had just wasted several hours. Alec's mother and sister were not willing to co-operate. They probably knew exactly where he was, and the cards Geraldine had handed to Judy had no doubt gone straight in the bin.

53

ALEC STOOD WITH HIS head pressed against the door, listening. He had been in hiding in his mother's house for days and he wasn't sure how much longer he could bear to remain holed up there. Listening at the door of his bedroom, he heard his mother going downstairs followed by what sounded like a woman's voice talking to her. He thought it might be the dark-haired detective who had questioned him in York. He was dismayed at the thought that she could have travelled all the way to Saddleworth to look for him. He wondered what Eddy had been saying about him, but reassured himself that it didn't really matter. Whatever the accusation, it would be Eddy's word against his. The police must realise that a jury were bound to consider Eddy unreliable, whereas Alec was articulate and self-assured, and knew how to appear trustworthy. So he was baffled that the police were still searching for him. Surely they had better things to do with their time.

There was no reason for the continued police interest in him now that Eddy had been arrested. After all, Eddy was the guilty one. Yet the police continued to search relentlessly for him, which made no sense. Thinking back over everything that had happened, it struck him that actually only one police officer had been pursuing him. The more he thought about it, the more convinced he became that she had been acting independently in her attempts to pin him down. He recalled her threatening him. 'If you had anything to do with this, we'll find out,' and 'You can't hide the truth from us forever.' But no one else had shown any interest in him at all. He wasn't officially a suspect. Convinced that just one officer was after him, he only had to silence her, and then he could start working out how to remove the one remaining stumbling block to the future he had been planning for so long.

The front door shut and his mother came back upstairs. Relieved, he went out on the landing to find out who had called. Seeing him, his mother flapped her hand frantically.

She addressed him in an urgent undertone. 'Get back in there. It's the police again. Asking for you.'

'Why didn't you send them away?' he whispered angrily.

'She wants to see Judy.'

'Bloody hell, mother. Get rid of them, can't you? Don't let them in.'

'Just get back in there and shut the door,' she hissed. 'I'll keep her out, but you need to stay out of sight. When I open the front door, she might be able to see up the stairs. We'll keep her outside, but you need to keep your door shut while your sister talks to her. And don't make a sound.'

He quizzed her urgently.

'I'd guess she's about thirty or forty,' his mother replied. 'She's tall, much taller than me anyway, and she's got short black hair and black eyes that seem to stare right through you.' She shuddered. 'I hope this is the last we see of her. She's a nasty bitch and she's got it in for you all right. But don't worry. She's never going to get hold of you, not while I'm here. You can stay as long as you like. The room's yours and there's no need for you to ever step out of the house if you don't want to. You're safe here.'

In that moment, Alec knew he couldn't bear to stay there any longer. Regardless of the risk, he had to get away. Living under his mother's roof, sleeping in that tiny bedroom, he might as well have been in prison, like Eddy. But he kept his plans to himself, saying only that he would be leaving as soon as the policewoman had gone.

'Don't be daft,' his mother replied.

'You can't go back to York anyway,' Judy pointed out unhelpfully. 'Not while they're looking for you.'

Concealing his irritation with his sister's stupidity, he bestowed an ingratiating smile on his mother.

'I really want to stay here and take care of you,' he lied, 'but I've caused you enough trouble as it is and it's not fair on you if I stay here anymore. As long as I'm living here, the police aren't going to leave you in peace.'

Even as he was speaking, Alec realised that he wasn't really making sense, because the police didn't actually know he was in Saddleworth. If his mother detected the flaw in his logic, she didn't mention it. As for Judy, she didn't appear to be listening to what he was saying. His sister wasn't interested in his situation, but his mother was always compliant. He ordered them both to be discreet and tell no one he had been there.

'This is between us,' he told her, taking her mother's hand and kissing it.

There were tears in her eyes and she nodded, and he knew he had her unquestioning obedience. It was always easy to get around her.

'You'd best get back down there,' he said.

He darted back into the narrow bedroom of his childhood, closing the door softly behind him. He flung himself down on the bed, which was too small for him now, and stared disconsolately at the wooden wardrobe which had once held all his clothes. He thought wistfully of the room where he had been sleeping in Eric's house, with its double bed and fitted wardrobes that stretched across a whole wall. He had spent ages emptying them, stuffing his aunt's clothes in bin bags. Even though he had covered his nose as he laboured, the smell of sweat and mothballs had nearly stifled him. Eventually he had discarded the bags at the council dump to be rid of them completely. And after all that effort, he had been forced to leave York. It was infuriating, being cooped up in one small room when there was a whole house standing empty, but he wasn't sure it would be safe for him to return to York. He had planned to take up permanent residence there, under the guise of taking care of the property for his cousin while he was away. With luck, Eddy would stay locked up for a very long time. Although Alec didn't wish Eddy any harm, he had to admit it would be convenient if Eddy were to die in prison.

At last his mother tapped on his door to assure him the police officer had gone. 'It's all right. She's a tenacious cow, but we got rid of her all right,' she said, her voice muffled by the door. 'You can come out now.'

Without stopping to kiss her goodbye, he ran out to the car he had recently acquired. It had cost him a lot to get the number plates changed, but he didn't care about that because before long he'd be loaded. No stupid bitch of a policewoman was going to get in his way. He felt in the inside pocket of his jacket for the all-important document and smiled. Thinking about the fortune he was about to get his hands on, he hunkered down out of sight to wait and watch from halfway up the hill. A few moments later, a car sped by. In the fading light he recognised the driver. Slowly he released his handbrake and eased out on to the road after her.

It wasn't too difficult to follow her, as he knew she was going back to York. He was tempted to try and run her off the road, but he knew that would be foolhardy. She might not even be injured, and he might be hurt or even killed. So he followed her, taking care not to get too close. The roads in the city were narrow and winding, but he managed to keep track of her as she drove through the city until finally she reached a street beside the river, where she turned into an underground car park. Now he had discovered the block where she lived, he just had to find out the number of her flat and he would be ready to strike. And the beauty of it was that she had no idea where he was, and no one had any inkling about his intentions.

54

Not long after Ian went out, the doorbell rang. Presuming he had forgotten his key, Geraldine hurried to open the door without pausing to check the security camera. As soon as she released the latch, the door was pushed open and a figure barged into her, catching her off guard. The intruder must have been watching the flat and waiting for his chance to enter, because he turned up soon after Ian left. Geraldine spun round and looked for something to use as a weapon. The first object she saw was an umbrella, but before she could reach for it her assailant lunged forward and pushed her against the wall, pinning her arms to her sides. The force of the movement dislodged his hood which slipped back to reveal his identity. She was not surprised to see who it was.

Alec leaned towards her and scowled, his face very close to hers. 'You know, you've become a nuisance,' he snarled.

She recoiled as a tiny drop of spittle appeared on his bottom lip. Involuntarily, she wondered whether any of his saliva had reached her, planting his DNA on her person for SOCOs to find. She pulled herself up short. She needed to concentrate all of her attention on subduing her assailant, not on analysing the situation as the scene of a murder with her as the victim.

'A real nuisance. Do you have any idea how much of a nuisance you are?'

'I don't know what you're talking about. Get off me.'

He continued talking, muttering more to himself than to her, jogging her viciously with each utterance.

'Always poking your nose in where it's not wanted. Never letting go. If it wasn't for you I'd still be living in York. It's your fault. I had it all, everything. And I deserved it. Do you hear me? It was mine.'

As long as he kept hold of her with both of his hands, he could only shake her and bruise her. At the very worst he might break her arms. If he was going to kill her, eventually he would have to let go of at least one of her arms. And as soon as he released his hold on her, she would subdue him. In the meantime, it was important she take the initiative and try to unsettle him. As long as he felt he had the upper hand, he was unlikely to lose focus. She hooked her foot around his ankle suddenly, in an attempt to unbalance him. With a sneer, he shoved her backwards, hitting her head against the wall.

'Not so fast,' he said. 'You're not going anywhere.'

'And you're on a fast track to prison for assaulting a police officer,' Geraldine replied quietly, hoping her composure would unnerve him. 'Listen to me, Alec. You've avoided any suspicion of involvement in Doreen's murder. There's nothing anyone can do about that, so you can just walk away. What you're doing now is madness. You must see that. Go home before you land yourself in trouble. If you don't let me go, you'll never get away with it.'

'Don't tell me, you've left a note on your desk at work that if anything happens to you, it was me what done it.' He sniggered, and in that instant Geraldine swung her leg up and kneed him in the groin.

With a yelp of pain, Alec loosened his grip, giving her just enough room to twist sideways and slip out of his grasp. He reached for her, but she had already escaped. Unable to get past him to the front door, she sprinted along the hall towards the bedroom. Frantically she glanced around, looking for her phone. Touching one key would summon help instantly, but the phone was in her bag on her bed. As she made it to the bedroom Alec burst in and launched himself at her, hurling her to the floor. Geraldine winced as she landed on her side with Alec on top of her. For an instant, she was too stunned to react. Recovering her presence of mind, she pushed against him with all her strength and succeeded in shifting him to one side. She was gathering her strength to push him away and clamber to her feet when he let out a growl of anger, and she felt the cold prick of a blade pressing against her neck.

Ian was out and would not be back for at least another hour. She was alone with a deranged killer and there was no one to help her. She doubted she could engage him in conversation for a few minutes, let alone for an hour, but she had to try.

She forced herself to speak calmly. 'Think about what you're doing, Alec. I'm sure you don't want to do anything stupid. Just stop for a moment. If you do anything to me, you'll never get away with it. Don't kid yourself that you can kill me and walk away. Your DNA is all over me and all over the flat. The police will track you down in no time. Everyone I work with has been looking for you, but now Eddy's confessed you're no longer wanted by the police. You're safe.' She wasn't quite sure what she was saying. 'Let me go right now, and we'll say nothing more about this. We'll keep it between ourselves. I know you don't want to hurt me. Things just got a bit out of hand. You lost it for a moment, but that's no reason to spend the rest of your life behind bars.'

The point of the blade traced a line across her throat, but there was no sharp pain. She didn't think he had actually cut her.

Yet.

She wondered how clean his knife was and shuddered. If he so much as broke her skin, the wound might prove fatal.

Forcing herself to speak, she ploughed on. 'You never wanted to hurt me, and you certainly don't want to kill me. Think about what you're doing. Why risk your liberty? And for what? As things stand, there's no evidence linking you to any crime.

You're free to walk away from all this. If you kill me, you'll be in prison until you die. You can't possibly murder a police officer and get away with it.'

'You think I'm crazy, don't you? You're wrong. I'm being perfectly logical and rational. The fact is, you have to be silenced,' he replied.

'What are you talking about?' she asked, desperate to keep him engaged in the conversation.

'You know too much,' he replied. 'But don't try and blame me. You brought this on yourself. You should have kept your nose out of my affairs.'

Pressing the knife against her throat, he dragged her up on her feet.

'Move!'

'You're going to kill me anyway. Why should I do what you want?'

'We need to get you on the bed,' he said, almost talking to himself. 'We can't afford to have you bleeding all over the carpet. Your duvet should do nicely.'

'Now that *is* stupid,' she said.

'No, actually it's perfect. I've got this all worked out. I'm going to wrap your body in the duvet and carry you out of here. You'll simply disappear. No one will ever find out what happened to you.'

Geraldine forced herself to laugh. 'You have no idea how much blood is pumped out of a body when you slice through an artery. There will be blood everywhere, sprayed on the walls, as well as the bed, and you'll be drenched too. You'll need to get rid of all your clothes and shower before you leave, but you'll still be convicted because you're shedding your DNA all over the flat. And,' she lowered her voice dramatically, 'you really don't want to be found guilty of murdering a police officer. You'll have every force in the country hunting you down. You won't be able to move without someone spotting you. You won't be able to breathe without someone hearing. There will be nowhere to run and nowhere to hide.' She nearly threatened his mother with police harassment, but she wasn't sure that prospect would particularly trouble him. Instead, she focused on Alec himself. 'You may think you've been frightened before, but this will be in a completely different league. You can't begin to imagine what your life will be like, hiding like a rat in a sewer, scared to come out in the daylight.'

'You're right. No blood,' he muttered. 'No matter. A pillow over your face will do it.'

With an involuntary movement, Alec drew back slightly, releasing the pressure of his knife blade against her neck. His hesitation didn't give Geraldine much space to move, but it was enough. Aware that she had very little to lose, in a flash she struck Alec's forearm with the edge of her hand, using all the force she could muster. With her other hand clenched in a fist she punched him on his temple, simultaneously kneeing him in the balls as hard as she could. Alec groaned, momentarily unable to move. Geraldine didn't give him time to recover. Rolling him over she twisted both his arms up behind his back until he yelped with pain. Her bag with her handcuffs and phone had fallen in the floor during their tussle and she couldn't pick it up without releasing her grip on one of his arms. Cursing under her breath, she hooked her foot through the strap of her bag and dragged it towards her. She gave one of his arms a vicious wrench as she lunged for her bag and pulled out her phone. Before Alec realised what she was doing, she pressed her alarm, alerting her colleagues to her plight.

Dropping her phone on the bed, she rummaged in her bag for her handcuffs, and gave Alec's wrists a final vicious jerk as she secured them behind his back. He cried out in pain and lay inert on the bed, moaning softly. Her ordeal over, Geraldine began to shake. She seemed to be waiting for a long time but at last she heard sirens approaching. Recovering her outward composure, she went to open her front door before her colleagues broke it down. A pair of burly constables dashed into her hall.

'He's in there,' she said, nodding at the open bedroom door. 'No need to treat him too gently. He came here to kill me,' she added, by way of explanation.

55

'WHAT THE HELL WERE you doing opening the door to him?' Ian demanded, glaring at Geraldine.

She understood his anger arose out of his fear for what might have happened to her, but she still struggled not to cry.

'Every ten-year-old knows not to open the door to strangers,' he raged. 'Even five-year-olds know that. We've got a security camera. Didn't you look at it? And we've got a chain on the door, for Christ's sake. Why didn't you put the chain on before you opened the door? What the hell do you think it's there for? Have you lost your mind?'

'I thought it was you,' she muttered.

'What? Me? How could it be me?' he spluttered. 'I've got a key.'

Miserably she tried to explain that she had opened the door, thinking Ian had left his key at home. 'I didn't want you to be late for your football practice.'

'Football practice?' he repeated, almost incandescent with indignation. 'What the hell has this got to do with my football? You could have had your throat cut. According to your own account, you very nearly did. What the blazes were you doing letting a crazy killer into the flat like that? What the hell is wrong with you?'

Eventually he calmed down sufficiently to understand what she was saying, but he continued to scold her for being careless. She let him rant on, knowing he was right. She had behaved with inexcusable negligence.

'Apart from anything else, it would have made a dreadful mess of the place if he had cut your throat,' Ian said at last.

With his return to an attempt at humour, Geraldine knew he was over his fit of temper.

'I know,' she agreed, relieved that he had calmed down. 'That's exactly what I told him. I warned him he would never get away with it. He was planning to kill me and cart my body away, wrapped in the duvet, and hide me somewhere I would never be found. I felt obliged to point out the massive flaws in his plan. First, there would be blood all over the bedroom and he would be drenched in it. Second, he wouldn't be able to get rid of the body. And finally, I warned him every police force in the country would be hunting him down. He'd never get away with it.'

'And that stopped him?'

'No. He came here to silence me and that was what he intended to do. I offered to keep quiet about the assault if he left, just to get rid of him, although of course once he'd attacked me, he'd condemned himself, but he was determined to finish me off. It was touch and go for a moment, but I managed to keep him talking for long enough to gain control of the situation. The problem was, I couldn't reach my bag with my phone and cuffs. Once he was distracted, I managed to get to them and that was that.'

'Well, I'm not going to say well done. You behaved like an imbecile. And I don't forgive you for putting yourself in danger like that.' He pulled her towards him and held her tightly. 'Now you have to promise me you'll never do anything so bloody stupid again. Ever.'

She smiled. 'Don't worry, I won't.'

'Don't worry, she says.' He drew away from her, shaking his head. 'I'm not sure I'll ever be able to sleep again.'

Geraldine told herself it was reassuring to know Ian cared so much about her, but she wished he had treated her with a little more sympathy and kindness. After her terrifying ordeal, she didn't appreciate him giving her such a hard time. Still, she didn't complain, aware that he was perfectly justified in everything he said. She had been careless for an instant, and as a consequence she had very nearly lost her life. She would have been equally angry with him, if he had put himself in danger.

'We ought to run a campaign about not opening the door without checking who's there,' she said as they drove to the police station to interview Alec the following morning.

Ian glanced quizzically at her. 'What's that expression about where charity begins?'

Geraldine had slept surprisingly well, and the sun was shining as she and Ian walked side by side across the police compound. She felt a wonderful sense of calm, despite the ordeal she had suffered the previous evening.

Alec was sitting bolt upright in the interview room, a duty brief at his side. Geraldine recognised the solicitor who had accompanied Eddy. His jacket was creased, as it had been the previous time she had seen him, and his hair was equally unkempt. Despite his scruffy appearance, he looked far more alert beside Alec than when he had been sitting with Eddy. Geraldine suspected he was more interested in Alec as a client than Eddy who was never likely to impress a jury favourably. Alec was a different proposition. Even after spending time in a cell, he looked cleaner and more respectable than his lawyer. He smiled at Geraldine in greeting, as though they were old friends. It was hard to believe that just a few hours earlier he had been threatening to slit her throat.

'Alec,' Ian began, 'there's no point in attempting to deny that you assaulted my colleague.'

Ian broke off, as his voice cracked.

'That is a complete misrepresentation of what happened,' Alec responded at once, his smile barely faltering. 'It was all just an unfortunate misunderstanding.'

'There was no misunderstanding. You held a knife to my throat and told me you were going to silence me,' Geraldine said. 'You were impressively thorough in your planning. You'd even worked out that you would need to dispose of my body somewhere it could never be found, which I suspect was going to prove tricky. Still, we'll never know how you would have managed that, will we?'

'Well, that's just your interpretation of our encounter,' Alec replied evenly. 'She always had it in for me,' he went on in a conversational tone, turning to Ian. 'She was convinced I'd murdered my aunt, and when she was proved wrong she turned on me. Some people are like that, you know. They can't stand being proved wrong. I don't deny I wanted her to shut up, but only because she kept on and on, accusing me of a terrible crime I had nothing to do with.' He shrugged, smiling in a manner that might have seemed charming in different circumstances. 'I wanted her to shut up, but that's not the same as saying I wanted to shut her up. I can see how you might have mistaken my meaning if you weren't paying attention to what I was saying.' His smile encompassed Ian and the lawyer. 'What man can honestly say he's never wanted a woman to shut up? We all know it wasn't me who killed my poor aunt. It was my cousin.'

Geraldine nodded. 'Let's talk about your cousin then.'

Alec threw a triumphant glance at his lawyer, as though to say that he had won; his equivocation had convinced his interlocutors to give up on the idea of charging him with assaulting a police officer.

'Eddy worked out a very clever plan to kill his mother,' Geraldine said. 'Only a brilliant mind could have come up with such an ingenious plan.'

'A devious mind,' Ian muttered.

But Alec was staring at Geraldine, as though mesmerised. 'It was very clever, wasn't it?' he agreed.

'Whoever dreamed that up was a genius,' Ian muttered

reluctantly, seeing where Geraldine was going with her line of questioning.

'It must be hard for you, having a cousin who's so much cleverer than you,' Geraldine went on. 'Don't you mind that everyone sees you as stupid, just because he's so much more intelligent than you?'

'Poor Alec, growing up in the shadow of his brilliant cousin,' Ian echoed Geraldine's goading.

'No, no!' Alec shouted, suddenly losing his self-control and banging his fist on the table. 'You've got it all wrong.' He turned to his lawyer. 'They don't know what they're talking about. I'm the clever one, me! Eddy's a fool, a stupid fool. Everyone knows I'm clever. Eddy's so stupid he killed his own mother when it was obvious he was going to be caught. How stupid is that?'

'We found his will, you know, in your car,' Geraldine said quietly. 'A car that, incidentally, had false registration plates. Eddy's will ties this up for us.'

She placed the document on the table, protected in a plastic evidence bag.

'Here it is. Eddy's will naming you heir to his estate if he dies or is convicted of any crime that carries a custodial sentence. Slightly unusual wording for a will, wouldn't you say?' she added, turning to the lawyer.

Alec lost his air of self-assurance and his expression darkened.

'Eddy signed it,' he muttered. 'That makes it a legal document.'

'Not without witness signatures, it doesn't,' Ian said.

Alec looked fleetingly stricken. Recovering his outward equanimity, he appealed to his lawyer who confirmed what Ian had said.

'We know why you encouraged Eddy to kill his mother,' Geraldine said softly. 'We know you set the whole thing up.'

Alec leaned back in his chair, his eyes narrowed. 'You can't prove that,' he drawled. 'You're always at it, trying to destroy my reputation with your filthy lies. None of it's true. Nothing you say is true. You won't get away with this, arresting an innocent man.'

He seemed to be rambling abstractedly, as though he had momentarily lost his confidence in his ability to talk his way out of the situation.

'Eddy's told us all about it,' Geraldine said, seizing on Alec's misgivings. 'We never believed he was clever enough to work out such a meticulously planned murder all by himself, but we got the truth out of him in the end.'

Alec frowned. 'Eddy's a liar. He wouldn't know the truth if it came up and slapped him in the face.'

'There's only one thing I don't understand,' Geraldine went on, ignoring Alec's outburst. 'Weren't you worried Eddy would tell us the truth?'

Alec shrugged, frowning. 'I thought he'd be too scared.'

'Of what?'

Alec sneered. 'Of me, of course. He always was a pushover.'

'You bullied him all his life, didn't you?'

Alec scowled. 'He didn't mind. I'm his cousin.'

'He was scared of you, wasn't he?'

Alec didn't answer.

'So you knew he would do whatever you told him to do?'

'He wanted to do it,' Alec said quickly. 'My poor aunt's death had nothing to do with me.' He sat forward, with a return of his earlier assurance. 'Eddy wanted to get rid of his mother so he could invite his girlfriend to go and live with him.' He snorted derisively. 'As if any woman would want to shack up with Eddy.'

'So you knew Eddy was going to murder his mother before he did it,' Geraldine said. 'How did you find out what he was planning?'

'Planning? Eddy? He couldn't plan anything to save his life.'

'So who did plan Doreen's murder?' Geraldine asked thoughtfully. 'It was worked out in such meticulous detail. Eddy had to work quickly. Who could have had the kind of influence over poor, stupid Eddy that would make him so efficient?'

The lawyer stirred. 'My client needs a break,' he said.

'One more question before you go,' Geraldine said. 'You cut Doreen's hair, didn't you?'

'Oh that,' Alec replied airily, but his eyes were suddenly cagey. He didn't know how much they knew about what had happened. 'Poor old aunty's hair was a mess,' he blurted out, 'so I offered to do it for her and found a knot.'

'That her carers had missed whenever they brushed her hair?' Geraldine asked.

'Yes, well, you can't believe a word those people say. They didn't look after her properly. Anyone could see that. It was her lucky day when I turned up to help. Aunty told me it hurt her when they combed her hair so I cut out the tangle for her. That's all. Really, you do a good deed, and where does it get you?' He stared at Geraldine, with a return to his earlier poise. 'It must be hard for you, being so horribly suspicious of everyone. Doesn't it ever occur to you that you might have this all wrong? I'm telling you, it was Eddy all along. You think you know everything about me, but you don't know anything.'

'I know you tried to kill me,' Geraldine replied quietly.

Alec began to reply, but the lawyer spoke over him and insisted on talking to his client in private.

'Take all the time you need,' Geraldine replied, breaking into a smile. 'Alec's not going anywhere.'

56

THE FOLLOWING DAY, GERALDINE went to see her sister. With both Eddy and Alec apprehended and charged, there was no reason for her to postpone their meeting. Helena had been importunate about seeing her, and Geraldine was reluctant to upset her. Previously they had always met in restaurants or cafés, but this time Helena insisted on Geraldine visiting her at home. She had recently moved, and Geraldine was curious to see Helena's flat. She was living in North London, not far from Highbury and Islington station, very close to where Geraldine had lived in North London before she had moved to York.

She found the house easily, a three-storey Victorian house in easy walking distance from the shops and the station.

Helena opened the high front door and took her into a ground-floor apartment where Geraldine admired a spacious front room with wood block floor and a polished black Victorian fireplace. Beige velvet curtains hung at the bay window, and there was a massive television screen fixed to the wall. They sat down on plush armchairs on either side of a wooden coffee table.

'Not too shabby, innit?' Helena crowed, looking around with a complacent smile.

Geraldine agreed that it was beautiful. She wasn't just being polite. From what she had seen so far, the apartment was comfortable and elegant.

'Yeah, I landed on me feet this time and no mistake,' Helena grinned. 'And this ain't all.'

She held out her left hand with a flourish to display a large diamond on her wedding finger.

'Does that mean you're engaged?' Geraldine blurted out.

'Don't sound so surprised,' Helena said. 'You knew about my fellah. I did tell ya.' She held her ring up, twisting her hand, admiring the gem sparkling in the light.

'I'm really pleased for you,' Geraldine said. 'If you're sure this is what you really want. I mean, are you sure he's going to make you happy? You're not letting yourself be seduced by the fact that he's got some money?'

'Some money? Geraldine, I'm telling ya, he's proper minted.'

'Are you sure? He could just be saying that to impress you.'

'You having me on? With all this?' Helena waved her hand around to indicate the apartment and the engagement ring. 'Seriously, what's not to like? I'm no fool, sis. I may have messed up good and proper in me time, but I been around and I know a blagger when I see one, and I can tell when I'm on to a good thing. He's loaded all right. How about you?' she went on, turning her attention from her diamond ring to Geraldine. 'Wouldn't you like a rock like this?'

'What? You mean a ring like that?'

Helena nodded. It was the first time in their lives Helena had owned something Geraldine didn't have.

'No,' Geraldine replied. 'That is, your ring is absolutely lovely, and it's not that I wouldn't like one, if it came up, but I'm perfectly happy as I am.'

'If it come up?' Helena asked with a shrewd stare. 'You mean you'd marry your fellah if he asked ya, but he hasn't asked?'

'We're neither of us that bothered about marriage,' Geraldine replied. 'We're perfectly happy as we are. Ian's been married before and it didn't work out. She made him desperately unhappy, and I think that put him off for life.'

'But what about you? Don't you want to get married?'

'Honestly, it doesn't bother me. We're together and that's what matters. But it would be nice to buy a place together one day, maybe get a dog.'

'A dog? What you want with a dog?'

Geraldine laughed at Helena's dismay.

'Just a little one,' she said. 'Although I think Ian would like an Alsatian.'

'Bloody hell, you need to ditch him and get yourself a sensible fellah.'

Geraldine shook her head. 'I wouldn't want anyone else.'

'Well, that's the best then, innit? You find the right fellah and you're sorted.'

'What about you? Are you sure he's the right one?'

Helena laughed. 'There ain't no right one,' she replied. 'But my fellah's a good sort, and he looks after me. After the life I've led, that's more than enough for me. See, I'm not like you, sis, I can't take care of myself. You know that as well as I do. Until you come along and pulled me out the gutter, I was lost. I wouldn't never have crawled out of that dark hole if you hadn't come along. You know that. I owe you everything.'

'You're stronger than you think,' Geraldine muttered, almost too overwhelmed to speak.

Helena shook her head. 'I'm not like you,' she repeated. 'I can't make it on me own.'

Geraldine wondered fleetingly what would happen to Helena if her fiancé died. Presumably she would be left financially secure. He was a lot older than her, but he might have children who would inherit his estate. She pushed that worry away. For now, Helena was settled and happy, and she and Geraldine were finally forging a positive relationship. When they had first met, Geraldine hadn't dared hope they would ever have a civil conversation, let alone grow close. She was relieved that Helena didn't appear to notice that she was temporarily too emotional to speak.

'Let's have some tea, then,' Helena said, with a flash of

the practicality Geraldine recognised as a facet of her own personality. 'Where do you want to go?'

Geraldine laughed. It had been too much to expect Helena to reinvent herself into a hospitable hostess. Maybe one day that would happen. For now, Geraldine was content to follow her sister to a smart café along Upper Street where, for the first time, Helena insisted on paying.

'I'm telling ya, I'm flush,' she said.

Geraldine wondered whether Helena expected her to continue paying her an allowance, but she decided not to raise the subject. She didn't want to risk spoiling their new friendly relations.

'So when are you getting married?' Geraldine asked when they had placed their order and were waiting for the tea to arrive.

Helena glanced at her hand resting on the table, diamond on display.

'We haven't fixed a date, but soon.'

'I thought you had to book these events months in advance.'

'Only if it's going to be a big bash, but our wedding won't be a grand do, just a quick visit to the registry office with a couple of witnesses off the street.' She hesitated. 'We're not inviting any of his family.'

'I take it they aren't thrilled about it then?'

Helena scowled.

'Have you met his children?'

'Yeah, filthy parasites the pair of them. They've scrounged off him all their lives and now they're shit scared he's going to leave his stack to me. It would serve them right if he left them nothing. They thought they had a meal ticket for life. Neither one of them has ever done nothing for him, hardly bother to see him, and they're bleeding him dry. Well, all that's changed now.' She glanced at her ring again. 'I told him, they should be treating him like royalty, and if they don't, he ought to cut them adrift to fend for themselves. That's only fair, innit?'

Geraldine refrained from pointing out that her own generosity had been supporting Helena for years. She wondered if Helena intended to invite her and Ian to the wedding ceremony.

'I'd like to know when it is,' she ventured.

Helena shrugged. 'We haven't fixed a date yet, not exactly. Nothing definite.'

Geraldine was sure she was lying but didn't say so. Instead, she asked when she could meet Helena's fiancé, but her sister was evasive.

'I don't want you to think I'm dodging your question,' Helena said.

She was, but it didn't really matter.

'As long as you're happy,' Geraldine said, with a smile. 'This isn't about me and my feelings, Helena. This is your life and you're free to do whatever you like. I'm happy about it all, as long as you're happy.'

Helena reached out and put her hand on Geraldine's arm.

'That's just what our mum would have said,' she murmured.

Geraldine had only met her birth mother once, shortly before her death. Helena had been raised by her. There was no question that Geraldine had experienced a far more privileged upbringing than her sister, who had been brought up by their alcoholic single mother. Life had been a constant struggle for them. But the woman Geraldine never knew had still been her biological mother. Knowing so little about her left a haunting gap in her life, but Helena had always refused to talk about her.

'Tell me about our mother,' Geraldine said.

'She was a mad cow,' Helena replied, with a wistful smile. 'I know I lived with her but I hardly knew her, not really. I mean, you never knew from one day to the next what she was going to be like. One day she was as reasonable as you are, never happy, exactly, but –' She broke off, searching for the right words to express what she wanted to say. 'There were times she was normal, ya know. You could talk to her and get a sensible answer back. But other days she was completely wrecked, as likely to slap you or throw up all over you as talk to you. Who was it said, "Shoot first ask questions after"? I tell ya, if she'd ever got her hands on a gun she'd have been taking potshots at everyone she saw, just for the hell of it. And next day she'd be sharing her sarnies with total strangers. You just never knew with her. It was the booze. That's what did for her. So I learned to stay away when she was off her face, you know.' She paused. 'I lived on the streets more often than at home when I was a teenager, just to keep out her way.'

'It must have been hard for you.'

Helena nodded. 'I guess. Because you love your mum, don't you? In spite of how much you learn to hate her, you still love her. I sometimes think it wasn't her fault, any of it. She was abandoned so young. But then I think, well, she should have sorted herself out once she had a child.'

'She had two children,' Geraldine reminded her.

Helena snorted. 'You were well out of it. I'd give anything to have had your luck, adopted by a decent family.' She stared intently at Geraldine. 'Your family were good to you, weren't they?'

'They were as kind and loving towards me as they knew how. But –' Geraldine hesitated. 'I never told you this before. I don't know why. I think at first I didn't want to upset you and then, after so much time had elapsed, it was difficult to share it with you. You would have been upset that I'd kept it a secret from you. Please, don't hate me for keeping it from you all this time.'

'What you on about?' Helena asked, but she looked tense. 'You're not gonna tell me you're dying or summat? That we got bad genes?'

'No, no, nothing like that.'

'What is it, then?'

'I was brought up with an adopted sister. She was my parents' daughter, their biological daughter. There were complications at

LEIGH RUSSELL

her birth and they couldn't have a second child, so they adopted me.'

Geraldine waited, afraid Helena would be furious at having been kept in the dark for so long.

'Oh that,' Helena brushed Geraldine's big reveal away with a sniff. 'I know all about Celia. I've known for ages. I wondered when you were going to tell me about her.'

Geraldine was dumbstruck. Before she could stutter a response, the tea finally arrived.

'But how did you know? About Celia, I mean?' Geraldine asked at length.

Helena chuckled. 'You ain't the only one can do a bit of digging. You might be a hoity toity police detective, but I got brains, same as you, and I can be a devious cow.'

Geraldine felt as though a weight had lifted from her shoulders. 'I wanted to tell you,' she said.

'Yeah, yeah,' Helena replied sceptically. 'I spoke to your Celia once, you know,' she added. 'We decided that if you was keeping us a secret from each other, you had your reasons. So we agreed to keep shtum. I think Celia was more upset about it than I was, but I told her it was all right. We'd met, you and me, and we never hit it off. She didn't have to worry about losing her sister to a stranger. That's what I told her, because I didn't want to screw things up between you and her. But I'm your real sister, not her,' she added, sounding almost angry. 'We're twins and that's about as close as we'll ever be to anyone. Don't you go forgetting that.'

'I won't forget,' Geraldine said, and smiled. 'I'm reminded of you every time I look in a mirror.'

Helena grunted, but she seemed satisfied. Geraldine felt elated. She no longer had a secret from either of her sisters, and Helena really cared about her. Life was good.

310

57

'YOU'RE VERY QUIET,' IAN remarked, as they sat down together the evening after Geraldine's visit to see Helena. 'Thinking about your sister and her fiancé?'

'No, actually. I was thinking about Beattie and what everyone's been saying about her.'

'What's to say? The woman's insane.'

'She was certainly desperate to get Louisa back. She couldn't bear being parted from her.' Geraldine paused.

'Are you thinking about your own mother, and how ready she was to give you away?' Ian asked.

Geraldine sighed and didn't answer.

'You know perfectly well it wasn't a straightforward decision for her,' he went on. 'It can't have been easy for her. If it had been, she would have given your sister up for adoption too. You must realise she didn't want to lose you. She just couldn't cope. And she wanted what was best for you. That's a generous kind of love.'

'Helena was a puny baby,' Geraldine said miserably. 'That's why she stayed with our mother. No one expected her to live long.'

'Whereas you were always strong,' Ian said, smiling, but she didn't smile back. 'Your mother gave you up so you could have the chance of a better life. Don't you think your twin would have preferred to be adopted into a normal healthy family, instead of staying with a smack head?'

'She wasn't a smack head. She was an alcoholic.'

'Drugs, drink, it's all destructive self-abuse in the end.'

Geraldine sighed. Heroin had threatened to destroy Helena but with Geraldine's support, her sister finally seemed to be sorting herself out. Alcohol had ruined their mother's life, but Geraldine hadn't traced her in time to help her as well.

'You can't save the whole world,' Ian replied when she confessed to him that she ought to have found her mother sooner, but had been afraid of what she might discover.

'Best not to dwell on what happened to your mother. Your sister seems to be managing to stay clean, and that's all thanks to you. She'd be dead too if you hadn't persuaded her to go to rehab.'

'And now she's engaged,' Geraldine said, smiling at last. 'She was sporting a ring with a diamond the size of her fist!'

'Well, that's exciting news, isn't it? What do you know about the man she's going to marry?'

'I haven't met him.'

'Oh. Well, maybe we can arrange to get together with them before the wedding. When is it?'

'I don't know. And I'm not sure we'll be invited.'

Briefly she related what Helena had told her about her fiancé and his family.

'Oh well, weddings always cause arguments,' Ian said cryptically. He turned to Geraldine suddenly. 'You don't mind, do you, that you never did? Because we could if you want. Get married, I mean. That is, I won't object if it's what you really want, although it wouldn't be my choice.'

Geraldine laughed. 'What woman could fail to be swept off her feet by such a romantic proposal? No, I've got no burning desire to dress up in white and throw a party where a roomful of people get sloshed, and I certainly don't intend to change my name.'

'What's the point of it then?' Ian asked, looking relieved.

'Exactly.'

Ian pulled her towards him and kissed her gently. 'Thank you for understanding,' he murmured.

Eddy and Alec were safely in custody with cases against them building. No jury was likely to acquit either of them. Nevertheless, the case continued to interest the investigating team, and the relationship between the two cousins, and the deaths of Doreen and Louisa, were the subject of ongoing discussion. One evening Geraldine joined her colleagues in the pub after work, while Ian was out playing football.

'There's a theme going on here,' Naomi said. 'Eddy killed his mother, and Louisa's mother killed her. There's a kind of symmetry to it, some sort of poetic justice, I think.'

'No justice at all as far as I can see,' Geraldine replied. 'And I think you've probably had enough to drink,' she added quietly. 'Did you skip lunch today?'

'Yes, ma'am,' Naomi replied sulkily, but she put her glass down and reached for a packet of crisps.

'There's no symmetry to it,' Binita replied. 'The two murders were unrelated, and totally different.'

'Beattie never intended to kill her daughter, but Eddy deliberately set out to kill his mother. That's a huge distinction,' Geraldine agreed.

'So you think Louisa's death was manslaughter not murder?' Naomi asked.

While Geraldine prevaricated about that, several of their colleagues joined in, all voicing different opinions.

'It's like a Greek tragedy, with Beattie killing someone she loved.'

'Funny way to express love, killing someone.'

'It happens all the time. Crimes of passion.'

'But she never meant to kill her.'

'Eddy's attack on Doreen had nothing to do with love,' Ariadne said firmly. 'It was unscrupulous and grasping. He did away with his own mother just so he could get his grubby paws on her property. It was unashamedly evil, and had nothing whatsoever to do with love.'

'But he only did it because he loved Louisa,' Naomi replied.

'Of course he didn't love her. He didn't even know her!' Ariadne retorted. 'You can't love someone you've never met.'

'He thought he was in love with her,' Naomi insisted.

'Insane delusion, maybe, but not love,' Ariadne said dismissively.

'Whatever anyone might think of him, we all agree he was insane,' Binita said.

'Isn't every act of murder an act of insanity?' Geraldine asked.

'Not when someone's killed for their money. That seems quite logical and rational to me,' a constable replied.

The colleagues sitting on either side of him assumed horrified expressions and made a show of moving their chairs further away from him. Everyone laughed at their antics.

'Eddy will be diagnosed with de Clérambault's syndrome, and taken into psychiatric care,' Ariadne said. 'You know, the condition where people suffer delusions thinking they're in love with a stranger.'

'Yes, I think we all know what it is,' Naomi replied.

'Isn't being in love always a delusion?' a constable muttered.

'He killed his mother because of some weird fantasy,' another constable remarked, shaking his head.

'If you ask me, Beattie is just as crazy as Eddy,' Naomi said. 'Can you imagine it, killing your own child?'

'But she didn't mean to kill her,' one of her colleagues said. 'Louisa fell down the stairs. We don't know that Beattie deliberately pushed her.'

'Even if she never meant her to die, she still attacked Louisa violently enough to kill her. In my book that's crazy, whatever the outcome.'

'Sane or insane, they both need to be locked up for good,' Binita declared. 'Which means we need to make sure our records are absolutely complete and the cases against them watertight. Alec in particular is a slippery customer. He might well try to convince a jury that he had nothing to do with his cousin's actions, but he's a dangerous psychopath. We can't let him wriggle out of a conviction because of some oversight in our records.'

Listening to her senior officer, Geraldine found herself comparing Binita's self-possession with Eileen's volatility. The new detective chief inspector would no doubt be easier to work with, but Geraldine understood that Eileen's outbursts expressed a passion for the job which Binita might not feel, a passion Geraldine shared. Eileen had given her a second chance after her demotion, and she felt guilty for the relief she had felt when Binita had joined the team. She determined to visit Eileen when she could.

The discussion continued as Geraldine stood up to leave. Ian would be on his way home, and it was her turn to cook. As she walked to her car, she thought how fortunate she was to have found a partner who understood her. In the wrong circumstances love could so easily turn to bitterness, but in her case, love had brought her not only happiness, but a sense of serene equilibrium. She smiled and walked faster, eager to get home.

Acknowledgements

I would like to thank Dr Leonard Russell for his medical advice.

My sincere thanks also go to the team at No Exit Press: Ellie Lavender for her invaluable help in production, Elsa Mathern for her brilliant covers, Lisa Gooding and Hollie McDevitt for their fantastic marketing and PR, Jayne Lewis for her meticulous copy editing, Steven Mair for his eagle-eyed proofreading, and Andy Webb and Jim Crawley for their tireless work at Turnaround, and above all to Ion Mills and Claire Watts. I am extremely fortunate to be working with them, and really happy that there are more books to come in the series.

Geraldine and I have been together for a long time, in the company of my editor, who has been with us from the very beginning. We couldn't have reached Book 18 in the series without you, Keshini!

My thanks go to all the wonderful bloggers who have supported Geraldine Steel; Anne Cater, Varietats Blog, Over the Rainbow Book Blog, The Book Wormery, Honest Mam Reader's Book Blog, The Book Lover's Boudoir, The Twist and Turn Book Blog, Books by Bindu, The Word is Out, Bookish Jottings, and Beyond the Books, and to everyone who has taken the time to review my books. Your support means more to me than I can say.

Above all, I am grateful to my readers. Thank you for your interest in following Geraldine's career. To those of you who write to me to ask when the next book is out, I am busy writing

Book 19 in the series right now, and there are more to come after that. So I hope you continue to enjoy reading about Geraldine Steel.

Finally, my thanks go to Michael, who is my rock.

A LETTER FROM LEIGH

Dear Reader,

I hope you enjoyed reading this book in my Geraldine Steel series. Readers are the key to the writing process, so I'm thrilled that you've joined me on my writing journey.

You might not want to meet some of my characters on a dark night – I know I wouldn't! – but hopefully you want to read about Geraldine's other investigations. Her work is always her priority because she cares deeply about justice, but she also has her own life. Many readers care about what happens to her. I hope you join them, and become a fan of Geraldine Steel, and her colleague Ian Peterson.

If you follow me on Facebook or Twitter, you'll know that I love to hear from readers. I always respond to comments from fans, and hope you will follow me on **@LeighRussell** and **fb.me/leigh.russell.50** or drop me an email via my website **leighrussell.co.uk**.

To get exclusive news, competitions, offers, early sneak-peaks for upcoming titles and more, sign-up to my free monthly newsletter: **leighrussell.co.uk/news**. You can also find out more about me and the Geraldine Steel series on the No Exit Press website: **noexit.co.uk/ leighrussellbooks**.

Finally, if you enjoyed this story, I'd be really grateful if you would post a brief review on Amazon or Goodreads. A few sentences to say you enjoyed the book would be wonderful. And of course it would be brilliant if you would consider recommending my books to anyone who is a fan of crime fiction.

I hope to meet you at a literary festival or a book signing soon!

Thank you again for choosing to read my book.

With very best wishes,

Leigh Russell